REVENGE

DI Jemima Huxley
Book One

Gaynor Torrance

SAPERE
BOOKS

REVENGE

Published by Sapere Books.

20 Windermere Drive, Leeds, England, LS17 7UZ,
United Kingdom

saperebooks.com

ISBN: 978-1-913028-47-3

Prologue

When the killings began, he had no idea that there'd be so many.

He'd freaked out in the hours leading up to the first abduction. Took himself off to a quiet spot and thought about not going back. But the solitude helped to clear his mind and re-evaluate his priorities.

When he returned, he still wasn't comfortable with what he was about to do, but as the moment arrived, he went ahead with it anyway. He changed that day. Life stopped being ordinary. He'd seen the terror on her face, watched as she'd struggled and pleaded. Wanted to look away, but couldn't. And until the day he died, he knew that he'd never be able to forget the screams.

There were times when he despised what he'd done. The monster he had become.

The ritual had been far harder than he'd ever imagined, and the moment of death was almost a relief. There had been so much blood. It was everywhere. A sick, wretched feeling had seeped through his pores as the life ran out of her, and its warmth trickled over his skin. Later, he'd scrubbed himself clean. Worried that he'd never rid himself of the smell of death.

He had been convinced that everyone would notice the change in him. Look at him and know what he'd done. Yet no one treated him any differently, and life went on.

He'd got away with killing someone, and after that, each murder became easier.

As he stood in the woods, shovel in hand, he cocked his head and listened to the night. Leaves rustled, an owl hooted, and unseen creatures scampered through the undergrowth. The place was full of predators, and prey. But he was the biggest predator of them all.

This corpse was larger than the others. It had taken more plastic sheeting to wrap it, and it had been a struggle to haul the lifeless lump into the car. When he parked up at the burial site, he'd opened the vehicle and dragged the body to a specially selected spot.

The next few hours would be back-breaking work as he dug a large enough hole. It didn't help that the ground was hard, and there were tree roots everywhere. But it only needed to be a shallow grave. Then he'd unwrap the corpse, dump it and leave it to rot.

Chapter 1

It was early May, and for thirteen days Britain had sweltered around the clock. Forecasters claimed the high-pressure system would sit over the country for the foreseeable future, meaning the unseasonably hot weather would continue. It didn't take long for officials to impose hosepipe bans over large swathes of the country as water levels dropped and there was fear of a drought. Daylight brought unrelenting rays, which beat down with laser-like intensity, searing the earth and causing the air to shimmer. The green and pleasant land was turning brown as plants wilted and shrivelled. Darkness brought little relief.

The Government issued health warnings for the young, frail, and elderly. Most people ignored them. For sun-worshippers it was a dream come true. After all, who needed the Mediterranean when you had weather like this at home?

Barry Island was crammed full of people as crowds of normally sun-starved sedentary couch-lovers took to their feet, spurred into action by the sun's rays. The seafront heaved and pulsed with activity as hordes of people headed for the beach. Local traders couldn't believe their luck as people scoffed cockles, candyfloss, and chips at an alarming rate. Bins overflowed. Seabirds screamed a relentless cacophony, their wings flapping rapidly and menacingly, as they swooped and fought for discarded scraps of food.

Up and down the country daily routines were abandoned. Businesses suffered as sick absences rocketed. Parents took their children out of school. There was a holiday atmosphere. It was time to kick back and enjoy life. The world and his wife were stripping off to top up their tan. Only the unfortunate few had no choice but to carry on with the daily grind.

Detective Inspector Jemima Huxley had not experienced the bonhomie brought about by the heatwave. She was a public servant, and someone had to be on duty. There was no crime requiring her immediate attention, but there were mounds of neglected paperwork to wade through. For the moment there was nothing to distract her from dotting the i's and crossing the t's, and the overly-hyped satisfaction she should experience from compiling well-documented orderly files. The day dragged, and the air-conditioning unit that had clanked ominously for the last few months finally shuddered and broke down. Jemima was hot, uncomfortable and resented every second of her confinement to a cluttered desk in a stuffy office. She would have loved to have been out there enjoying the sunshine. But no such luck. Her request for leave had been laughed at and denied.

She looked around, saw the coast was clear and so reached down and extracted a *Mothercare* catalogue from inside her bag. She knew she shouldn't be doing this in work time, but it wasn't as if there was anyone around for her to set an example to, so she flicked through it. The baby clothes were adorable, and she already had a pram and cot in mind. The pregnancy testing kit was in the bathroom cabinet at home, and she planned to use it the following morning.

The end of the shift eventually arrived, and it hadn't come a moment too soon. Jemima was already planning her evening as she walked to the car, but her enthusiasm didn't last long. She noticed the first faint whiff of an unpleasant odour when she had less than a mile to go, but failed to realize its significance as she was too busy fantasizing about sitting on the decking at the far end of the garden, while she and Nick enjoyed the evening sun.

As she pulled up on her drive, the smell was undeniable, and a wave of nausea swelled inside her. She grabbed her bag, locked the car and hurried to the front door as she unwillingly inhaled the stench from the nearby fields, and fought the urge to gag. She had no choice. She had to breathe. But as she did so the fumes from the recently spread fertilizer seeped through her nostrils.

Jemima had to hand it to the farmer; he certainly knew how to choose his moments. It was probably his way of sticking two fingers up at the residents of the housing estate. Four years earlier he'd been forced to sell off part of his land to a building contractor. It was either that or risk going under, and he'd had a chip on his shoulder ever since. Jemima knew nothing about agriculture, but she was sure the farmer could have waited until the weather cooled before fertilizing his land.

If it hadn't been for the unbearable heat, she'd have kept the windows closed, but they'd already been shut all through the day. Every room was like a furnace, but as Jemima opened windows throughout the house, she realized she might as well have camped out on the farm.

Nick arrived home at almost seven o'clock. Neither of them had much of an appetite. Thoughts of relaxing on the decking turned into watching reality TV while eating beans on toast, drinking chilled lemonade and sharing a tub of Ben & Jerry's.

That night was a test of endurance, and the only reason Jemima finally decided to venture upstairs was that the sofa wasn't quite long enough for her to comfortably stretch out. The bedroom was still ridiculously hot. There was no hint of the rose and vanilla potpourri that lay uselessly in a bowl on the bedroom windowsill and Jemima shuddered at the thought of having to spend hours in a room where the stench of chicken manure filled the air. Jemima tried not to breathe too deeply, and as she lay there in the dark, she ran through her relaxation techniques, though it seemed that on this occasion nothing was going to work. She couldn't conjure up the image of the meadow, with its clusters of orange and yellow wildflowers interspersed amongst the grass. Her favourite butterflies had disappeared, but there was plenty of cow dung with large, ugly flies buzzing around it. She just couldn't shut out the smell of the farm. It was overpowering. She was angry and exhausted. It was no wonder she couldn't sleep.

As she tossed and turned, the fitted sheet loosened and bunched uncomfortably beneath her, its cotton fibres damp and limp with sweat. Miraculously, Nick seemed immune to the effects of the heat and managed to fall asleep almost immediately. He lay on his back, mouth slightly open. His slow regular breath whistled, and after a while gave way to a series of protracted rumbles, which Jemima soon began to anticipate and resent. To make matters worse, Nick held his edge of the duvet in a vice-like grip, preventing her from tossing it to the floor. Jemima had thrown the covers off herself on three occasions, only to wake bathed in sweat as Nick had heaved the duvet back over her. She just couldn't get comfortable, and whichever way she lay some part of her body ached.

Jemima eventually fell into a fitful sleep, waking to look at the clock at alarmingly regular intervals. As the hours crept by and Nick continued to sleep she got increasingly frustrated. There was no breeze, and the stillness of the air seemed to amplify every sound. The clock ticked. Nick breathed. Jemima felt herself beginning to lose it.

Jemima's thoughts turned to imagining what it must be like to be pregnant. She'd wanted to have a baby of her own for so long. She and Nick had been trying for almost two years and had been disappointed so many times. As it was, she was way beyond desperate. She'd willingly give up almost everything she had just to have a child of her own but tried not to think about it too often, as she knew stress was counterproductive and would decrease her chances of conceiving. But the more she struggled to distract herself, the more her thoughts turned to pregnancy.

There were times when Jemima felt cursed. Her sister Lucy had just announced she was pregnant with her third child. Lucy was an Oxford graduate. Lucy was a successful business woman. Lucy was the most fertile woman on the planet. She only had to flutter her eyelashes at her husband, and there was another baby on the way. Jemima had spent most of her life in her sister's shadow as Lucy had consistently outperformed her at every turn.

Even Dan Broadbent had recently become a first-time father. Broadbent, Huxley's less than sharp sergeant, who she was considering keeping on a leash to minimize the chaos he caused wherever he went. And since the birth of his son, Harry, Broadbent's intellectual capacity had diminished even further, when almost overnight he transformed into a perpetually exhausted spongy-brained blob.

The more she thought about it, the more fertile everybody apart from her seemed to be. There were at least two pregnant female officers at the station, and three male officers were expectant fathers. Jemima knew she should think about something else. She should picture the meadow, with its flowers and butterflies. The meadow was safe, comfortable and peaceful. The meadow made her happy. The meadow relaxed her.

Chapter 2

At some point, Jemima managed to fall asleep again. Then as dawn broke, the birds began to wake. As luck would have it, scores of them nested in a large oak tree at the bottom of the garden. Jemima would have happily cut the tree down had it not been for a very inconvenient preservation order. She hated that tree, even though it had been there far longer than their house. Unfortunately, it was large, strong and healthy, and provided shelter for hordes of birds and squirrels. And if that wasn't bad enough, every autumn their guttering was blocked by leaves shed by the tree, and this caused Jemima lots of angst as she steadied the ladder for Nick to climb. She'd press her weight against it for all she was worth, holding her breath as she looked upwards, praying Nick wouldn't fall off, as he stood unsteadily near the top of the ladder and scooped mounds of moss and rotting foliage into a bucket.

The oak tree was also the favoured spot for the birds' regular choir practice, which invariably took place at first light. For any human who happened to be a light sleeper, it was like being subjected to an avian version of the X Factor. The persistent chirrups and screeches made her want to scream, and Jemima thought anyone who claimed to love the sound of birdsong hadn't been forced to listen to it when they'd had less than an hour's sleep themselves.

With choir practice finally over for the day, Nick muttered something unintelligible, turned over in his sleep and threw the duvet back over Jemima. It was 7:02, and the sun already felt like a furnace. Jemima knew she might as well get up, as there was no point lying in bed. As she swung her legs over the edge of the mattress, she noticed an all too familiar ache in her stomach, and immediately knew what it meant. She swallowed hard, forcing herself not to cry when all she wanted to do was curl up into a tight ball, close her eyes, and wake up in an alternative universe where she had a baby of her own.

The monthly cycle of hope and grief was steadily chipping away at her sanity. She'd always been an optimist, but it was becoming increasingly difficult to believe she'd ever get pregnant. After all, she hadn't up until now. She knew she had a good life, a successful career, a happy marriage, and a financially stable background, but with every passing month, it got harder to count her blessings and stay positive.

Jemima looked at Nick as he slept contentedly, oblivious to her latest disappointment. He was everything she wanted in a husband. They'd met quite by chance at a Cardiff Blues match, and there'd been an instant attraction between them. Nick was a sports journalist with the *Daily Wales* newspaper, and after the game, he'd taken her to meet the rugby team. He had an easy way with people. Everyone liked him. It was a strange experience for Jemima, who was used to people treating her with suspicion. She'd been wary about telling Nick she was a police officer, but when she finally plucked up the courage he hadn't shied away, and they'd been married for almost seven years.

When she first decided she wanted to have a baby, they'd had sex at every opportunity: indoors, al fresco, the back of the car and even the toilet cubicle of an InterCity train. It was fun, exciting, and they'd never been more in love. But as the months passed and Jemima failed to conceive, the fun went out of their lovemaking, and science took over. There were thermometers, charts and urgent dashes across the city just to have sex at the so-called optimum moment. It was challenging and awkward as they both had busy schedules, and it didn't help that Jemima's work pattern was always unpredictable. Their sex life became stressful, contrived, and almost a chore.

During her spare time, Jemima had studied so many articles on pregnancy and conception that she believed she could write a thesis on it. They'd changed their diets, cut out caffeine, and Nick even wore loose pants and trousers. She'd taken up yoga to de-stress and give her body the best possible chance to conceive. Full marks on the theory, A plus for effort, but an absolute failure on the practical.

Jemima knew they'd have to discuss the possibility of seeking professional help. They'd both seen documentaries about couples struggling to conceive a child. Neither of them relished being poked, prodded, and asked the most intimate of questions. She was sure Nick would object to the indignity of sitting in a cubicle with a selection of well-thumbed magazines while he produced a sample to order. After all, as Nick already had a son from his first marriage, the fault must lie with her.

Jemima padded across the landing, opened the bathroom door and locked it behind her. Once inside, she switched on the radio and turned on the shower. She was about to have a meltdown and didn't want Nick's pity. So she sat hunched beneath the spray, hugging her knees as tears streamed down her face.

Other women made it look so easy, and it seemed particularly unfair that women who didn't want kids got pregnant all the time, yet Jemima was unable to do the most natural thing on earth, and she hated herself for being so useless. Her shoulders shook, and gut-wrenching sobs made her stomach ache even more with the effort it took to stifle the sound. It had become a well-worn ritual, a routine part of her life. One she refused to share with anyone. Life had become a constant battle of emotions and mood swings. It was exhausting and frightening.

Finally, the feeling of desperation receded as an all too familiar surge of anger, frustration, and self-loathing surfaced. Jemima stood up, stepped out of the shower, opened the cupboard door and reached for the razor blade concealed in a box of tampons.

The metal glinted tantalizingly. It was such a small implement, yet powerful, one which gave relief time and time again. She spent a few seconds turning the blade between her fingers before leaning forward to force the edge of it into her leg and expertly dragging it across to tear the flesh.

She knew the secret was to make the cut short and shallow. That way Nick wouldn't get suspicious, and if he happened to notice it, she could explain it away as a shaving mishap. Last month's scar had already healed as had fifteen others before it, and they now looked little more than ugly stretchmarks.

Blood flowed from the new wound. It hurt, but the pain felt good as it was a pain she had control over. It was a choice she had made for herself. Not something which her body had imposed upon her.

Jemima stepped back into the shower before the blood had a chance to reach the floor. Her heart rate slowed as she raised her face towards the showerhead allowing jets of water to pummel her skin. She scrubbed herself vigorously, using far too much shower gel to wash away the evidence of this month's failure.

Jemima heard Nick call her just as she was returning the freshly wiped blade to its hiding place. She felt a flash of irritation at his untimely interruption, as she hadn't had a chance to conceal her wound with an Elastoplast. 'What'd you say?' she asked as she opened the bathroom door.

'Your boss is on the phone. Says it's urgent,' said Nick holding out the receiver for her to take.

'Sir?'

'Huxley, get over to Llys Faen Hall a bit sharpish,' said Detective Chief Inspector Ray Kennedy. 'The owners, a Mr. and Mrs. Tremaine, discovered a body buried in their woodland. The forensic science team is already on their way. I'll get on to Broadbent and tell him you'll pick him up at his house. Give me a ring as soon as you know what's happening up there.'

Chapter 3

There was no time to discuss things with Nick. As usual, work came first, and personal problems had to wait. Jemima rushed to the kitchen, drank a glass of orange juice and grabbed a banana, munching mouthfuls of the fruit as she got dressed and dried her hair. It took less than fifteen minutes from putting down the phone to leaving the house. Who said women couldn't get ready in a hurry?

As she drove to Broadbent's house, she hoped she wouldn't have to come face to face with his wife and baby. She knew it was ridiculous; after all, it was only a woman and a three-month-old child. She even liked Caroline Broadbent. They'd spent many an evening in the pub together. But if Jemima were to see Caroline now, she knew it would push her over the edge. She was only just about managing to keep a lid on her emotions. It was the baby, the damn baby.

The more she allowed thoughts of Broadbent's family to enter her head, the faster her heart raced. Before she knew it, her breath was shallow and rapid. Somehow she still had the presence of mind to realize she had to react quickly or risk having a full-blown panic attack right there in the car. So she forced herself to inhale deeply through her nose, felt her lungs expand, and slowly released the breath through her mouth.

A glance at her hands showed her knuckles to be white with tension. Her grip on the steering wheel was so intense that it was almost impossible to maintain it, but as she tried to relax her fingers, she realized she needed the feeling of discomfort. It grounded her. Kept her focused, stopped her from letting go of the here and now. She had to calm herself, and do it quickly.

No matter how bad she felt, she was determined not to let Broadbent see just how fucked-up she was.

Over the last few months, Jemima had had concerns about her emotional fragility. She was on edge but knew she couldn't afford to let the cracks show at work. It didn't do for a police officer to lose it in public. Especially a female Detective Inspector.

Women had a hard enough time in the force as it was, and there'd be a queue of people ready to label her as a liability and claim she couldn't handle the pressures of the job. It wouldn't matter that their accusations were unjustified. They'd be sympathetic to her face and stick the knife in her back. Worse still, they'd shunt her off to some dead-end job. No one wanted to work with a basket case. There were times when you had to trust your colleagues with your life. And how could you do that if they started acting irrationally?

Jemima knew she had to compartmentalize her life. There were rules, and they were there for a reason. Your work life and private life were two incompatible entities. Like the grape and the grain. If you were sensible you didn't mix the two, else you could end up regretting it. You should never get emotional at work, as emotion was seen as weakness and made it difficult if not impossible for you to make sound decisions. You had to earn respect. For a woman, it was doubly hard to gain but exceptionally easy to lose. A murder inquiry needed a strong DI, and that was Huxley's role.

The bottom line was, Jemima had a job to do, and if she wanted to continue as a respected DI, she bloody well had to get on and do it. She'd worked hard to get where she was, and continually felt she had to outperform her male colleagues for anyone to take her seriously. She'd clawed her way up through the ranks and wasn't about to let all her hard work and determination go to waste by acting like a broody mother hen.

She pulled up in front of Broadbent's house and sounded the horn. Within seconds he was at the door. Thankfully there was no sign of Caroline or the baby. He held up his hand to acknowledge Huxley then turned to shut the door carefully behind him.

Jemima couldn't help but notice Broadbent's hair looked as though it hadn't seen a comb, and this was the third day in a row he'd worn the same shirt. She sighed, knowing she'd have to say something soon. Heat and stale sweat weren't a good combination, but right now it was a conversation she could do without. She had enough on her plate, and Broadbent's recently questionable personal hygiene regime was one aggravation too many. If he took offence and had a go at her she'd probably burst into tears, and how would that look? She decided to see how things panned out throughout the day. Perhaps she'd broach the subject with him later.

'Bad night?' she asked as he fastened his seatbelt. She indicated to pull out. All thoughts of falling apart in front of him were now firmly out of her mind. She was the SIO, and he followed her orders.

'You know how it is, not getting much sleep at the moment,' he said, struggling to suppress a yawn. 'Someone's found a body then?'

'Yeah, out at Llys Faen Hall.'

'Great, couldn't ask for a better start to the day,' said Broadbent. 'Never mind, I s'pose the fresh air'll do me good. I must've only got about three hours sleep last night. I know he can't help it, but the little fella always seems to drop off just when I'm getting up for work. I'm telling you, Gov, you don't know how lucky you are not to have kids. You and Nick should make the most of your time together, 'cos once you've got a kid, that's it for the rest of your life. No money. No sleep. And no bloody sex. Caro doesn't even wash my clothes at the moment, and I can't remember the last time she cooked dinner for me. I sometimes wonder what I'm getting out of this relationship. She'd better buck her ideas up soon. I can't take much more of this.'

'My heart bleeds for you,' said Jemima, forcing a sympathetic smile to her lips.

'D'ya mind if I get my head down for a couple of minutes?' asked Broadbent.

'Be my guest,' she replied, relieved she didn't have to make further conversation or listen to more of Broadbent's parental woes.

It was a good time to be on the move. As traffic was reasonably light, with the only tailback being on the main route into the centre, it didn't pose a problem as they headed across the northern fringe of the city. The air conditioning unit blasted out cold air which helped mask the stale smell of Broadbent's armpits, and Jemima was relieved to feel the breeze on her face as it stopped her from feeling drowsy. She glanced across at Broadbent who sat there, eyes closed, his slow rhythmic breathing testament to the fact he was already asleep, and Jemima experienced a sudden stab of envy. He had what she wanted: a baby.

Broadbent snorted. As he did so, a small slug-like trail of drool crept from the corner of his mouth and slowly edged its way towards his cheek. It reminded Jemima of Nick and was too intimate a moment for colleagues to share. His head slumped towards her, and she got a waft of morning breath. It made her want to slap him. He was pathetic. Broadbent and his wife needed to get their act together. Their baby was three months old, and they still hadn't managed to organize a routine. He was going to have to interview people today. The very least he could have done was to wear some clean clothes.

As the thought entered her head, Jemima could hear Lucy's voice saying, 'Honestly, Jem, you've got no idea what it's like to look after a baby. You just think they're small and cute, but in their first year, they take everything you've got and then some. They're parasites. Think of the hardest thing you've ever done then quadruple it, and imagine having to do it twenty-four-seven. I'd swap you your job anytime. You get paid, and you get time off, whereas I'm firefighting all the time just to stand still. I never get a moment to myself.'

Jemima bit down hard on her bottom lip. Her sister was right. She didn't have a clue what it was like to look after a baby, and the way things were going she probably never would. Almost instantly, she felt pressure building behind her eyes and knew she'd start to cry if she didn't snap out of it quickly. She couldn't let that happen, so she forced herself to concentrate on her breathing technique, in through her nose, out through her mouth. Luckily it was effective.

The traffic became heavier as she approached Llanishen, with cars backed up at a junction as drivers struggled to turn right. Jemima inched forward in the queue until she was eventually able to turn left up Station Road, heading towards Lisvane. As she took the road towards Rudry, she noticed the familiar smell of chicken manure and realized that Broadbent's body odour wouldn't be an issue, at least while they were outside.

Chapter 4

Llys Faen Hall had been built on the side of a hill about a mile to the north of Lisvane, where it enjoyed views across Cardiff, the Bristol Channel, and on a good day the Somerset coast. The Hall, as it was known locally, was set a long way back off a country lane, with a high dry-stone wall marking its boundary. There were numerous signs fixed to the wall, advising passers-by that beyond it was private property. It was evident the Tremaines were people who valued their privacy. Jemima didn't blame them. Up ahead there was a gap in the wall, and Jemima reduced her speed to manoeuvre the car through the open space where eight-foot-high electrically operated gates demarcated the end of the public highway and the entrance to the Tremaines' private estate.

A young-looking PC stood guard at the entrance. Jemima recognized him as Kevin Williams, an eager and likeable recent recruit. 'It's going to be another hot one, Marm,' said Williams, as she stopped the vehicle and presented her warrant card.

'I see you drew the short straw?' said Jemima.

'Yeah, must've done something bad in a previous life,' he joked. 'Been here for about an hour now, and I've only just got used to the smell. Talk about fresh country air; I'd take traffic fumes over this any day. At least I've got some mints to take the taste away, else I'd upchuck. Heavy night?' he asked, nodding at Broadbent who was still fast asleep.

'Something like that,' said Jemima. 'Which way is it?'

'Carry on down the driveway. Take the next right and head on up to the woods. The SOCOs are already there.'

It was a wide driveway lined with a few deciduous trees and a variety of rhododendron bushes, which would have been in full bloom a few weeks earlier. As it was, there were only a few remaining flowers, and they were well past their prime.

The driveway veered off to the left, and after travelling a few hundred yards, there was still no sign of the house. Eventually, a single-lane track branched to the right and headed up towards the wooded hillside. Jemima slowed down and eased the car into the turn. It was a steep incline. She drove carefully, wary of damaging the suspension even though the surface was in a better condition than many sections of the public highway.

In the distance, Jemima spotted a collection of police vehicles, and as she approached, she could see that this was where the track ended. The ground was rougher and had been cleared to form a large turning area, but today it was an impromptu car park. She found a gap, pulled in, engaged the handbrake and switched off the engine. There wasn't much room to open the doors, but it would have to do.

Broadbent was still fast asleep, head resting on his right shoulder, mouth slightly open, and the trail of saliva had stained his shirt.

'Time to go,' said Jemima as she undid her seatbelt and reached across to tap his shoulder.

'I changed him last time,' spluttered Broadbent as he opened his eyes and slowly wiped his mouth with the back of his hand. 'Oh, it's you,' he said as Jemima's face came into focus. 'Thank God for that. I was dreading the state of the nappy if it smelt like that. That smell's not you, is it?' he asked wrinkling his nose in disgust.

'No, it's bloody well not. It's chicken shit. The farmer spread it on the fields yesterday,' said Jemima as she turned to acknowledge a burly officer walking towards their vehicle carrying a couple of sets of disposable overalls and overshoes.

They set off at a brisk pace. Broadbent was only just managing to keep up. He didn't make any attempt to speak. He looked exhausted, his eyes bloodshot, and skin almost grey. It was easy to see how someone could think he'd been on a bender the night before.

'You look like shit. Are you sure you should be at work?' asked Jemima.

'Work's the only place I get any peace,' said Broadbent in a flat tone. 'I can't cope with the constant crying. It's doing my head in, but I'll be OK. You don't need to worry about me. I'm up to the job.'

The crime scene had already been taped off, and the blue and white plastic shimmered in the sunlight. Jemima was surprised at how far apart the trees were. From a distance, it looked as though they had been planted close together, but it wasn't the case. Roots bulged from the ground, yet much of the surface was surprisingly even. She could tell by the leaves that there were different types of deciduous trees. Most of the trunks were thick and tall, which probably meant the trees were old. They looked healthy, and the foliage provided a welcome respite from the sun, even though some of the rays managed to find their way through the gaps, giving the ground a mottled effect of light and shade.

There were four forensic officers hard at work. They'd already marked out a grid and were in the process of digging and sifting soil. Part of a corpse was visible.

'DI Huxley, and DS Broadbent,' said Jemima, holding out her ID. 'We've got ourselves a body then?'

'I'd prefer it if you didn't come any closer,' called Jeanne Ennersley, as she stood up and stretched. 'You know the drill.

We have to do our best to preserve the crime scene. And it's not a body. As things stand, it's two and counting. The ground's disturbed in a few places, so we've undertaken an initial scan of the immediate area with the ground penetrating radar. It suggests there may be more corpses up here. On our first sweep, we've identified potential locales. The GPR is a pretty reliable indicator, so I'd say we're going to be here for a few days yet. And if these first two corpses are anything to go by, I'd say we're not going to have to dig down too far to find the others.'

'Any chance of this being an ancient burial site?' asked Jemima.

'It's unlikely. The two we're working on at the moment have been in situ less than a year, and the first one has probably been in the ground for less than a month. The graves are shallow, suggesting that someone was in a rush to dispose of the bodies and wasn't too bothered about anyone finding them. My guess is we've got ourselves a serial killer.'

'Have you found any ID on the victims?' asked Jemima.

'Not so far. The only thing I can tell you at the moment is that one is female. Not sure about the other one yet, as we haven't had time to uncover much of that body. It's going to be a while before we finish with these two. When we do, we'll ship them over to John Prothero at the University Hospital. He's on standby for the autopsies, and he's assured us they'll be given priority. I'm sorry, but I've got to get on. As I said, there are probably more bodies, and it's not as if you can do anything to help.'

'You're right,' said Jemima. 'No point in us hanging around; it's time we went down to the Hall and spoke to the Tremaines.'

Chapter 5

'What do you know about the Tremaines?' asked Broadbent, as Jemima manoeuvred the car in the overcrowded parking area.

'I've never met them, which is hardly surprising as people like us don't fraternise with the likes of them. But I've read some magazine articles about the history of the Tremaine family, and how the house came to be built,' said Jemima.

'Typical of you to be clued-up from the get-go,' chuckled Broadbent. 'Come on mastermind, give me a potted history, so that I'll know the type of people we'll be dealing with.'

'Well, as far as I can recall, Llys Faen Hall has been in the Tremaine family for five generations,' said Jemima. 'It was designed and built in the mid-nineteenth century, for Henry Tremaine. He owned three local coal mines and got rich from the blood, sweat, and tears of his workers.'

'I'm talking about the height of the Industrial Revolution, when everyone wanted coal, and the hillsides of the Welsh Valleys had it in abundance. Men like Henry Tremaine got rich at the expense of the poor. There were plenty of people living hand-to-mouth just to survive. Locals had no choice but to risk their lives bringing it to the surface. If they didn't work, they didn't eat. Even children had to earn their keep. The alternative was starvation or the shame of the poorhouse.'

'So the long and the short of it is that Henry Tremaine was a hard-nosed rich bastard who was more than happy to exploit and abuse his workforce. Seems as though the Tremaine family already has blood on its hands,' said Broadbent.

'Oh, get over yourself, Dan! How'd you like it if people judged you on how your ancestors lived their lives?' asked Jemima.

'I wouldn't, but that's not the point,' he replied, a little too defensively.

'Anyway, back to the quick history lesson,' Jemima continued. 'It was a well-known fact that the Tremaines were a greedy, selfish, and ruthless family. Henry Tremaine got off on lording it over the peasants. He ordered the construction of Llys Faen Hall to celebrate his wealth and increase his social standing.

'Things began to go pear-shaped for the Tremaines in the late nineteenth and early twentieth centuries. There was a catalogue of mining disasters in this area, followed by the Great War and subsequent depression. The Tremaines lost three of their own on the French battlefields. Successive generations had squandered much of the family fortune.

'When David Tremaine's father became head of the family, it marked a fresh start for the Tremaines. Armstrong Tremaine was ashamed of the way his ancestors had carried on and was determined to prove that he was different. At first, there was a great deal of suspicion over his motives, but he worked tirelessly to improve life for the locals. Armstrong built up a business in the brewing industry which went from strength to strength, allowing him to open a chain of public houses. His son, David Tremaine, the current owner of Llys Faen Hall, diversified the business to encompass the restaurant and hotel trade.'

'And he's one of the richest men in the country,' added Broadbent. 'I've seen him on the news a couple of times, but I've never seen his wife. I think they're a very private couple.

Still, I don't suppose you get to be that successful without making quite a few enemies.'

'Are you suggesting someone's buried those bodies up there as some sort of revenge for David Tremaine's business dealings?' asked Jemima.

'Well, it's a possibility,' said Broadbent. 'I'm not saying that's what's happened. It's just a theory.'

'Worth considering, but let's keep an open mind for now,' said Jemima. 'We'll find out what happened this morning, take their statements, and have a look around the grounds. It's a big place. We need to get a feel for it, do some background checks on the Tremaines, and their staff.'

When they reached the main driveway, Jemima turned right and continued towards the house. Within a few minutes, the landscape changed, and open parkland appeared. On the left was a small pretty looking cottage. It was set back at least ten yards from the drive and surrounded by a garden. The windows were wide open, and the sound of Abba's 'Mamma Mia' could be heard coming from inside.

The approach to Llys Faen Hall turned out to be quite spectacular. Formal rose gardens gave way to various bushes trimmed into the shapes of animals, which in turn led to a circular forecourt with a large ornate fountain at its centre, cascading gallons of clear water into its base. The still, sultry air made the sound of running water very appealing, and Jemima had to stop herself from walking over to the fountain and splashing some of the water on her face. It was such an idyllic setting that it was hard to reconcile it with the corpses in the woods.

A volley of piercing screams sounded to their right, causing them both to jump.

'What the hell was that?' asked Jemima, her heart suddenly pounding again.

'I dunno, but it didn't sound human,' said Broadbent, scanning the area. 'Ah, there are the culprits,' he said, pointing at some peacocks. 'They're better than guard dogs. Scare you to death when they screech like that. By the look of it there're three of them, all Indian Blues. Good choice if you ask me, less susceptible to infection than green peacocks, and easier to breed. Oh, and look at that!' he said as one of them opened out his tail feathers. 'What a beaut! I wish I had my camera.'

'You're not here on a bloody nature trip,' snapped Jemima. 'And anyway, what's with the peacock trivia?'

'Aw, you've gotta love 'em,' said Broadbent. 'I mean look at him, those feathers are magnificent. I don't know why, but I've had a thing about them ever since I was a kid. They're beautiful birds.'

'Get a life for fuck's sake,' muttered Jemima as she left Broadbent admiring the bird. She headed towards the main entrance, shaking her head in disbelief.

A smallish middle-aged man appeared from nowhere. He was wearing a dark grey suit, highly polished shoes, white shirt and royal blue silk tie. He looked overdressed for the weather, and beads of perspiration were visible on his forehead. His features were pointy, and his blue eyes darted around deviously, refusing to rest on anything. Jemima couldn't make up her mind whether he was shifty or shy, but when he spoke his voice was deep and resonant. This wasn't a shy man. His speech was clipped and self-assured, with the slightest hint of a Welsh accent.

'Police?' he asked.

'Detective Inspector Huxley and this is Detective Sergeant Broadbent,' she said as she held out her warrant card and Broadbent caught up with her.

'Alistair Williams, estate manager,' he replied. 'The Tremaines are expecting you, so if you'd be so kind as to follow me.'

Chapter 6

Llys Faen Hall was a stunning home that had recently featured in *Luxury Lifestyle*, a magazine where the homes of the rich and famous were displayed for ordinary people to drool over and provided criminals with a blueprint to plan a visit. The residence was an interior designer's dream, full of exquisite features, furnishings, and artwork. Four granite steps at least thirty-foot-wide led the way to an impressive set of solid oak double doors, which were both high and broad enough to easily allow a large transit van to be driven inside without risk of damaging either the vehicle or the property. On either side of the steps was a marble plinth on which stood a life-sized stone lion, a seemingly bizarre choice for such a setting.

The inside of the house was even more impressive. The entrance hall was the size of a typical modern apartment. It was rectangular, and the floor was solid marble. A generous staircase gave access to a galleried landing area, and directly overhead was the largest crystal chandelier imaginable. For an old property, it was surprisingly light and airy. The walls were a neutral tone, adorned with modern artwork displayed in simple, understated frames which drew the eye to the paintings themselves. Five doors led off the vestibule. Each was closed, and everything was quiet.

'I'll take you through to the drawing room,' said Alistair Williams, as he opened the second door on the left and marched ahead without looking around to ensure they were following him.

They entered the most beautiful-looking room Jemima had ever seen, and despite the purpose of their visit, she found herself unable to stop acting like an overenthusiastic visitor to a stately home. She was fascinated by the high ceiling, which although mainly white was elaborately decorative. The central focal point was a large flower with a delicate sky blue ovary encircled by pale yellow stamens, surrounded by sixteen white petals, each edged in gold leaf. Radiating from this flower were forty-eight small blue Carolina roses in bunches of three, set along eight spines decreasing in size the further away they were from the centre. Moss green tendrils linked these roses together, painted to resemble the outline of an urn. The floral design was enclosed within a mottled effect gold leaf band, and the design was repeated in a modified form at each corner of the ceiling to take account of the right angles.

The walls were a pale yellow, and the floor a highly polished oak. French doors led to an outdoor seating area and the garden beyond. The room was large enough to look sparsely furnished despite it containing a grand piano, three Louis XIV style sofas, a chaise longue and an elaborately carved occasional table. A large Grecian urn stood in each corner of the room, and a painting of Heracles and Athena dominated the area over the fireplace. A magnificent display of freshly cut freesias filled a large vase upon the table, and their scent brought a fragrant freshness to the room.

David and Helen Tremaine sat together on one of the sofas, and it was apparent that Helen Tremaine had been crying as her cheeks looked unnaturally red and puffy. As the Tremaines stood to greet them, Jemima noticed how attractive Helen Tremaine was, for a woman who was most likely in her mid to late fifties. She'd managed to maintain a svelte figure. A few white strands were visible in her otherwise light brown hair, which was tied back off her face in a loose French plait. She wore a minimal amount of cosmetics, her lips pale, and the skin around her eyes slightly smudged with mascara. Her open-toed flat sandals displayed unpainted toenails, and Jemima noticed that Helen Tremaine's fingernails were also bare. A fitted short-sleeved cream blouse showed off her toned arms to perfection, and her dark brown summer trousers ended mid-calf to reveal slender ankles. The only pieces of jewellery she wore were a small cross, which hung from a simple gold chain around her neck, and a plain gold wedding band on her left hand. The whole ensemble was simple yet effective.

Unlike his wife, David Tremaine looked as though he spent little time keeping himself in shape. His ruddy complexion suggested he enjoyed a drink, and his waistline also bore out the assumption. He was completely bald, yet his eyebrows and arms, which were visible only below the elbow, suggested that he once had blonde hair. He wore a dark blue paisley shirt with the sleeves rolled up, tan coloured casual trousers that could have done with being a larger size, and well-worn training shoes. Given his physique, it was an unattractive look.

'I'm sorry we have to meet under these circumstances,' said David Tremaine, after they had introduced themselves.

'Have you any idea whose body it was?' asked Helen Tremaine, wringing her hands together.

'It's too early to say,' replied Jemima. 'We're just here to make some initial inquiries, have a look around, and take statements from you.'

'Well, I'm not sure we can be of much help,' said David Tremaine. 'Corbett, our Staffie, discovered the body while we were out on our morning walk. We don't often get up to the wood these days. Usually, we do a few circuits of the lake to the far side of the house. The thing is, they've been spreading that damn muck on the fields, and the smell is bloody awful, so we thought we'd head up to the wood for a change. Thought it might not be so strong up that way.

'We never confine Corbett to the leash — he's an obedient old thing. But for some reason, when we got up there he just took off. It was so out of character, but I suppose he must have picked up the scent. I kept whistling and calling for him to come, but he ignored me and kept barking. It wasn't his usual bark either. It was more high-pitched, excited. Helen thought he must have found something. We expected it to be a rabbit or some other vermin, never expected it to be human remains.'

'I don't think I'll ever forget it,' said Helen Tremaine as she took up the story from her husband. 'I could just see the hand at first, sticking up out of the ground, fingers curled, grey and lifeless. It was as if my brain couldn't process what I was seeing. I remember staring at it, and on some level, I knew it was a human hand, but I kept telling myself it was my mind playing tricks on me. It's our land. It's an idyllic place to live. Things like that don't happen around here.

'We were both rooted to the spot. I suppose we must have been in shock. Then David had one of his angina attacks, and I had to go through his pockets to find his spray. I couldn't stop my hands from shaking. For an awful moment, I thought he'd forgotten to bring the spray out with him, but I eventually managed to find it. I got him to lean back against one of the trees, and when I was sure he was all right, I called the police on my mobile phone.

'I had a devil of a job to get Corbett on the leash. He hates it at the best of times. The silly thing was very excitable and didn't like me dragging him away from the body. He can be stubborn when he wants to be. After David had recovered, we headed down to the main gate to meet the officers so we could direct them to the spot. Do you think it was a transient who just happened to die up there?'

'Oh, Helen, you can be so naive at times. The body was buried,' said David Tremaine. 'Someone had to have done that.'

'You mean the person had been murdered?' asked Helen Tremaine, in a high-pitched voice, as she twisted a limp cotton handkerchief tightly around her left index finger.

'It's too early to say,' said Jemima, sensing Helen was close to tears. 'It's likely the forensic team will be there for a few days. Is it just the two of you who live here?' she continued, trying to garner as much information as she could before Helen lost it completely.

'That's right,' said David Tremaine.

'And what about the cottage we passed on the drive?'

'Alistair Williams lives there with his wife and daughter,' said David Tremaine. 'The cottage comes with the job.'

'Do you have any other staff?' asked Jemima.

'A gardener, gamekeeper, housekeeper, and a cook,' said David Tremaine.

'And do any of those live on the estate?' asked Jemima.

'No, they come in during the day, Monday to Friday, that is. We rarely ask any of them to work weekends,' said David Tremaine. 'Alistair's the estate manager. I'm sure he'll be happy to arrange for you to speak to the staff. You can use the library if necessary.'

'Before we talk to any of them, we'd like to take a look around the grounds,' said Jemima. 'We need to get a feel for the place.'

'I'll get Alistair to contact Isaacs. He's our latest gamekeeper. Only been with us for a couple of months, but he should be able to show you around,' said David Tremaine.

'Are you aware of any strangers having accessed your land in the last few months?'

'No. As far as I know, the main gate is secure, but the grounds are so extensive it wouldn't be that difficult for someone to get in at some other point, and we'd be none the wiser if they got into the wood. There are no security measures in place up there; it'd be impossible for us to install them,' said David Tremaine.

'Do either of you know of anyone who may have a grudge against you?' asked Jemima.

'Not that I know of,' said David Tremaine, surprised at being asked such a question. 'You don't think this is personal, do you? Because I can assure you you're way off the mark if you think someone has buried a body in our wood as a warning to us. We don't move in such circles, Inspector. I may be a successful businessman, but we lead very boring lives. I don't deal with criminals. There's no place for coercion or dodgy deals in my business. I don't hold with that sort of thing. Everything I do is completely legitimate. I've never even filed a late tax return. This body hasn't got anything to do with us.'

'I had to ask,' said Jemima. 'One more thing: are you aware of anyone who's gone missing recently?'

'No,' said David Tremaine. 'I'm not.'

'What about you, Mrs. Tremaine?'

'Missing? No, no,' she faltered.

Chapter 7

Peter Isaacs turned out to be a man of few words, who gave the appearance of being more at ease with nature than with his fellow man. He had close-cropped hair, rugged features, and it was evident from his toned physique that he regularly worked out. Jemima thought he was probably somewhere in his thirties, though his tanned, almost leathery skin aged him considerably. A military tattoo was visible on one of his muscular forearms. Isaacs was far from being a handsome man and looked as though he may live life on the wild side. A pale scar extended for almost three inches along his left cheekbone. His nose had been broken at some stage and had set at an unfortunate angle, which emphasized a pronounced lump on its bridge.

An old Jack Russell terrier walked dutifully at his heel. It was a scruffy-looking mutt: thin, wiry, with a mean face. Unlike his owner, the dog was not afraid to make eye contact and looked as though it was spoiling for a fight if the opportunity were to present itself. As they approached the animal, a low guttural sound resonated from the back of the dog's throat. It was somewhere between an overt growl and a death rattle, and neither Broadbent nor Jemima were keen to feel those sharp little teeth on their flesh.

'Quiet, Jock!' ordered Isaacs, as he shot a warning look at the dog. 'He don't like strangers. Not very sociable, but a good ratter. Earns his keep though. He'll give you no trouble as long as you keep your distance.'

'He looks old,' said Jemima.

'Plenty of life in him yet,' said Isaacs defensively. 'Boss said you want me to show you round. I ain't got long. Gotta fix the wall at the far end of the estate. So, what ya wanna see?'

'We just want to get a feel for the place,' said Jemima. 'See the estate for ourselves.'

'Boss said they've found a body up in the woods. I'm tellin' you straight, ain't nuffin' to do with me, and I ain't been 'ere long, so I won't be much 'elp to you.'

'You're a bit defensive,' said Broadbent.

'With good reason,' snapped Isaacs. 'I grew up on the Ely estate, so I've seen your lot fit the likes of me up. Don't matter to you if I'm guilty or not. You'll just want someone to go down for it. But I'm tellin' you straight; I'm not your man.'

'I won't try to deny there've been miscarriages of justice in the past, Mr. Isaacs, but I haven't been responsible for any of them,' said Jemima. 'At the moment, we've no reason to suspect you of anything. We just want to take a look around. Are you ex-military?'

'Yeah, noticed my tat, did you? Served in Afghanistan 'til they wrote me off. Patrol got caught up with a landmine. Three dead, and me injured. Got the scars to prove it,' he said, raising his vest to reveal an angry-looking scar on the left side of his torso. 'Touch and go for a while, but it's up 'ere where it gets you,' he said, tapping his head with his forefinger. 'Still get flashbacks. Never forget it. Never. That's what I likes about this job. I can spend time out in the open and keep to meself. I'm not too good round people anymore. Don't like confined spaces. Get a bit jumpy if there's too much noise.'

The estate turned out to be larger than Jemima and Broadbent had anticipated. Alistair Williams had already told them its acreage, but for anyone born and brought up within the confines of a city, it was virtually impossible to imagine the amount of land in question.

'Ever have trouble with poachers?' asked Broadbent.

'All the time. They're a pain in the arse. Over that way's a favourite place for 'em to set their traps,' Isaacs said, pointing in the distance. 'Not many weeks when I don't come across some. Vicious things they are. After the rabbits, see. Don't stand a chance if they get caught up in 'em. They hides 'em in the rough grass. Break your ankle no problem. Never managed to catch any of the scum laying 'em, though.'

'So it's not that difficult to get onto the estate then?' asked Jemima.

'Nah, plenty of ways to get in, 'specially after dark,' said Isaacs.

'Do you spend much time up in the wood?' asked Broadbent.

'Some — I cover the whole estate at least once a week, got to check out the boundaries for damage and the like. Don't mean I check all through the wood, though. Me and Jock 'ave our little routines, but there's too much land for us to cover. There's certain things we 'ave to do, and others as and when.'

'Why did your predecessor leave?' asked Jemima.

'No idea. No one talks 'bout 'im. Just know they were desperate for a replacement, so I don't think 'e gave 'em much notice.'

'What do you think?' asked Broadbent as they left Isaacs and headed back towards the house.

'I think he's right. It'd be easy enough for anyone to get into that wood,' said Jemima. 'Apart from the wall separating it from the road, there're no security measures up there. It's not a busy road at the best of times, so there'd be plenty of opportunities to get a body out of a vehicle, but it'd be a bit of a struggle to get it over the wall. Once you're in the wood though, you're almost home and dry. There's not much chance of anyone seeing you there, even if you had a torch. It's too far away from the house and completely sheltered from the road. If you're going to dispose of a body, it's a pretty good place to do it.'

'But you'd have thought the corpses would have been buried a bit deeper,' said Broadbent.

'I suppose — it depends on what it's like up there,' said Jemima. 'The tree roots could have made it difficult.'

'So, wouldn't you look for somewhere else to bury the bodies? There's plenty of common land, and it's not exactly a popular walking route. Why would you make things hard for yourself when you could probably dig a deeper hole somewhere else, and not have to negotiate a wall?' said Broadbent.

'Good point, but I don't know the answer,' said Jemima. 'The only thing I can say with any certainty is that this was someone's preferred spot. As for their reasons, I haven't got a clue. For now, I think we need to check whether they routinely lock the main gates at night. Just because they have security gates doesn't mean they always use them. People get complacent. And it'd make things a hell of a lot easier if you could just drive in with the body.'

Chapter 8

When Jemima and Broadbent returned to the main house, they came across David Tremaine sitting on a small wooden bench beneath a wisteria-strewn pergola. He looked preoccupied but nodded a welcome with a slight dip of his head. 'Did Isaacs show you everything you needed to see?' he asked as they approached.

'Yes, thank you,' said Jemima. 'I didn't appreciate just how much land you own. It's also made us realize just how easy it is to access your estate.'

'I suppose it is if you're determined enough,' said David Tremaine. 'I've never really given it much thought. We have a reasonable amount of security in place, but most of it's focused on and around the house. The land always seemed incidental. You see, I've always lived here, and we've never had so much as a break-in, which is quite amazing come to think of it. This awful incident has highlighted that it's easy to become complacent if you've lived a relatively charmed life. It's been a wake-up call. Things are going to change from now on.'

'Is your wife not around?' asked Jemima.

'She's in bed,' he replied, as he sipped from a glass of brandy. It was apparent that he was still in shock from discovering the body. Perhaps the light in the drawing room had given his complexion a ruddy glow, but in the natural light, albeit shaded by the wisteria, he looked pale and drawn. He sat hunched forward, arms resting on his thighs. His pudgy fingers clasped loosely around a crystal glass, as he absentmindedly swirled its amber contents. 'Helen worries too much, bless her,' he continued. 'She called the doctor out to take a look at me. He said I was fine, but prescribed her a sedative. I'd already told her she needed to rest. She doesn't sleep well at the best of times. She was very shaken up after finding the body like that, such a sensitive soul. Always tries to see the good in everyone. Not a bad bone in her body. Likes to think she's the strong one, but she's not. She needs looking after.

'It's the shock of someone deliberately doing this on our land. This is our home. It's not as if someone dropped dead up there in the woods. Someone deliberately chose to dispose of a corpse on our land. And what if it was murder? It's too close for comfort. If we've had a killer wandering around, then we could be at risk. Who's to say they won't come back? You've got to find whoever's responsible and lock them up.

'The Hall has been my family home for generations. I'm ashamed to admit my ancestors were tyrants. They abused the people they should have protected, and it's that abuse which increased their wealth. But my father worked hard to make amends for what our ancestors did, and I think he went a long way towards showing that we've learned from the past and come out of it as better people. My father gave us back our dignity, and throughout my lifetime this has been a happy place. Now it feels tainted again. Have they removed the body yet?' he pressed.

'No. The forensic officers are still working up there,' said Jemima. 'It'll be a while. They'll have to take it slowly. They've got to preserve evidence and record it accurately. It's an important part of any investigation. There aren't any shortcuts. I'm afraid it's a slow hard slog.'

'Well, they can take as long as they need, if it means you find whoever's behind it,' said David Tremaine.

'When we spoke earlier, you mentioned Isaacs had only recently come to work for you?' said Jemima.

'That's right. He's been with us for about two months. Before that, we had Barton, Tony Barton. He was with us for about six years. Likeable chap, quite popular down at the Black Goat by all accounts. I believe he was the captain of their darts team. I always had the impression Barton was happy here, but then he suddenly upped and went. When it came down to it, he didn't even have the decency to come and say goodbye. Alistair said it was some family emergency, but it seemed a bit odd. I'd spoken to Barton once or twice, you see. Always like to know a bit about the people we employ, but I can't say he ever mentioned any close family. I got the impression he was on his own.'

'Has anyone approached you for references since he left?' asked Jemima.

'I wouldn't know about that. You'd have to talk to Alistair. He deals with that side of things. I just have the final say on any hiring and firing. I've got my hands full with Tremaine brewery and pubs, and of course, there's the chain of DHT hotels and restaurants.'

'I understand,' said Jemima. 'I'll ask you again, though, do you or your wife know if anyone has a grudge against you?'

'Not me personally, though it's possible someone's taken against my wife. She's not likely to tell you herself. She likes to keep a low profile, but just over four years ago she founded a women's refuge in Cardiff. It's a much-needed service. It's surprising how much domestic violence there is. She helps out there four days a week. She never said she'd had any concerns about it, but by all accounts, the men those women are running from are capable of anything.'

'Where's the refuge located?' asked Jemima.

'It's in Cyncoed.'

'Sorry, sir, I thought you were alone,' said Alistair Williams as he walked rapidly towards the pergola.

'Perfect timing, Williams,' said David Tremaine. 'The officers were asking me about Tony Barton.'

'Tony Barton?' Williams said, raising his eyebrows.

'We're just gathering information, Mr. Williams,' said Jemima.

'Well, he was our gamekeeper, left about three months ago. It was all a bit sudden. We never got to the bottom of it, and it caused a lot of problems. We found ourselves without a gamekeeper, and a good gamekeeper isn't easy to find these days. It's not as though they train them up in the schools and colleges, at least not around these parts. I ended up having to recruit a replacement through the job centre. Of course, most of the applications went straight in the bin. They just seem to apply for jobs so they can keep getting their benefits, but most of them don't want to work. Isaacs was different. He showed some aptitude, and he's not afraid to get his hands dirty. You've probably noticed he's not a people person, but that's not what the job requires. He's a bit rough around the edges, but he's made a promising start.'

'So what reason did Tony Barton give for having to leave so suddenly?' pressed Jemima.

'He didn't,' said Williams, looking skyward. 'It was all a bit vague, as I recall. He just said he had personal problems, and needed to leave immediately. He came to see me after work one day and looked quite distressed. It wasn't like him. He seemed agitated. He didn't go into specifics, and I didn't like to push him on it. He was determined he had to go and said it would be impossible for him to work out his notice. To be honest, I saw no point in arguing. He'd obviously made up his mind. So I gave him what we owed him in cash. That was the last I saw of him.'

'You told me he had family problems,' said David Tremaine.

'Did I? I can't say I remember,' said Williams, refusing to meet his employers gaze.

'Did he have any family?' asked Jemima.

'I don't know. We never spoke about personal matters,' said Williams, shrugging his shoulders.

'Do you have his last known address?' asked Jemima.

'It'll be on the computer. I'll get it for you.'

'Has anyone asked you to provide a reference for him since he's gone?' asked Broadbent.

'No,' said Williams, staring at his hands as he picked at some loose skin around a thumbnail.

'Don't you think that's odd?' asked Jemima.

'Well, now you come to mention it I suppose it is, but he could have won the lottery or something.'

'He could have done,' said Broadbent, 'but you just told us he seemed upset and said he had personal problems. That's hardly the way you'd expect someone to act if they'd just come into some money.'

'I wouldn't know,' said Williams, his tone of voice barely masking the irritability he clearly felt at them pushing him on the circumstances surrounding Tony Barton's departure. 'I'm only telling you what happened; I can't say more than that.'

'We'll need the names and contact details of everyone employed at the Hall during the last twelve months, including any contractors you may have used. We'll have to interview everyone,' said Jemima. 'Perhaps we could start with you, Mr. Williams?' Jemima turned her attention back to David Tremaine. 'And I'd appreciate it if you could tell your wife we'll need to speak to her again, perhaps later this afternoon. It'd be useful if she could compile a list of names for us, as we'll need to check them out.'

'I'm not sure that will be possible,' said David Tremaine. 'She may tell you otherwise, but as I understand it, some of these women don't use their real names.'

Chapter 9

Jemima and Broadbent followed Alistair Williams as he walked rapidly towards his office. The soles of his shoes connected with the path in a quick, efficient succession of rat-a-tats. As he walked, he made no attempt to speak to them, or even check they were still there.

Williams' office was far from impressive. It was a room you could easily mistake for a walk-in cupboard and was just as welcoming as the man himself. The space was barely large enough to accommodate the cheap-looking desk, chair and four metal filing cabinets that were shoehorned into the cramped area. What little floor space remained was cluttered with what Jemima presumed were Alistair Williams' personal items: a worn-looking briefcase, a plastic lunchbox and a pair of wellington boots. There was barely room for them to stand comfortably, and Jemima found herself wondering how the estate manager could manoeuvre his chair into a suitable position to be able to sit down in the first place.

It did not give a good impression of the way the Tremaines treated their workforce, as it was such a stark contrast to the lavish living quarters inside the Hall itself. Everything was old and shabby. Presumably, cast-offs no longer required by the Tremaines, and it was clear that little money had been spent on their estate manager's workspace. The metal filing cabinets looked old enough to be antiques. The drawer fronts were scratched and dented, while over-stuffed dusty cardboard folders were piled precariously on top. The desk was an old wooden type, its visible surface scarred by numerous scratches and white rings where hot mugs had scorched the wood. The chair was torn down the left side of the backrest, revealing a small quantity of nicotine-stained foam padding.

'You'd be better off waiting outside, while I print the list,' said Williams. 'It's like a sauna in here at the best of times. As you can see, there's nowhere for you to sit. I shouldn't be long, five minutes tops. There's a courtyard on the right. The sun won't have got there yet, so it should still be cool.'

'Do you think there could be a link with the women's refuge?' asked Broadbent, as they sat on one of the three wooden benches in the courtyard.

'It's possible,' said Jemima. 'We'll look into it, but we still need to speak to everyone on the estate, and it seems too much of a coincidence that Tony Barton suddenly upped and left. We need to follow up on him. He could have a legitimate reason for leaving like that, but he could be responsible for those bodies. After all, no one would pay much attention to a gamekeeper if they saw him up in the woods late at night. He'd have the perfect excuse for being there. He'd even be able to drive his car up there without arousing anyone's suspicions.'

'I don't know about you, but I'm getting to the stage where I can't think straight,' said Broadbent as he yawned and stretched, revealing huge sweat stains on his shirt and releasing a waft of body odour as his hands reached for the sky. 'I need something to eat. There wasn't much food in the house this morning. I only managed a piece of toast with the last scrapings of marmalade, and that was over five hours ago. I'm bloody starving. I've heard the Black Goat's got a decent lunchtime menu, and since we're up this way, it'd be a shame not to try it out.'

'Go on, then,' smiled Jemima. 'I've noticed your stomach rumbling. I could do with something to eat myself, and we can ask around about Tony Barton since he's supposed to be the captain of their darts team. At least if we do that we won't need to feel guilty about taking time out for lunch.'

Jemima had just decided to find out what was keeping Alistair Williams when the estate manager hurried into the courtyard. 'Mind if I smoke?' he asked, already in the process of lighting a cigarette.

'How long have you been the estate manager?' asked Jemima.

'Must be about fifteen years,' said Williams as he took a long drag and tilted his head upwards, slowly letting the smoke drift out of his mouth. 'Fifteen years loyal service, and they still haven't seen fit to give me a decent size office. I bet you wouldn't work in conditions like that?'

'Wouldn't be allowed to,' said Broadbent. 'They take Health and Safety seriously in public service.'

'They value their employees,' said Williams.

'It's not that,' said Broadbent. 'They just can't afford to be seen to be breaking the law. People get away with whatever they can.'

'Tell me about it,' said Williams. 'Once you work here for a while, you realize the only money the Tremaines are happy to spend is on themselves. Anyway, I've printed the list for you. The official visitors were easy enough. Most of them are regulars, but you've had a look around — anyone could have got into the woods without being seen.'

'Have you noticed any unusual activity on the estate?' asked Jemima.

'No. I spend most of my time cooped up in that bloody rabbit hutch. I'm either staring at my computer screen or on the phone. I occasionally get to go into the house, but they don't encourage it, and when I come outside it's usually to one of these benches so I can have a fag. I've got a cottage on the estate, and I cycle there and back, but I've never noticed anything odd.'

'What about your wife and daughter?' asked Jemima.

'What about them?' said Williams with a sudden edge to his voice.

'Have they ever noticed any strangers hanging about?'

'Doubt it,' said Williams. 'The wife's in a world of her own most of the time. Obsessed with those fitness DVDs of hers, Zumba or whatever the latest fad is these days. My daughter's at school during the week, and then it's either homework, or she's out with her friends. She wouldn't notice anybody or anything unless Justin bloody Bieber was standing in front of her. That girl's got her head in the clouds. You won't get any sense out of her.'

'We'll need to talk to both of them,' said Jemima.

'You'll be wasting your time,' Williams replied.

'We'll still need to speak to them,' Jemima insisted.

'Well, in that case, I'd like to be there when you talk to my daughter. I don't want her getting upset. A girl of her age shouldn't get dragged into anything like this.'

'We have procedures for dealing with children, Mr. Williams, but you're welcome to be there when we talk to her. What's your daughter's name?'

'Tess — my wife loves those Thomas Hardy books. Outdated romantic nonsense in my opinion. Tess Eustacia Williams. I ask you, what sort of name is that? Anyway, they're not there at the moment. Melanie, that's my wife, she's gone shopping with some of her friends. She should be back at about three o'clock, in time for when our daughter comes home from school. You can call around then. I'll take an hour off and be there when you arrive.'

'There's no need for that. As long as your wife's there when we speak to your daughter then it'll be fine,' said Jemima.

'Well, I think there is a need for me to be there,' replied Alistair Williams sternly.

'Do any of the staff hold a grudge against the Tremaines?' asked Broadbent.

'I wouldn't have thought so. I know I moan about the size of my office, but they're all right really. They're decent employers.'

'What about the contractors, any complaints recently?' pressed Broadbent.

'No more than usual, but they deal directly with me. They'd have nothing to do with the Tremaines. I'm sure this isn't some grudge. David Tremaine's a decent man.'

'I noticed the electronic gates when we came in,' said Jemima. 'Are they usually locked?'

'No. Those damned things are more trouble than they're worth. I always have to call someone out to fix the bloody things. These gadgets always sound so good, but you just don't realize what can go wrong with them. Since we've had them installed, there's hardly been a week when they haven't malfunctioned. The truth is, anyone can drive in here unnoticed, especially up to the wood, and we'd be none the wiser.'

Chapter 10

The air-conditioning had barely had a chance to kick in by the time Jemima and Broadbent pulled into the car park of the Black Goat. Jemima had surprised herself at how quickly she'd driven there, taking some of the bends at almost breakneck speed. Luckily there had been nothing coming in the other direction. Even Broadbent had been worried but knew better than to say anything to Jemima when she drove like that. Instead, he just gripped the edge of his seat, closed his eyes and said a silent prayer or two.

Jemima parked the car in one of the few remaining spaces. As they opened the doors of the vehicle, they were blasted by even hotter air. The entrance to the pub was only a few yards away, but in the short time it took them to get inside it was like walking through a furnace. Once inside the building, the temperature was noticeably cooler, and the shade came as a welcome relief.

'I'm surprised it's this busy,' said Broadbent as he looked around. They made their way to the bar, zigzagging through the various groups of customers. 'There's a table in the corner if you want to grab it. I'll get us some drinks and a couple of menus. What do you fancy?'

'Lemonade with ice and a slice,' said Jemima as she dropped her bag onto the empty table and flopped into a seat. She turned her face upwards to make the most of the cooler air being agitated by one of the building's large ceiling fans. But her relief was cut short when she heard a slight commotion and opened her eyes to see a heavily pregnant woman waddling towards a nearby seat.

'I thought you'd have dropped by now,' called a middle-aged woman.

'You and me both,' smiled the mother-to-be giving her abdomen an affectionate rub. 'Nine days over. Can't wait to get the little bugger out. They're going to induce me if nothing's happened by Monday. This heat's a killer, though. No matter what I do, I just can't seem to get comfortable.'

Jemima instinctively wrapped her arms across her own flat, empty, useless abdomen. She immediately envied this woman even though she knew nothing about her life, as here was someone who would soon feel the satisfaction of holding a child she had created.

It seemed there was no escaping the feeling of failure that dogged Jemima wherever she went. There were times when it was more manageable, and she could lose herself in her work. But at the moment, it was proving impossible to give this case her full attention. She knew she had to rise above it, as she needed her wits about her. She wished she'd said no when Broadbent suggested coming to the pub, but they were here now and there was nothing she could do about it without looking like a complete fuckwit.

Broadbent eventually returned with the drinks and a couple of menus tucked under his arm. 'Grab them,' he said indicating to the menus.

Jemima gave him a half-hearted smile, reached out and took the laminated menus hoping they wouldn't smell of his sweat. They sat in silence as they made their selections, and all the while Jemima kept taking sneaky looks across at the pregnant woman. Suddenly, she realized Broadbent was saying something to her. He wanted to know what she wanted to eat. She chose a chicken and bacon club with a side order of fries as it was the first thing she saw on the menu.

She fished in her purse and extracted a twenty-pound note. 'My treat,' she said, thrusting the money into his hand. Broadbent looked surprised, but didn't argue about the unexpected display of generosity, and went to order the food before she had a chance to change her mind.

'Sorry, did you say something?' Broadbent sat across from her. She hadn't even noticed his return.

'I asked if you fancied being Harry's godmother?' he said in a cheery voice.

It was the last thing Jemima had expected him to say, and she couldn't hide her surprise. She swallowed a mouthful of lemonade the wrong way, which made her cough and splutter. 'You want me to be godmother?' she asked when she eventually got her breath back.

'Don't sound so surprised. I can't think of anyone I'd want more. I'd say we've got to know each other well over the years. You and Caroline get on. She wants you to be Harry's godmother just as much as I do. You never know — if you spend a bit of time with the little man, he may make you realize what you're missing.'

'I'm flattered. Look, I think I just tipped some of this on my top. I need to go and do something about it before it stains,' Jemima said, quickly pushing her chair away from the table.

As she rushed through the door, Jemima bumped into a woman who was just coming out of the Ladies. 'Sorry,' she muttered as the heavyset woman grunted and gave her a disapproving look. Thankfully all of the cubicles were vacant, and Jemima pushed open the nearest door, locked it behind her and leaned back heavily against it. She couldn't take anymore. The breath had caught in her throat before she let out a shuddering sigh. She was shaking as she pulled down her trousers and ripped off the plaster. The newly-made wound had scabbed over, but Jemima dragged her nails over it reopening the cut. A trickle of blood ran down her leg, and she exhaled slowly, savouring the feeling it gave her.

The relief proved to be short-lived, as there was a moment of panic when Jemima suddenly thought she didn't have any more plasters. She'd have a hard time explaining why there was a bloodstain on her trouser leg, and someone would be sure to notice it. She fumbled with the zip on her bag and emptied the contents onto the floor of the cubicle. Lipstick, compact and purse clattered onto the tiles along with a couple of pens, a small notebook, scrunched up tissues and a small Elastoplast. It wasn't an ideal size, but it would have to do. She fixed it in place. It barely covered the cut, and Jemima knew it would hurt like hell when she came to pull it off later that day, but perhaps that was so much the better.

Jemima was still crying as she hurriedly packed away the contents of her bag. She'd worked so hard at controlling her emotions today, especially after the way she'd cried earlier that morning, but here she was again, still blubbing about her inability to have a child. What was Broadbent thinking of? How could she be Harry's godmother when all she wanted to do was to run off with the child and claim him as her own? But she couldn't tell Broadbent that. She couldn't tell anyone. They'd all think she was mad. And what would Caroline think if she turned them down?

She was trapped. She'd have to go back out there, accept the offer, smile and enthuse about it until lunch arrived. Then hopefully she could forget about it for a while, and they could concentrate on the case. She'd give it a few days then make her excuses. Hopefully, within that time she'd be able to come up with a believable excuse as to why she couldn't be Harry's godmother, and Broadbent would never need to know how horrified she'd been by his offer.

By the time Jemima returned to the table, the pregnant woman had gone. Their food had already arrived, and it tasted good. At first, she just picked at a few chips, but the more she ate, the more Jemima realized just how hungry she was. Broadbent ate quickly and messily, like a pack animal who didn't know when he would see food again. He was staring at the dessert menu trying to decide whether to have profiteroles or strawberry cheesecake when the landlady came to remove their empty plates.

'Could you spare a few minutes?' asked Jemima, flashing her warrant card.

'Yeah, but I haven't got long. We've got a big party booked in this evening, so there's a lot to do. What do you want?'

'Is Tony Barton one of your regulars?' asked Jemima.

'Haven't seen him for a couple of months. He used to come in here most evenings. Nice guy, a bit of a charmer, easy on the eye if you know what I mean. He was captain of our darts team, but he let us down badly. Didn't show up for the game against the Four Cocks, and worse still didn't let anyone know in advance. He hasn't been in here since. Probably just as well. We lost the match, and they're not a very forgiving lot.'

'Do you remember the date?' asked Jemima.

'Um, I don't know exactly. Hang on a minute,' she said, turning to face the bar. 'Oh, Dai, what date was the darts match against the Four Cocks?'

'You trying to be funny?' asked the short, rotund man behind the bar.

'Oh, get over yourself,' said the woman, casting her eyes to the ceiling. 'Come over here will you? These police officers want to know. He's my husband,' she said, turning back to them. 'The darts team's his baby. They're a competitive lot.'

'What're you asking about that match for?' asked Dai as he waddled over towards the table, readjusting his trousers as he went.

'We're trying to locate Tony Barton,' said Jemima. 'Your wife just told us he didn't turn up that night and hasn't been in since.'

'Aye, that's right. He cost us the match. We've had a drop in profits since Tone upped and left us. He was one of our best regulars.'

'So what was the date of the match?' pressed Broadbent.

'Let me get the diary,' said Dai. 'The old grey matter's not what it used to be.' He returned moments later with a small grubby-looking book and quickly thumbed through the pages. 'Eleventh of March,' he said.

'Do you know Tony Barton well?' asked Jemima.

'Probably better than most,' said Dai. 'I always thought he was the reliable sort. Dead competitive with the darts. He had a bit of a talent for it. He's not in any trouble, is he?'

'Not as far as we know,' said Jemima. 'We just need to speak to him.'

'Well, he works up at Llys Faen Hall. He's their Gamekeeper. I always used to joke with him. I said we should call him Mellors, from *Lady Chatterley's Lover*.'

'Are you suggesting that Tony Barton had an eye for the ladies?' asked Jemima.

'He most certainly did. I told him he could fill a book with all his chat up lines,' laughed Dai. 'Mind you, some of the things he used to come out with made me cringe. Dead corny like, but fair do's; they seemed to work for him.'

'Was there anyone, in particular, he was friendly with?' asked Jemima.

'Do you mean women, or just generally?'

'Both,' said Jemima.

'Couldn't say. He used to chat to anyone at the bar. That was his seat over there,' he said, pointing to a bar stool to the left of the counter. 'As for women, well it was all stories and innuendos. You know the sort of thing —' he turned to Broadbent. 'Typical Jack the Lad, only with him, I got the impression most of what he boasted about was true.'

'Anything in particular stick in your memory?' asked Broadbent.

'Well, he told me he was having the best of both worlds with a mother and daughter, claimed neither of them knew about the other. He said it made it all the more exciting. Playing with fire if you ask me. I think he used to take them up to that wood of his. He liked a bit of al fresco, did Tone. Said it gave things a bit of an edge. I'm a bit too old for that sort of thing myself. Don't think my back would stand it. But good on him, that's what I say. It's nice to know someone's getting a bit.'

'We've got Tony Barton's address on Alistair Williams' list, haven't we?' asked Jemima, as they walked back to the car.

'Yeah,' said Broadbent. '27a Broadley Close, Llanishen.'

'One of the flats on the estate?'

'Probably,' said Broadbent.

'Let's pay him a visit before we head back up to the Hall,' said Jemima. 'If he's not there, we'll see if we can speak to some of the neighbours.'

Chapter 11

The estate was by no means the worst one the city had to offer, but it was a known trouble spot. It was usually safe enough to walk around in daylight, but best avoided after dark. Most of the people who lived there were fine, but the area was dragged down by a handful of teenagers who were hell-bent on making everyone's life a misery. The police were always getting callouts from residents targeted for no apparent reason. It was fast becoming a training ground for younger kids, as there was no shortage of teenagers willing to teach them the ropes. They cut their teeth on bullying, moved up to petty theft, and if they were left unchecked, they moved on to car crime, dealing and housebreaking.

The local police were up against it trying to keep on top of the callouts, but even if they managed to make an arrest, the kids were bailed and back out on the streets in next to no time. It was one of the frustrations of modern life. The system didn't work. The offenders knew they could get away with it, and every time they did they gained a bit more kudos, which encouraged them to take things that little bit further. It was all about pushing the boundaries and sticking two fingers up at the establishment.

It was evident when they arrived at the address that Tony Barton wasn't at home, as the windows of his ground floor flat were boarded up. As Jemima got out of the car, she saw a young woman with a pushchair walking towards a nearby house. The sight of the pushchair made Jemima's legs feel a bit wobbly, but this was work, and she didn't want Broadbent to pick up on the fact that something was wrong, so she took a deep breath and called out to the woman.

When she returned to the car, Broadbent was dozing, and he lurched forward as Jemima slammed the driver's door. 'Nice to see you're as alert as usual,' she said.

'Sorry. Just closed my eyes for a couple of minutes, that's all,' he replied, failing to stifle a yawn.

'Well, it seems as though Barton moved out at the end of March. Didn't tell anyone where he was going. The neighbour said he'd been attacked. She didn't know where it happened but was fairly sure it wasn't on the estate. Apparently, he spent a couple of nights in the hospital. A few weeks later, she saw him loading some of his stuff into the back of his car, and that was the last she saw of him. The council were around a couple of weeks ago and emptied the flat. They're doing it up for new tenants.'

'Sounds as though someone had it in for him,' said Broadbent.

'The question is, who?' said Jemima. 'I'll drive us back out to the Hall, and you get on to the station. Find out if Barton ever reported an assault.'

'Do you think there's a link to our case?'

'Dunno, but we need to check it out,' said Jemima.

As Jemima and Broadbent pulled up at the gates of Llys Faen Hall for the second time that day, they were greeted by a different police officer. He was older than the one who had been on duty that morning and was clearly finding the heat uncomfortable. His forehead was slick with sweat, and his face looked very red.

'Has there been much activity?' asked Jemima, after they'd shown him their warrant cards.

'It's been fairly quiet. I've been expecting the press to turn up, but so far so good. It looks as though they haven't got wind of it yet. I've heard that they're just about to move the second body. Should be coming out any time now.'

'I don't envy you standing around in this heat,' said Broadbent. 'When's your relief due?'

'I've a few more hours to go yet,' said the officer. 'On the plus side, it'll do my diet good. Should sweat off a couple of pounds at this rate.'

'Here, take this water,' said Jemima, leaning over to get the bottle from the glove compartment. 'It's a bit on the warm side, but you look as though you need it. Don't want you getting dehydrated. You won't be of much use if you've passed out.'

As Jemima and Broadbent headed through the gates, they could see the vehicle which was being used to transport the second body coming slowly towards them. Once it had passed, Jemima took a right and headed up the track. When they arrived at the crime scene, they found the forensic team taking a break. They'd removed their protective clothing, which was uncomfortably hot at the best of times, and now looked more like a group of friends enjoying an afternoon in the country as opposed to a team of skilled forensic scientists at a crime scene.

A small table was laid out with refreshments, and everyone sat around on foldaway seats. Three of them including Jeanne Ennersley were playing cards, while another sat reading a magazine.

'As you can see, we weren't expecting company,' said Jeanne, as she placed her cards face down on the table. 'In our defence, we've been hard at it since first thing this morning, and we'll be here until the light goes.'

'You don't need to justify yourselves to us,' said Jemima. 'I wouldn't do your job if they paid me ten times what you guys get. How's it going?'

'Just removed number two, so we broke for a late lunch. And we also came across our first article of clothing. We found a pair of ladies knickers, not on a body, but snagged on a bush about fifty yards from here. Can't say whether it belonged to one of these corpses, but we've bagged it and sent it for testing. We'll be making a start on number three soon. How's it going with you?'

'Just doing the usual groundwork,' said Jemima. 'Come across anything interesting with the bodies?'

'Only thing we noticed was they both had something pushed into their mouths,' said Jeanne.

'What sort of thing?' asked Jemima.

'I'm not sure,' said Jeanne. 'Possibly some food. Prothero should be able to tell you more when he's carried out the post-mortem.'

Chapter 12

As Jemima and Broadbent approached the Hall, a middle-aged looking man could be seen trimming one of the bushes. He stood precariously on a stepladder which had clearly seen better days, snipped a few leaves, descended, surveyed his handiwork from various angles and climbed the steps again, clearly not satisfied with what he'd achieved.

'Must be Philip Davies,' said Broadbent.

Jemima parked the car. They walked to the front of the house and rang the bell. There was the sound of footsteps, along with David Tremaine's voice, somewhat muffled by the closed door.

'Laurence, you're just going to have to deal with it. I can't leave Helen alone at the moment. If it's that urgent, you'll have to sort out a video conference link… It's not as if it's the first time you've had to do something like that… I've got to go. There's someone at the door. I'll speak to you later.'

David Tremaine opened the door as he slipped his mobile phone into his trouser pocket.

'Problems?' asked Jemima.

'Oh, you know how it is,' he sighed. 'You leave your right-hand man in charge, and he suddenly decides to have a major wobble and not show any initiative. I've reminded him it's not the first time he's taken the helm. He's usually dependable, but every so often the pressure gets to him, and he's afraid of making a wrong decision. I suppose it explains why I'm in charge and he doesn't run a successful company of his own. Anyway, where are my manners? Come in. Have you come to speak to Helen?'

'Yes,' said Jemima.

'Do me a favour, and go easy on her,' said David Tremaine. 'She's distraught. She's in the TV lounge. I thought a bit of mindless afternoon television might help.'

The TV lounge turned out to be more like a home cinema, with a seventy-inch screen suspended on the far wall, and six leather chairs positioned for optimum viewing. The curtains were drawn to keep out the light and prevent glare. Helen Tremaine sat on one of the chairs, and despite the oppressively warm temperature she was covered in a silk throw. A cookery show was playing on the television, and when she realized it was not just her husband entering the room, she switched it off and removed the throw from her legs.

'Open the curtains, darling,' she instructed, and immediately apologized to Jemima and Broadbent. 'Please, do sit down,' she insisted.

'How are you feeling?' asked Jemima.

'I'll get over it,' said Helen Tremaine with a weak smile. 'It was just a nasty shock, that's all.'

'Well, I'm afraid it's worse than we first expected,' said Jemima. 'They've found three bodies already. Two have been removed and taken for post-mortem. There'll be a police presence on your land for some days, possibly even weeks, and as that particular area is now a crime scene, you'll not be allowed to go up there until our investigations are complete and the forensic team is happy there's nothing else to be found.'

'Three bodies?' mumbled David Tremaine, slowly shaking his head in disbelief. 'So it wasn't just a one-off. It must be murder then. Do you have any idea how long they've been there?'

'The only thing I can say is that we believe the woman you found this morning has been dead for less than a month. As for the others, I don't know at the moment.'

'Have you any idea who they are?' asked David Tremaine.

'Not yet,' said Jemima. 'Mrs. Tremaine, we'd like you to tell us about the women's refuge.'

'You don't think there's a link to the refuge, do you?' gasped Helen Tremaine.

'I've no idea. Is your involvement with this refuge well known?' asked Jemima.

'Not really,' said Helen Tremaine. 'We keep things very low key. The women we help are at risk, and we're well aware of the danger their former partners pose to them. I don't openly discuss the refuge with anyone.'

'In that case, it's unlikely these bodies have anything to do with it. But I'm not going to rule it out at this stage, and we'll have to look into it. Have any of your residents gone missing recently?' asked Jemima.

'I wouldn't know,' said Helen Tremaine. 'They just turn up, stay awhile, and we help them relocate to other parts of the country. They find it hard to trust anyone. You've got to understand, many of them have been victims of abuse for a very long time. Their confidence is at rock bottom, and they don't trust themselves to be a good judge of character. Most of the time, we don't even get to know their real names.

'We aren't able to do enough for them. We're short of space and funds, so the only thing we can provide is a short-term bolthole. It gives them a bit of breathing space for a while. We offer counselling and a safe place to stay while they're with us. We link up with a network of similar groups operating throughout the country. We try to co-ordinate our efforts. Our aim is to help these women realize they have a choice about their future. We try to help them start a new life.

'It's such a worthwhile cause, and we've had some successes. Of course, some of the women return to their husbands and partners. I've never understood why they go back. After all, they know what they're returning to, and they'll probably get punished for having left in the first place. It's disillusioning when that happens, but who am I to judge? I just wish they'd value themselves more and have the courage to start again. Have you got photographs of the dead women's faces? I'd soon be able to tell you if they stayed with us.'

'I'm afraid it's not that easy,' said Jemima. 'The bodies are bloated and discoloured. They wouldn't look like anyone you know. In your opinion, how easy would it be to abduct a woman from your refuge?'

'It couldn't happen. We've spent an absolute fortune on security, and there's always at least one member of staff on duty at all times of the day or night.'

'Who else helps out there?' asked Jemima.

'Vanessa Bolton's there most days. She's my number two. And during the nights and weekends, we have Mair Longton and Harriet Breen.'

Chapter 13

As the pathologist already had two of the bodies, and Jemima had managed to establish the first post-mortem was well under way, she decided they should go round to see if he could give them any useful information.

Post-mortems were one of the unpleasant parts of the job, definitely up there with being the first at the scene of a violent crime. Mangled corpses, severed body parts, the smell of rotting flesh, blood, urine and faeces, were all things any sane person would choose to avoid. The trouble was, when you dealt with murder and violent crimes, you rarely had a choice. Every violent death was shocking in its way, and no matter how hard you tried to desensitize yourself to the horror of what had happened, the victim always managed to evoke an emotional response in you.

Over the years, Jemima had been to enough post-mortems to know that the smell of formalin and putrefying flesh stayed with you long after you walked out of the room. It clung to your clothes, seeped through your pores and made you long for the moment you could take a hot shower and scrub the touch of death away. Nothing prepared you for the first time you saw a blade slicing through a corpse. You know it's going to happen, yet your stomach still lurches as you watch bodily fluids drip through gloved fingers as handfuls of slimy internal organs are scooped out, dropped unceremoniously into containers, weighed, dissected and shoved back inside the cadaver.

Jemima enjoyed the intellectual challenge of solving a case: gathering the evidence, sifting through the facts, applying logic to reach a reasoned conclusion. And if it wasn't for the stark reality of the situations she found herself having to deal with — psychopaths, warped minds, dead bodies, smells, filth, and human detritus — then working a murder investigation would have been quite a pleasant way to challenge her mind. But the job wasn't like a game of Cluedo. She'd never yet come across a Reverend Green in the library with the candlestick. And reality had a way of grinding you down. Fear and disgust could easily fuck with your mind, but you needed to detach yourself, lock those thoughts and emotions away and get on with the task of making the world a safer place.

Jemima was secretly in awe of pathologists. She always had been. They never had any easy or good days, just days when there were fewer corpses. She often wondered how they could maintain a professional detachment when they had to examine the body of a child or a murder victim. Of course, their findings could give a whole new perspective to a case, but no matter how you dressed things up, the process was gross. She couldn't understand why people chose it as a career path, yet plenty did, and it surprised her how many pathologists were so passionate about their work. John Prothero was no exception.

'Jemima, my dear, and Daniel,' smiled Prothero as he held his arms aloft in a welcoming gesture. He was a short man, in his late fifties, potbellied, with thin hair combed over in an abysmal attempt to hide an otherwise shiny pate. He reminded Jemima of the late actor Arthur Lowe, and she secretly lived in the hope that one day he would look up from whichever corpse he was examining and say something stupid like, 'Don't tell them your name, Pike.' But he never had, and she hadn't dared comment on his likeness to the actor in case it caused offence.

'Come in, come in, I've been expecting you,' continued Prothero. 'We've got an interesting one here. Not a run-of-the-mill sort of death. Care to take a closer look?'

'No thanks, John,' replied Jemima, shaking her head. 'I'm fine over here.' But she wasn't. She rummaged through her bag to find a packet of mints and realized to her dismay that she'd left them in the glove compartment of the car. It was a bad start. Even leaning up against the wall, she could see too much of what was going on.

The body had a greenish hue, and the corpse's tongue protruded from the mouth. Jemima put her hands in her pockets, and stared hard at her shoes, as she battled against the bile rising in her throat, spilling a hot, bitter taste onto the back of her tongue and making her cheeks tingle. She could feel her lunch churning in her stomach and hoped she wouldn't show herself up by having to rush out of the room, as she knew Broadbent wouldn't be able to resist laughing about it back at the station.

As usual, Broadbent seemed quite composed and appeared to have found something of interest on one of the ceiling tiles. He was getting to be quite predictable. Whenever they came into this room, his eyes always seemed to fix on some elusive point on the ceiling, and Jemima knew he wouldn't look away until it was time to leave.

'You coppers are all the same,' laughed Prothero. 'Never want to get your hands dirty. I haven't come across one of you yet that has the stomach for looking at the real evidence.' He worked quickly and competently, recording his findings as he spoke, and Jemima ascertained the victim was white, a natural blonde, sixty-three inches tall, with a small tattoo of a dolphin on her left buttock. She had most likely been in her early to mid-twenties.

'She's had quite a few injuries in her short life, either very accident prone or more likely a victim of abuse. There are old breaks to the left wrist and ulna, and plenty of scar tissue to her back and abdomen. It looks to me as though someone wanted to hurt her but didn't want to leave any obvious signs on display. She's looked after her teeth, though, and had some recent dental work, so with a bit of luck you should be able to identify her that way. I'll get the x-rays sorted out and send them over as soon as I can.'

'When did she die?' asked Jemima.

'At the moment, I'd say she's been dead for less than ten days. Come and take a look,' encouraged Prothero, allowing himself a wicked smile. 'There are maggots on the body, but no pupae. I'll have to do further tests to be more precise. It was murder, though. There's fresh bruising on the wrists, ankles, and forehead consistent with her having been restrained. The cause of death was asphyxiation. There're petechiae visible in the eyes, and there's bruising under her chin and on her cheeks. In fact, there's still evidence of a few of the finger-marks if you look carefully.

'The odd thing is, she's got the remains of fruit in her mouth. Pomegranate seeds, if I'm not mistaken. But I don't think she ate any of them. There're a few lodged in the oesophagus, but there's no evidence of any having entered the stomach. It looks as if the killer poured them into her mouth, and then someone clamped her jaws shut and held their hands over her mouth and nose. She wouldn't have been able to breathe.

'The poor girl was also subjected to a horrific sexual attack. There are severe internal injuries consistent with a jagged blade being forced up inside her. Come over here — if you look carefully, you can see the tearing goes all the way through the vagina, womb, and even punctured the lower intestine, so the

70

weapon must be a fair size,' he added, gesturing for her to move closer.

'I'll take your word for it,' said Jemima. 'Just photograph the injuries and send me a set of prints. So are you telling me we should be looking for a serrated knife?'

'Not necessarily,' said Prothero. 'The injuries aren't consistent with any serrated knives I've come across. Whatever's been used is not of a uniform width, but it's a flat blade. What's interesting is the tissue damage shows an odd pattern. There's tearing on two sides as though whatever it was had large, exaggerated asymmetric protrusions, but I've got no idea what it could be. I'd hazard a guess at it being a custom-made weapon. It was a ferocious attack. It'd take a lot of force to inflict injuries like these. I can guarantee that there would have been a lot of blood at the attack site.'

'Could it have been a ritualistic killing?' asked Jemima.

'That's for you to determine,' said Prothero. 'I just report on what I find, and leave the rest to you.'

'Do you think she was killed in the wood?' asked Jemima.

'I can't say for sure, but I wouldn't have thought so,' said Prothero. 'Your forensic team may find something to suggest where it happened, but it's out of my remit. As I said, I can only tell you how, not why or where. The second body's also arrived. I've taken a quick look. It's in a more advanced stage of decomposition, and Jeanne's warned me there're more to come. It's going to be a busy time. I'll let you know my findings.'

As they left the building, Jemima found herself wishing she'd kept the bottle of water she'd recently given away. She needed to rinse her mouth to get rid of the bad taste post-mortems always left behind. At least the mints were still in the glove compartment.

They headed back to the station and arrived to find the room unusually busy, as Kennedy was talking to a group of strangers. 'Ah, Huxley, Broadbent, meet the new team,' he said.

'You managed to get extra resources?' Jemima asked, raising an eyebrow in surprise.

'Uh-huh,' he nodded. 'It wasn't easy, but as we've got at least three corpses, there was no way the powers that be could refuse my request. The introductions will have to wait I'm afraid. I want a word in my office, Huxley. In the meantime make yourself useful, Broadbent, and familiarize your new colleagues with the layout of the station.'

Ray Kennedy was a traditional no-nonsense copper of the old school, who despised the slipshod attitudes of some of the younger officers, especially those who entered the force as graduates. He knew some of them were all right, but quite a few of them had a bad attitude and openly looked down their noses at less qualified officers who'd spent a damn site longer on the job, and had more common sense than they were ever likely to have.

In Kennedy's opinion, a good copper was someone who worked hard, cultivated decent contacts and did what was right, which was not necessarily something that would set you in good stead for the next promotion. As far as he was concerned, experience counted for a lot more than any worthless piece of paper saying you'd been clever enough to pass an exam. Though that was not the way the force seemed to be operating these days.

Kennedy was fanatical about getting results. He obsessively and meticulously gathered and collated evidence on all his cases, and would have been a prime candidate to write a book on good practice. He saw it as his mission in life to put criminals away, and his dedication and success rate had seen him rise through the ranks. Opinions on Ray Kennedy were divided: highly regarded by those above him, but often thought of as a pedant and stickler for irrelevancies by some of the lower ranks.

'I don't need to tell you this is going to be a high-profile case,' said Kennedy as his oversized frame flopped into the well-worn snug chair which creaked ominously under the weight. 'It looks as though we've got ourselves a serial killer, and once the press gets wind of it, they'll be milking it for all its worth. It's a first for Cardiff. We've never had a serial killer operating in this city, but I suppose it was only a matter of time. We need to find out who those women were and quick before he has a chance to kill again.

'The only thing I know for certain is that the longer this case remains active, the more pressure we'll be under. Chances are we'll find ourselves on the front page of every national newspaper whether we like it or not. So we have to make sure we're on top of this from the start. We can't afford to cut corners. No one talks to the press about this case. Everything goes through the official channels. And that goes for you as well. I don't want any pillow talk with that husband of yours. You all know the procedure. All media inquiries go through the press office.

'I expect notes to be written up and progress documented by the end of each day. No excuses. You've got to make this new team gel, Huxley. Make sure they do the job and do it right. I don't want any gung-ho coppering coming back to bite us on the arse. I've only been able to get four extra officers. I've known Sally Trent for a while. She's bright, dependable and thorough. Ashton's her sidekick, and I've heard good things about the lad. In fact, I'm surprised he hasn't made it to sergeant yet. I'm more worried about Will Sanders. By all accounts, he's not a team player. I've heard he's a bit lazy at times and has a reputation for putting it about with the women. He wouldn't have been my first choice, but he was the only other sergeant they were prepared to let me have. Keep an eye on him and rein him in if necessary. Peters has worked with him for a couple of years, but I don't know anything about him. Have you seen Prothero?'

'We've just come from there,' said Jemima. 'It wasn't a straightforward killing, and I'm wondering whether it was ritualistic. The victim had restraints around the forehead, wrist, and ankles. Pomegranate seeds were poured into her mouth, then her jaws were clamped shut and her airways blocked. She died from asphyxiation. An asymmetric blade was repeatedly pushed through the vagina, and perforated her womb and intestine.'

'Nasty. You're right. It doesn't seem like the run-of-the-mill type of killing. Search the internet and see what you can find. Have you come up with anything so far?'

'No, but the gamekeeper went missing up at Llys Faen Hall. He disappeared back in March, never to be heard from again. Neighbours say he'd taken a beating. Of course, it could be a coincidence, but we'll have to check it out,' said Jemima.

'OK, get out there and organize your team. We need to identify the victims and find the killer before he has a chance to do it again,' said Kennedy.

Chapter 14

The last thing Jemima needed at the moment was to have to babysit a new team. It would take a lot of effort to transform them into an effective unit, and in her current state of mind, the timing was lousy. She understood why Kennedy had arranged for the extra resources. She would have done the same thing in his place. The number of victims made this a high-profile and challenging case. It needed a quick result, but Jemima knew she didn't have the energy or patience to deal with these added complications right now. At least she was familiar with the way Broadbent worked, knew his strengths and weaknesses. They trusted each other. But now there were four other people to worry about. She'd have to ensure they worked well as a team, gain their respect and ensure they didn't cut corners. It was too much pressure.

She returned to the incident room to find Broadbent sat at his desk. Most of the others had gathered round him. She could just about make out the baby photos he was enthusiastically showing off. One of the men had isolated himself from the others and was slumped in Jemima's chair, mobile phone to his ear, idly doodling on a scrap of paper. He was engaged in a private conversation, his voice low and guarded. When he saw her walking towards him, he winked and grinned cheekily at her.

Jemima felt her hackles rise. 'Get out of my seat, and sort your social life out on your own time,' she snapped.

'Gotta go, speak to you later,' he said, before disconnecting the call and pocketing the phone. He stood up slowly, pushing her chair back from the desk.

'Time's moving on, so let's make a start,' shouted Jemima, trying to make herself heard above the chatter at Broadbent's desk. 'Let's have some quick introductions, so we all know who's who, and then we'll go straight into the briefing session. It's possible that this is the biggest murder investigation this force has ever seen, so we've got to hit the ground running. For anyone who doesn't know me, I'm DI Huxley, and this is the sixth murder case I've run. I expect some of you may never have worked a murder. So when you introduce yourselves, I'd like to know your background and what expertise you bring to the team.'

'DS Sally Trent,' said a large, middle-aged woman, holding up her hand. She was obviously a heavy smoker. All the signs were there, from the strong smell of cigarettes, nicotine-stained fingers on her right hand, the hacking cough, and the lines around her mouth which made her look far older than she probably was. 'I'm based over at Fairwater. I haven't got any experience with murder, but I've worked plenty of sexual assault cases. I don't have any specialist skills apart from being good with victims and their families.'

'DC Finlay Ashton,' said the only mixed-race officer in the room. At well over six foot, it was impossible not to notice him, especially as he spoke with an accent you'd expect to find at an elite private school. 'I've partnered Sally for the last eighteen months, but I've never had the privilege of working a murder case before. I'm a computer forensics graduate. There hasn't been much call for my skills so far, but if you need any technical input then I'm your man.'

Jemima suddenly noticed the man who had recently sat in her chair was now sitting on her desk. She knew he was going to be trouble, but before she could say anything he jumped off and said, 'I'm sure I don't need to introduce myself, but for the record, I'm DS Will Sanders.' He was arrogant, confident, too well-dressed for work and his aftershave was overpowering. 'I've worked many different types of enquiries, including one stint with murder. I know the ropes, I take calculated risks, get results, and I'm an asset to any team.'

'Well you won't be taking any risks on my team,' said Jemima, rather too forcefully. Will Sanders was pushing her buttons. It was time to assert her authority. 'I'm not having any maverick fucking up this investigation. Get this into your heads now: you all work for me. I take the decisions, and I'll allocate tasks. You'll report your findings to me, and I expect progress to be documented by the end of each day. And Sanders, just so we're clear, you don't get to fart without asking my permission. And never sit in my chair or on my desk again.'

'Time of the month,' muttered Sanders.

'What did you say?' demanded Jemima.

'Nothing, Marm,' said Sanders in a surly voice.

'Good. Just keep it buttoned, and do as you're told. Right, who's next?' she asked, looking at Gareth Peters.

'DC Gareth Peters,' said an officer whose eyes were the most intense shade of green Jemima had ever seen. They gave life to a face which was otherwise thin, sallow and pock-marked. His voice was almost musical, gentle and soothing like a lullaby played on a harp. A strong Welsh lilt made you want to listen carefully to what he was saying. Jemima could tell he was young, probably no more than mid-twenties. But his thin blonde hair was already receding, and she felt sorry for him having to work alongside a prick like Will Sanders. 'I worked on a murder inquiry when I was attached to the North Wales police. It was gang-related, very messy.'

'I'm sure your experience will come in useful,' said Jemima.

Broadbent completed the introductions, and then Jemima updated them on everything they knew so far.

'What's the latest body count?' asked Peters.

'Three, but they haven't finished searching the area, so it could increase,' said Broadbent.

'OK,' said Jemima. 'As we've got multiple unidentified victims, we'd better allocate names to them. We'll work through the alphabet. This one's Annie. We know she was buried at Llys Faen Hall within the last ten days, so we need to take statements from everyone who was on the estate during the last two weeks. Let's get the names up on the board. Broadbent, call them out,' ordered Jemima as she picked up a marker pen and stood in front of one of the large whiteboards that would be used to record their progress.

'We've got the owners, David and Helen Tremaine. Alistair Williams the estate manager. Peter Isaacs the gamekeeper. Philip Davies the gardener. Marie Frontenac the cook. Janet Bleasdale the housekeeper. Williams lives on the estate with his wife and daughter, Melanie and Tess Williams,' said Broadbent.

'We also have a missing gamekeeper, who may or may not have anything to do with these murders,' said Jemima. 'His name's Tony Barton, formerly of 27a Broadley Close, Llanishen. Broadbent and I went there today. The place's currently unoccupied, and a neighbour confirmed Barton had been beaten up. Barton was a regular at the Black Goat. He was also the captain of their darts team. He didn't turn up for a match on 11th March against the Four Cocks and hasn't been back to the pub since. The landlord told us Barton had been boasting about having a fling with a mother and daughter.

'Is that what led to him being attacked? Broadbent's already checked, and it seems as though Barton never reported an assault despite having spent a few nights in the hospital as a result of it. So it's safe to assume something's gone on that he doesn't want us to know about. Are this mother and daughter he was allegedly having affairs with now two of our corpses? Is this why Barton's gone to ground? We need to check him out and fast. If only to rule him out of the investigation. Sanders, I want you and Peters to check with the council to see if they have a forwarding address for Barton. It takes a while to get a council property, so you're unlikely just to walk out on one once you've got it. Talk to the neighbours. Someone may know something useful. Broadbent and I will see what we can find out tomorrow when we go back to Llys Faen Hall.

'Ashton, I want you to look into the sexual assault aspect. Compile a list of anyone with form. Whoever killed these women is likely to be experienced, but it doesn't necessarily mean we'll have a record of them. They may have stayed under the radar until now. Then again, we may get lucky and find them in the database. Widen the search to include anyone with form for rape, sexual assault or violence against women. It's an unusual MO. The killer repeatedly thrust a jagged piece of metal into Annie's vagina. It was a frenzied attack which punctured her womb and intestine. It took a lot of force. So the perpetrator has to be strong. Prothero said the weapon was large, and it's likely to have been custom-made. If this was the case, then who made it? Was it a local commission or was it ordered from a specialist?

'Annie also had a mouthful of pomegranate seeds, and some had reached her oesophagus, but there weren't any in her stomach, so she wasn't eating them. Prothero believes they were placed in her mouth during the attack. He said that marks around her nose and mouth suggest that someone held her mouth closed. So is this a sexual thing? Is it symbolic or ritualistic? What does it mean to the killer? Trent, I want you to go through the missing persons records to try to identify Annie.

'Broadbent, you contact local metalwork specialists and find out how easy it would be to obtain a weapon like this. I've got a few calls to make, and then I'll give Ashton a hand. I want everyone back here by six o'clock for an update, then we'll call it a day.'

Chapter 15

When Jemima finished her telephone calls, she found Ashton already hard at work, confidently interrogating the database, selecting relevant criteria to eliminate unlikely suspects, leaving only those known offenders who may have been responsible for the deaths of these women. It was evident that he didn't need any supervision. She felt a small sense of relief. At least there was one new member of the team she'd probably be able to trust.

'I've restricted the initial search to South Wales and Gwent,' said Ashton as Jemima perched herself on the edge of the desk. 'Sex offenders tend to be creatures of habit. They tend to operate within an area they know. Of course, there're always the exceptions. I've made the assumption that if death didn't occur in the wood, the perpetrator would want to minimize the risk of discovery when transporting the body to the burial site. Taking these factors into account, I've come up with fourteen names of known offenders at large within the last month. Given time, I'll be able to eliminate quite a lot of these, but if he's already known to us, I don't want to risk overlooking him at the start.'

By five o'clock they'd established three of the men were already dead, while another six had gone on to reoffend and were currently serving time. As each of these six had been inside for at least the last eighteen months, it ruled them out of killing Annie. That left five possible suspects. From here on in, the database wasn't going to tell them anything they needed to know. The only way of establishing whether or not any of these men were linked to the case would be by good old-fashioned police work.

Jemima dragged a chair up to Ashton's desk, and they made a start.

William Underwood was first up on their list of suspects, but his record showed he was a long shot. He was twenty-eight years of age and had been convicted seven years earlier for a series of sexual assaults on four different women. He'd targeted his victims in supermarket car parks late at night, followed them to their cars, before pinning them up against their vehicle and assaulting them.

Each of his assaults had been opportunistic. He'd been out of prison for almost six years and had had no other convictions since his release. There was no evidence to suggest a predisposition towards violence. It seemed Underwood just liked touching his victims, and unless he'd significantly changed, it was doubtful he would have made such a leap.

His records stated he had a low IQ, which made it unlikely he could have committed these murders by himself as they would have required some level of organizational skills. However, it didn't rule him out completely. Underwood could have linked up with someone who had the necessary skills to commit these murders, and who wanted a submissive partner. So they still needed to interview him.

Peter Jacobs was a real contender. He was thirty-five and had convictions for the rapes of three women, all in their early twenties. The prosecution proved Jacobs stalked each of the women before breaking into their homes to rape them. He bound and gagged his victims, and threatened them with a knife, even though he never actually used the weapon. He served time until 2007 and had no convictions since then.

Terence Lane was found guilty of exposing himself to a couple of female colleagues at an office Christmas party and subsequently raping one of them. It wasn't a cut and dried case. The women claimed he walked into their toilet area where he exposed himself. He said he'd had too much to drink, thought it was the men's bathroom and had his penis out before realizing he was in the wrong place. He had a lot of support from some of his male colleagues saying the woman who accused Terence of rape had been flirting with a lot of men throughout the evening. They reckoned she was up for sex with anyone who would have her. Lane admitted having sex with the woman later that night at the back of a nightclub but insisted it was a consensual act.

The jury was divided, but the judge agreed to take a majority verdict, and Lane was convicted ten to two in favour, though it seemed his family believed his version of events as his wife and children stood by him, and he moved back home after his release. Reading the case history, it seemed Lane was extremely unlikely to have been involved in these murders, and they agreed it wasn't worth interviewing him at this stage.

Dwayne Richardson was a particularly nasty piece of work. By the time he was thirty-seven, he had three separate convictions for rape, and the level of violence used had escalated with each attack. His latest sentence had been for seven years. He served twenty months and somehow managed to convince the prison authorities he was no longer a significant threat to the public. They transferred him to the open prison at Usk almost four years ago. Two months after his arrival, he disappeared and hadn't been seen since.

Simon Quinn was a thirty-two-year-old with two previous convictions for violence against women. He was sent down for GBH against two known sex workers, working the docks area.

He was a regular punter, known for liking things a bit rough. Most of the girls refused to go with him, but there were two who were still prepared to take his money. He attacked both women on the same night, having picked them up two hours apart.

The first woman was left with a three-inch gash on the left side of her face and was lucky not to lose the sight in her left eye. The second sex worker had multiple cuts to her palms and forearms, as she tried to defend herself against him. Luckily for her, Quinn was spotted picking her up in his car and was arrested while the attack was taking place. A drug test showed him to be high on cocaine. He served his time and was released about eighteen months ago. Since then he'd been spotted picking up girls in the area, but there were no further complaints made against him.

It was now almost six o'clock, and time to gather around the whiteboard and pool information. There was no sign of Sanders or Peters, and neither of them answered their phones.

'We'll just have to start without them,' said Jemima as she glanced impatiently at the clock on the wall. 'How did you get on with the missing persons?' she asked Trent.

'I've got four possibilities. This is the first one,' said Trent, holding up a photograph.

'She looks young,' said Jemima.

'She is. Her name's Amy Wright. She's the youngest of the four. Her mother reported her missing three weeks after her seventeenth birthday. No one had seen or heard from her for three days. Her mother initially thought Amy was staying with her boyfriend, but she later found out Amy had ended that particular relationship the day after her birthday. I've tried getting in touch with Amy's mother but there was no answer, so I've left a message on her answerphone.'

'What about the others?' asked Jemima.

'Kylie Trinket's twenty-nine. She lived alone in a house on the Glenfields Estate in Caerphilly. One of the neighbours reported her missing seven weeks ago when Kylie's dog, Kaiser, didn't stop barking all night. She said Kylie was devoted to the dog, and would never have gone away without him. I've confirmed Kylie worked at the local Asda, and their HR department says she turned up for work on the day she went missing, but no one seems to have seen or heard from her since. They described her as conscientious and reliable. They're worried about her.'

'Why does Glenfields ring a bell?' asked Jemima.

'It's where Terence Lane lives,' said Ashton.

'I don't believe in coincidences,' said Jemima. 'Put him back on the list. We need to bring Lane in for questioning. Was Kylie in a relationship with anyone?'

'The file says she was dating someone called Harry, but I don't have his details on record, and I haven't had enough time to look into it.'

'What are the names of the other two missing women?'

'Victoria Larkin and Rachel Hawley,' said Trent. 'I've got a photograph of each of them, but I haven't had time to read through their files. I've managed to request dental records for each of them, though.'

'Good work. You can pick up where you left off in the morning,' said Jemima. 'What's the news on the weapon?'

'There're not many places that would do that sort of work,' said Broadbent. 'I managed to find specialist metalworkers in Pontypridd and Cwmbran, but they both confirmed that a piece like that would be a special commission. It wouldn't come cheap, and it's not the sort of thing they'd do. There'd have to be a custom-made mould for it, and that's what would put the price up. But there're plenty of ways someone could acquire a blade like that, especially through the internet. It could have been shipped halfway round the world.'

'Sorry we're late, Gov. Got caught up with some of Tony Barton's old neighbours,' said Peters as he jogged into the room, his forehead damp with sweat.

'Why didn't you answer your phone?' asked Jemima. 'And where's Sanders?'

'My battery died, Gov. Forgot to charge it last night. Won't happen again. Sanders is parking the car. He shouldn't be long.'

'So what did you find out?' asked Jemima.

'Someone seemed to think Barton's gone to stay with his brother in Uttoxeter. He didn't leave a forwarding address, but they thought the brother's name's either Dan or Dave. He works for Bombardier in Derby; they build trains or something. I'll put a call through to Staffordshire in the morning. See if they can trace him for us.'

'Has Peters given you an update?' asked Sanders as he strolled into the room, drinking from a can of soda.

'Why is your phone off?' asked Jemima.

'Didn't want any interruptions,' said Sanders. 'I noticed a few missed calls, but as you didn't leave a message, I thought it couldn't be urgent.'

'Well in future, make sure you keep it switched on,' snapped Jemima. 'This is a fucking murder investigation. Anything could happen, and we all need to be contactable. And if you're going to be late for a briefing session, then at least have the decency to let me know. Have you contacted the council about Barton?'

'Not yet,' said Sanders.

'Well, it's too late now, they'll have gone home. Make sure you do it first thing in the morning. Let's call it a night. I want everyone back in the morning by eight. Broadbent, a word in private,' said Jemima, lowering her voice so only he could hear. 'Do yourself a favour and stick some earplugs in tonight. It'll be a long day tomorrow, and I'll need you to be firing on all cylinders. Oh, and make sure to shower and change your clothes before you turn up. I know you're finding it tough at the moment, but while you're at work, you have to maintain an acceptable level of personal hygiene.'

Within minutes, the room went from bustling to eerily quiet. Apart from the low hum of machinery, the only other noticeable sound came from the wall clock as the hand clicked out seconds like a mechanical heartbeat. Jemima was the only one left, and unlike the others didn't feel inclined to rush home. She was drained but knew that when she walked through her front door and saw Nick, she'd feel compelled to tell him she still wasn't pregnant.

Jemima knew he'd be sympathetic, but the way she felt at the moment she didn't trust herself not to break down in front of him, and his sympathy would just make things worse. From the time she'd got out of bed that morning, her emotions had yo-yoed. Now the pressure of work was off for a few hours, and she was close to breaking down again. She didn't want to come across as pathetic and needy, even though that was exactly how she felt.

Jemima needed some time to herself to clear her head and put things into perspective. So instead of heading home, she made herself a cup of green tea. As she let it brew, she closed her eyes and did her best to think happy thoughts. But it proved to be impossible. She saw shapes in the darkness but struggled to recognize what they were. Suddenly she was surrounded by dead women, their faces almost within touching distance as they screamed, howled and clawed hopelessly at the air. They were so close she could feel them pressing in on her, their arms tightening around her chest, making it impossible for her to breathe. At that moment, she jerked herself awake.

She'd only been asleep for a couple of minutes, but her heart was pounding, and she felt unsettled. She needed to calm down, so kicked off her shoes and stood in front of the evidence board. Placing her hands on her hips, she rolled her head slowly in a circular motion, horrified by the crunches and cracks rasping beneath her skin. She leaned forward, feet slightly apart, legs straight and touched her toes with her fingertips. It hadn't seemed so long ago that she could bend like this and place her palms flat on the floor. It was yet another sign the aging process was catching up with her, and she was past her prime. What if she was one of those women who had a premature menopause? If that were to happen, she might never have the chance to conceive a child. It was time to make an appointment with her doctor to discuss the options.

She silently chastised herself for being so weak. There were more pressing things to deal with at the moment. The case had to take priority. As Jemima stood up straight her eyes locked on to the photographs of the four missing women, and she immediately felt ashamed of herself. This board displayed real heartache. Families were missing loved ones. Women had been tortured then murdered, and their bodies had lain undiscovered until today. If ever Jemima needed a wake-up call to put her own problems into perspective, then this was it. There were far worse things in life than being unable to conceive a child. She had options, whereas these women didn't.

Jemima yawned and realized she couldn't fight her feelings of exhaustion any longer. Her limbs felt heavy, and she sensed the starting of a headache. She needed to go home, get something to eat, have a shower and sleep.

Chapter 16

Jemima arrived home to find Nick's car already on the drive. As she headed towards the front door, Jemima could hear the Kaiser Chiefs' 'Ruby' blaring from the deceptively small, yet incredibly powerful Bang & Olufsen sound system Nick had recently installed in the living room. Although he denied it, it was a testament to the fact that he was not as impoverished as he liked to make out.

As she opened the door, she could see steam rising from pans, and a waft of freshly cooked chicken carbonara filled the air. Nick was in the process of pouring a dressing on a salad of mixed peppers, tomatoes, and baby spinach leaves, holding his hand high in the flamboyant theatrical style she often mocked.

'Hi, Babe, just in time,' he said as he blew her a kiss. 'It'll be ready in five.'

'I'm glad you've cooked. It's been a hell of a day, and I just need to slob out and get an early night,' replied Jemima, dropping her bag on the floor as she headed over to kiss Nick.

'Sounded bad when you took the call this morning. I suppose you're going to be working long hours for the next few weeks?' asked Nick.

'Be lucky to get time off at weekends,' sighed Jemima. 'It's my biggest case so far, so we won't be having many evenings like this for a while.'

'No point in me asking if you want to come to the cricket on Saturday then?'

'Love to, but I can't.'

'In that case, I'll just take James.'

James was Nick's nine-year-old son from a previous marriage. Nick was only allowed to spend time with him when it suited his ex-wife. James lived in another part of the city with his mother, Wendy, who categorically refused to get a job. Wendy insisted she needed to be a stay-at-home mother, even though James was in a school that had a perfectly good after-school club. Whenever Nick challenged her about her reasons for not getting a part-time job, she claimed that even working a few hours a week while their son was still at school could have a detrimental effect on him for the rest of his life.

Jemima had grown to despise Wendy for the way she unashamedly bled Nick dry and had tried to point out to Nick that there was no proven scientific basis for Wendy's assertion that James would suffer if she were to go out to work. Jemima even listed off names of couples they knew where both parents worked full-time, and their children hadn't shown any signs of neglect or gone on to develop aberrant personality traits. It was an irrational argument by a woman who just didn't want to have to work for a living, and although he refused to acknowledge this as being the case, Jemima was sure Nick felt this too.

At one time, Jemima had even looked into how much child support Nick would be legally obliged to pay his ex-wife, which ended up being far less than the amount he paid into her bank account each month. But Nick was a decent man who wanted to be a good father to his son. Wendy often made it awkward for Nick to spend time with James, and Nick felt an overwhelming sense of guilt about not playing a more traditional fatherly role in James' life. To compensate for this, he paid his ex-wife an exorbitant amount of money each month to support his son. Jemima was sure that Wendy didn't spend the money on James, and used it instead to enable her to have expensive haircuts, regular manicures, and to pay the ridiculous monthly fees at a private health club.

Despite being brought up by his manipulative mother, James was a delightful child who was a joy to be with and fun to be around. Like many children his age, he seemed to take pleasure in the simplest of things. He was always happy kicking a ball around, riding a bike or climbing trees. Jemima found his exuberance for life infectious, and a perfect antidote to the darker side of life she experienced at work.

Jemima wished James was her son. He was so easy to love, with his big brown eyes, goofy teeth, a smattering of freckles and a mop of unruly brown hair. Whenever she looked at him, she thought he was the most perfect child she had ever seen. He was at that age where he hadn't reached the self-conscious stage and still enjoyed having hugs without worrying what his friends would say if they ever found out. Jemima knew things would change long before he started high school, so she made the most of every cuddle and did her best to ensure James had a good time whenever he came to visit.

That evening, Jemima failed to find the right moment to discuss things with Nick. She wanted to tell him how useless she felt but didn't know how to broach the subject. It seemed too big and far too important a matter to raise it when she was in this frame of mind.

Although the pasta smelt wonderful, she found she didn't have much of an appetite. She spent more time moving things around her plate than actually eating the food. Nick knew the routine by now — whenever Jemima worked a murder case, it always affected her in two ways; her appetite became birdlike, and her social skills became almost non-existent. By the time he'd cleared his plate, Jemima was still distractedly picking up forkfuls of spaghetti and letting the pasta drop back to the plate before she'd even opened her mouth.

Nick reached over and ruffled her hair. 'I'm gonna watch a DVD,' he said.

'Uh-huh,' she replied without looking at him.

It was almost thirty minutes later when Jemima realized she was alone at the table. As she headed out of the kitchen, she could hear shouts and explosions coming from the TV. She'd seen enough violence for one day and headed upstairs to run herself a bath, as the thought of having to stand in the shower seemed like far too much effort.

The smell from the farm was still noticeable. But after the day she'd just had, the stench of chicken manure didn't seem so important. So Jemima pulled down the blind, lit some scented candles and lay in the water until it turned cold and the skin on her fingers had puffed and wrinkled. She felt drowsy and slept fitfully that night, but at least there were no long periods of wakefulness. She drifted from one dream to another, and in the morning couldn't recall any of them.

Chapter 17

The following morning, Jemima arrived at the station at 7:45. Despite having slept through most of the night, she still felt exhausted. Even her early morning shower had failed to refresh her. She thought she might be coming down with something, as her head was fuzzy, and her throat had a thick, gritty feel to it. She'd already drunk a carton of orange juice in the hope that the vitamin C would ward off any virus she may have, but so far, she didn't feel any better.

Broadbent was already at his desk. For once he looked rested, more like the way he used to be before the reality and responsibilities of fatherhood had taken their toll, transforming him into one of the living dead. Jemima was relieved to see he'd washed his hair and was wearing a different shirt. It was bright yellow, rather baggy, and looked as though it was fresh from its packaging. Visible fold lines ran the length of the material, and the sleeves had a crumpled look about them. The choice of colour seemed a bit too informal for a murder inquiry, but Jemima was just glad she wouldn't have to put up with the smell of stale sweat for a while.

'I take it you had a good night's sleep?' she asked.

'Yep, slept in the spare room. The earplugs worked a treat. Don't know why I didn't think of it myself. Can't remember the last time I had this much energy. I feel like a new man. And such an amazing thing happened last night. Harry smiled at me. I'd only just got in, and he looked up at me with those big blue eyes of his and I swear he smiled at me.'

'Probably just wind,' said Jemima, a little too dismissively as a stab of jealousy tore through her. Seeing a look of disappointment flicker across Broadbent's face, she immediately felt churlish, but at the moment there was only so much feigned happiness and enthusiasm she could show for other people's family life.

'That's what Caro said, but I swear it was a smile. The little chap recognized me. I know I'm out at work all day, but he feels the bond between us. He knows I'm his dad. It's wonderful.'

'I'm sure it is. New shirt?' asked Jemima, in a desperate bid to stop Broadbent talking about his child.

'Yep, and before you say it, I know it's not the best colour, but I didn't have much choice. It was the only clean shirt in the house. Oh, and Prothero rang to say the second body they pulled from the woods has similar injuries to the first. She had pomegranate seeds in her mouth. He thinks she's been dead for about three months and is a similar age to Annie. He'll let us have the post-mortem findings and the x-rays of the teeth later today.'

'Has he sent anything through on Annie's teeth?' asked Jemima.

'I've got it here,' said Broadbent, pointing at a folder on his desk.

'Sanders can chase up the dentists this morning.'

The sound of idle chatter and laughter marked the arrival of Trent, Peters, and Ashton. 'Right, let's make a start,' said Jemima. 'Has anyone seen Sanders this morning?'

No one had.

'Well, we can't afford to wait. We've just had confirmation that the second body was that of a female with similar injuries to those inflicted on Annie. Her murder predates Annie's. Prothero reckons she's probably been dead for about three months. She's a similar age to Annie, and until we identify her we'll refer to her as…'

'Sorry I'm late,' shouted a red-faced Sanders, as he crashed through the door and headed towards them. 'Taxi driver jumped the lights at the North Road junction with Crown Way. Caused chaos. Three cars involved. They've had to set up a diversion until they can get the vehicles moved. Have I missed much?'

'Don't make a habit of being late, Sanders,' said Jemima. 'As I was about to say, until we've identified the second victim, we'll refer to her as "Bethany." At the very least we've got ourselves two murdered women, and it's likely that the other bodies are linked to this case. So I want Trent and Ashton to continue with their tasks from yesterday.

'Due to his proximity to Kylie Trinket, I want Terence Lane interviewed this morning. No excuses. Pull him out of work if necessary. As yet we don't have anything concrete to link her disappearance to any of these corpses, but I don't want us to be a few days into the case only to find out she's one of our women, and he's responsible for her disappearance. I also want William Underwood, Peter Jacobs, Dwayne Richardson and Simon Quinn interviewed by the end of the day. Coordinate the effort with uniform, and get them to round up the suspects.

'Broadbent and I are going back to Llys Faen Hall. We need to interview the staff, and we're going to show Helen Tremaine the photographs of the four missing women. If any of them were at the refuge, she should be able to recognize them.

'Sanders, I want you to do your best to get a match on Annie's dental records. Trent's already requested the records for the four missing women, so put some pressure on their dentists and get those records here by the end of the day. We need to identify Annie.

'Peters, I want you to continue following up on Barton. We need to establish whether he's linked to this case. I expect you both to let me know when you've completed your tasks so that I can decide where you'll be of most use. It shouldn't take either of you more than an hour or so, and by that time we may have more leads to follow up.

'Whoever's responsible for murdering these women is experienced and confident enough to dispose of their bodies. At the moment they may not know that we've found them, so that gives us a bit of an advantage, but we can't keep this under wraps for long. Someone will talk, and once the press gets hold of it, the pressure will be relentless. We've got to identify Annie and Bethany and find a link between them. Psychopaths usually build up to murder. Chances are he may already be known to us for other offences, such as sexual assault, or rape. But it doesn't necessarily mean he'll have a conviction. He's building on tried and tested methods to minimize his risk and has been at it for a while. This killer is confident, and he's got a taste for it. There were less than three months between the deaths of Annie and Bethany, and I don't want him to have a chance to do it again.

'We've got a lot of ground to cover today, so let's get to work. Keep me informed of any developments. Other than that, we'll meet back here at six o'clock to reassess the evidence.'

Chapter 18

Jemima and Broadbent arrived at Llys Faen Hall to find it looking much the same as on the previous day. Despite the earliness of the hour, the officer on guard already looked uncomfortably hot; his shirt was limp with perspiration. He informed them that the forensic team had been on site since first light, and another body had recently been removed, with a further two located.

Sprinklers sprayed tiny jets of water across the grassed areas along the approach to the Hall. It seemed the hosepipe ban didn't apply to the wealthy. The gardener was kneeling beside one of the larger flower beds, diligently removing the smallest of weeds before they had a chance to take hold and spoil the magnificent display of hardy fuchsias. Broadbent, who was a keen gardener himself, admired the pink and violet shades of the Margery Blake and the lavish petals of the Dollar Princess. Jemima shook her head in exasperation. She was beginning to doubt she knew him at all.

Janet Bleasdale escorted them to the drawing room. She bore more than a passing resemblance to the actress Wendy Craig. Janet was courteous and professional but uneasy with their presence. It wasn't an unusual reaction, as more often than not even those with nothing to hide seemed to feel awkward around the police.

Although her voice remained steady, her face and neck gave away her obvious discomfort as her pale skin flushed despite the interior of Llys Faen Hall being pleasantly cooler than the external temperature. As she spoke, she avoided making eye contact with the pair of them. Janet asked them to take a seat in the drawing room while she informed Mrs. Tremaine of their arrival. Before either Jemima or Broadbent had a chance to say anything, the woman turned on her heel and scuttled out of the room without a backward glance, shutting the door firmly behind her.

After a few moments spent idly gazing around the room, they were joined by Helen Tremaine. Jemima noticed how pale and gaunt the woman's complexion had become. The deterioration in the last twenty-four hours was remarkable. She'd made little effort to groom herself, though her hair was neatly brushed. As she walked towards them, there was a faint waft of floral perfume, but she still wore yesterday's clothes, which were slightly crumpled, having lost their crisp freshly laundered lines. Her eyes were bloodshot, as though she'd recently been crying. The redness was accentuated by dark patches of puffy skin around the eyelids. A slight tremor was noticeable to either side of her mouth as Helen Tremaine did her best to force a welcoming smile to her lips.

'I'm afraid I'm alone at the moment,' she said in a high-pitched unsteady voice. She wrung her hands as though seeking comfort from the touch, and did her best to speak slowly and clearly. Her voice cracked as she said, 'My husband's taken Corbett for a walk. He shouldn't be long. He promised to be back by ten. May I offer you some refreshment?'

'Perhaps later. I wondered whether you recognize any of these women?' asked Jemima as she produced the photographs of Amy Wright, Kylie Trinket, Rachel Hawley, and Victoria Larkin.

'Are these the women buried in the wood?' asked Helen Tremaine, taking the photographs in a trembling hand.

'No,' said Jemima. 'These women were reported missing by members of their families. As yet we've nothing to link them to the bodies.'

'I don't recognize her or her, but that's Tara Fenton,' said Helen Tremaine, holding out the photograph of Rachel Hawley, 'and that's Charlie Jones,' she added, pointing at the image of Victoria Larkin. 'They stayed at the refuge, and both went without telling us where they were going. They weren't there at the same time, though.' The little colour on Helen Tremaine's cheeks had drained away, ageing her further, and Jemima noticed tears in her eyes.

Helen Tremaine lowered her gaze and gulped loudly. 'Now, if you'll excuse me, I have to go,' she said, and without further hesitation, she rushed from the room. There was a dull thud as her shoulder collided with the door frame. It made her stagger slightly, but she kept moving and did not look back.

Jemima's phone rang as Helen Tremaine rushed from the room. It was Sanders. Just the sound of his voice repulsed her, and Jemima recoiled in disgust. She wished Kennedy hadn't told her about Sanders' reputation as a womanizer, as it had coloured her judgement. She'd formed an instant impression of him and didn't like what she'd seen. He made her skin crawl. She couldn't risk him having any direct contact with the women at the refuge. After what they'd been through, they could do without an insensitive idiot like Sanders trying it on. He could bolster his ego elsewhere.

'I've managed to ID Annie through her dental records. She's Rachel Hawley,' he said.

'Good work,' said Jemima grudgingly, wishing anyone other than Sanders had made the breakthrough. 'Actually, I was just about to ring you, because Helen Tremaine's just confirmed that Rachel Hawley stayed at the women's refuge. They knew her as Tara Fenton. So we've linked the victim, Helen Tremaine, and the refuge. Has Trent managed to locate Rachel Hawley's family yet?'

'Yes, she's given me the mother's address,' said Sanders.

'In that case, I want you and Peters to go and talk to her. Find out as much as you can about Rachel. I want to know who she was running from. Keep me updated, and tell the rest of the team that Broadbent and I will be at the refuge.'

'OK. By the way, Ashton asked me to tell you they've just brought in Terence Lane,' said Sanders. 'He's about to interview him with Trent.'

Chapter 19

To the casual observer, there were no visible indications that the refuge was anything other than a large, well-maintained family home. It looked architecturally unremarkable and blended in with the neighbouring properties, located in an area of the city where most householders were financially comfortable. The large Victorian house had been sympathetically renovated and was set back from the road behind a substantial set of electrically operated wrought iron gates, as were most of the houses. It seemed residents in this area of Cardiff valued their privacy. This part of the city was one of the few well-established residential areas where the majority of properties had remained as large family homes instead of being bought up by developers and converted into apartments.

Jemima pressed an intercom button that crackled to life. There was a short delay before a woman's voice asked who was there. Jemima explained the purpose of their visit, and they were told to hold up their warrant cards to be viewed on the monitor.

'You can call the station to verify our credentials,' said Jemima.

'That won't be necessary, Inspector. I've already spoken to Helen Tremaine, so I've been expecting you.' A buzzer sounded. There was a deep clunking sound as the gates slowly began to open. Jemima and Broadbent walked across the gravel driveway, small stones crunching beneath their shoes. The door to the refuge remained shut until the gates had fully closed behind them.

The door was eventually opened by an attractive woman who ushered them both inside. She introduced herself as Vanessa Bolton. At thirty-eight years of age, she could easily have passed for ten years younger. She was tall, with sparkling green eyes and well-cut shoulder length blonde hair that framed an attractive face.

Jemima's heart missed a beat as she noticed the swell of Vanessa Bolton's stomach. The woman looked as though she was almost full-term. Thankfully, Jemima was now more self-composed and focussed on the case, and even though it was still a blow to see another pregnant woman, it had far less of an impact on her than it would have done had she met her on the previous day.

The interior of the refuge was surprisingly cheerful. It was clean, bright and homely. There was an assortment of comfortable sofas and large plump cushions that gave a welcoming feel to the lounge area. Every piece of furniture was different in style and age, which somehow added to the charm of the room. The floor was stripped pine and the walls a combination of pale greens, yellows, and creams. A panic button was visible on the wall, as were movement sensors. A washing machine could be heard trundling away in the distance.

'Helen rang me earlier and told me about the bodies. She said you showed her photographs of two of our former residents who'd been reported missing by their families.'

'That's right,' said Jemima. 'But since our conversation with Helen Tremaine, we've discovered that the woman you knew as Tara Fenton, but whose actual name was Rachel Hawley, was one of the women buried up at Llys Faen Hall.'

'Tara!' shrieked Vanessa as her hand shot towards her mouth. She staggered slightly and slumped into a nearby chair. 'Oh my God, that's awful. Are you sure?'

'As sure as we can be, so we need to know anything you can tell us about her. Such as any friends, who she had contact with, and whether she ever felt threatened while she was here. It doesn't matter how trivial or insignificant you think something is. The smallest detail could still be helpful,' said Jemima.

'I understand, but I'm afraid there's not a lot I can tell you,' said Vanessa. 'As you can imagine, the women who come here are desperate. Sometimes they've suffered years of abuse, and I don't just mean the odd slap when an argument gets out of hand. Many of them have sustained a catalogue of severe injuries. They're often lucky to be alive. They've finally found the courage to walk out on their lives. Most of them have had to leave everything behind because they've finally come to their senses and realized it's their only chance of survival. These women don't trust anyone.

'Try to imagine what it must be like to live with someone who regularly beats, rapes, or humiliates you. Never knowing one day to the next what will set them off again. It could be as simple as the wrong song playing on the radio, their favourite shirt not being ironed, or just because they've had a bad day at work. And it's not just the physical abuse. Some of the women genuinely believe they're to blame for their partner's behaviour.

'Most of them don't have a job or an independent source of income. They were totally dependent on the men who abused them. These women were isolated. They've had little chance of social interaction, and few opportunities to raise their self-esteem. They feel ashamed, worthless and terrified. The bottom line is, if you don't have money you have very few choices. That's what perpetuates the cycle of abuse. They were trapped. Until they came to us, they couldn't see a way out. I'm sure Helen must have told you we sometimes don't even get to find out their real names. You can't blame them for being so cautious. Few of them are willing to risk revealing something which could allow their partner to find them.'

'I understand these women are scared,' said Jemima.

'I'm sure you do, but I don't think any of us can appreciate just how deeply their experiences have affected them. We can only imagine what it must have been like for them,' said Vanessa. 'Anyway, you were asking about Tara, sorry, I mean Rachel. What I can tell you is that she was no different to any of the others. She was withdrawn, and desperately wanted to start a new life somewhere else. She didn't bring any children with her. So presumably she didn't have any. She'd been with us for about four months. As far as we know, no one from her past knew where she was.

'She was doing well during the counselling sessions. Her self-confidence was growing. We were teaching her basic computing skills to make her more employable. She was bright and keen to start over again. We were in the process of sorting her out at a halfway house just outside Edinburgh. I don't know whether Helen mentioned it to you, but we're part of a nationwide scheme where we do our best to relocate the women and help them change their names and find jobs. Tara, I mean Rachel, disappeared about a week before she was due to leave, and we never saw or heard from her again.'

'Were there any signs of a struggle?' asked Broadbent.

'No. The security measures in place keep unwanted visitors out. Of course, the women are free to come and go as they please. But no one came in and abducted her, if that's what you're getting at — she left here of her own free will. Something must have happened to her after that.'

'Did she leave any possessions behind?' asked Broadbent.

'No. Most of the women only tend to have the clothes they're standing in, and they discard them shortly after they've arrived. We want to help them move on, give them a fresh start. It's a very different world, Sergeant.'

'Do you happen to know what she was wearing when she left here?'

'Jeans, trainers, and a navy jumper,' said Vanessa. 'I can give you similar items if it would help. You see, we buy in bulk to kit them out. Our only rule is the clothes must be serviceable, and not be the sort of thing that would attract attention to the women.'

'It would be useful to have a sample of the clothes. And do you by any chance remember the date she disappeared?' asked Broadbent.

'Let me look at the register… Ah, there it is,' said Vanessa as she thumbed through the pages. 'She signed out at about ten o'clock on the morning of May 23. All our residents have to sign in and out. It's one of our house rules.'

'We'll need to speak to the night wardens, and also any of the residents who were staying here at the same time as Rachel,' said Jemima.

'I'm afraid that won't be possible at the moment,' said Vanessa. 'I'm the only one here. Harriet Breen will be back on duty at seven. Mair Longton's on holiday. She's spending a week in Majorca, lucky thing. As for the residents, I think only two of them were here at the time. The turnover's quite fast with most of them. Rachel was unusual in that respect. I'll ask them if they're happy to speak with you about Rachel, but I can't force them to.'

'I'd appreciate it if you'd tell Harriet Breen that we'll call back tonight. And I'd like the names of the two residents you mentioned,' said Jemima.

'Tania Stockbridge and Faith Jones, but as I've said, I don't know whether they'll be prepared to talk to you,' said Vanessa. 'It goes against everything we stand for to force them to do something they don't feel comfortable with.'

'I understand, but you'll appreciate this is a murder inquiry and one of your residents is a victim. There are still bodies we haven't yet identified. So it's possible some, or even all of the others, have spent time at this refuge. You have to make your residents realize it's in their best interest for them to speak to us. How long do you keep your security tapes?'

'Only a week,' said Vanessa. 'Money's tight, and that's one way we keep our costs down. But I can't remember the last time we had an incident here. You've seen what it's like; it's not going to be easy for any unwanted visitors to get in. This building is possibly the safest place these women have ever lived.'

Chapter 20

Jemima and Broadbent returned to Llys Faen Hall, and Janet Bleasdale's face clouded over as she opened the door to find them standing there. A scowl of disapproval narrowed her eyes and dropped her mouth to a determined moue. Even her voice conveyed annoyance, and as her speech quickened, so her accent thickened. 'Can't you call back another time?' she snapped. 'Mrs Tremaine's in a right state, and Mr Tremaine's having to comfort her.'

'Where's Mrs Tremaine now?' asked Jemima.

'She's in bed. Not that it's any of your business,' said Janet. 'I'm worried about her. I've never seen her like this. I don't know what you said to her, but she was as pale as anything and shaking like a leaf by the time you'd finished with her.'

'It was actually you that we came to speak to,' said Jemima. 'It shouldn't take long, and then you can get back to whatever it is you're doing.'

'Why do you want to speak to me?' Janet asked, a look of surprise spreading across her face. 'I won't be able to tell you anything. I never go up to the wood.'

'That's as maybe, but as the housekeeper, you know who comes and goes. I need a list of everyone who's visited the Tremaines in the last four months,' said Jemima.

'Alistair Williams could give you that information,' said Janet. 'You don't need to trouble me with that.'

'Mr Williams is providing us with a list of official visitors,' said Jemima. 'But his list won't include any social callers.'

'The Tremaines aren't the sort of people to have many visitors,' said Janet. 'The only person who visits regularly is Mrs

Tremaine's sister-in-law, Sylvia Shackleton. Of course, Mr and Mrs Tremaine socialize a lot, but it's usually elsewhere. They attend formal dinners and that sort of thing, but thankfully they never seem that keen on having people call to the house. It makes my life a lot easier.'

'Is Sylvia Shackleton married to Mrs Tremaine's brother?' asked Jemima.

'She was. They've been divorced for many years now, but she's remained friends with Mrs Tremaine,' said Janet.

'And what about Mrs Tremaine's brother, does he ever visit?'

'I wouldn't know about that. I'm not aware he's been here since his split with Mrs Shackleton, but that's not to say he hasn't been,' said Janet. 'I don't live in, so I couldn't swear to what goes on after I've finished for the day.'

'So you're saying they could have any number of visitors in the evenings, and you wouldn't know about them?' pressed Jemima.

'Exactly,' said Janet. 'They don't talk to me about personal matters. It wouldn't be right. You'll have to ask Mr and Mrs Tremaine if you want to know about their visitors. We're all shaken up by what's happened. You don't expect that sort of thing around here. Now is that all? Only I must get on.'

'One last thing: have you seen anyone acting suspiciously around the grounds, or any strangers hanging around?'

'I haven't noticed anything, but then I wouldn't. I drive in and out each day, but whenever I'm here, I'm always in the house. It's a full-time job looking after this place. You've seen the size of it. It's hard work for just one person. Now I have to go, or else I won't have time to finish my duties.'

Jemima and Broadbent left Janet Bleasdale and headed out in search of Philip Davies, the gardener.

'Sounds a bit odd about the brother. Janet Bleasdale implied the Tremaines don't have anything to do with him. Why would you turn your back on your brother, yet keep in touch with his ex-wife?' asked Jemima.

'Families fall out all the time,' said Broadbent. 'My mum and her sister haven't spoken to each other for almost a year now. They had a stupid argument over something and nothing. Neither of them is prepared to be the first one to apologize. I tell you what, though; I bet you anything Philip Davies hasn't seen anything suspicious. He doesn't look the type to notice anything that's not firmly planted in the ground.'

Chapter 21

Philip Davies was turning over the soil in an empty bed. It was hard physical work at the best of times, but in the current temperature, it was an unenviable task. Davies was in his early fifties but looked a good deal younger than his age. His scalp was covered with thick wavy dark hair, flecked here and there with the occasional strand of grey. He wore knee-length cotton shorts and a loose fitting checked shirt, which looked old and faded. His skin was tanned, but not leathery-looking like Isaacs'. It was a fair assumption that Davies was a man who looked after himself. He looked reasonably fit. His body was lean, and his muscular limbs glistened beneath a covering of damp, dark hairs.

As they approached, Davies forced his fork into the ground and casually leaned on it, causing it to move deeper into the already aerated soil.

'Wondered when you'd get around to talking to me,' he said, taking a hand off the fork handle to extract a grubby looking piece of cloth from the pocket of his shorts so he could wipe away the sweat trickling down his forehead.

'I'm Detective Inspector Huxley, and this is Detective Sergeant Broadbent. We'd like to ask you a few questions.'

'You ask away. It's a bad business. The sooner you've found whoever's responsible, the safer the women in these parts will be. It appears that the devil is amongst us, so it's essential we remain vigilant. We need to come together now as a community and banish the evil in our midst.'

'Are you a religious man, Mr Davies?' asked Broadbent.

'Yes, I'm a Methodist minister at the local chapel. Used to be a position of respect, but these days, oh I don't know…'

'Have you noticed any strangers hanging around the estate in the last four months?' asked Jemima.

'No,' replied Davies. 'If I had, I wouldn't have waited for you to ask me. I'd have come straight to you. It upsets me to think of those poor women lying up there in that godforsaken place. Speaking as a father myself, my heart goes out to poor Alistair. It doesn't bare thinking about what could've happened.'

'What's it got to do with Alistair Williams?' asked Jemima.

'Well, it's not him exactly,' said Davies with a sly glint in his eyes. 'It's more his daughter. My youngest boy, David, he's just a bit older than Alistair's girl. They go to the same school, you see. Well, David had this silly crush on her, but I told him to stay away. I don't want him getting involved with that family, but he wanted to ask her out. You know what boys of that age are like; there's just no telling them. Anyway, nothing happened between them because the girl was already seeing someone else. Now I don't know if there's much truth to it, but my David has been brought up not to lie, and he said that one of Tess Williams' friends told him that the girl was involved with an older man. Apparently, it was common knowledge at the school that they regularly came to these woods for sexual intercourse. If you ask me, it's immoral. I mean, she's only a child.'

'Did you tell Alistair Williams about this?' asked Jemima.

'No, I did not! I thought it was best to stay out of it. I'm not one to gossip, and it's not as though I'd seen anything with my own eyes. I'm sure you've already discovered Alistair's not the most approachable of men,' said Davies. 'You've got to tread carefully with him. He does the hiring and firing around here, and he enjoys the power it gives him. Tony Barton, the previous gamekeeper, got on the wrong side of him and Alistair gave him his marching orders. It's not easy to find a decent gamekeeper these days, but that didn't matter to Alistair. He doesn't care how many years you've worked here. He believes everyone's dispensable. I like my job. I'm good at it, and I need the money. But I don't want you thinking I took the decision to keep quiet lightly, because I didn't. I asked the Lord for guidance, and he told me it was better to keep my own counsel. So that's why I didn't tell Alistair Williams about his daughter's fornicating ways.'

'Do you know who this older man is?' asked Jemima.

'Not for certain,' said Davies. 'But I did notice an over-familiarity between the girl and Tony Barton. She was always flaunting herself around the place, with far too much of her body on show. She used to follow Barton around like a little puppy, and he did nothing to discourage her, but then he wouldn't. He's always had a bit of a reputation with the women.'

'So did you ever see Tess Williams and Tony Barton together in the wood?' asked Jemima.

'No,' replied Davies. 'I don't go up there. I come in, get on with my work and go home. I only saw the way the girl acted when she was parading about round here. But after what my son told me, I wouldn't have been surprised if the older man was Tony Barton.'

'Do you think the knickers they found in the wood could belong to Tess Williams?' asked Broadbent as they headed towards the kitchen.

'Quite possibly,' said Jemima. 'We'll talk to her later. She's probably still at school at the moment. Let's have a quick word with the cook first.'

They could hear Marie Frontenac's voice long before they reached the kitchen, as she sang along enthusiastically to Westlife's 'You Raise Me Up'. It was a stark contrast to the sombre quietness of the rest of the house. The kitchen smelt wonderful. There was something baking in the oven, and a large quantity of fairy cakes and macaroons were cooling on four wire racks set out on a well-worn wooden table.

It seemed as though Marie Frontenac was a good cook. She could easily have become a model. Her long brown hair was tied back from a face which would not have looked out of place on the cover of a glossy magazine. She had expertly applied cosmetics, but Jemima could tell that even without make-up this woman was stunning. She had long slender legs, an unimaginably small waist, and large breasts, to which Broadbent's eyes were drawn.

Jemima felt uncomfortable. It was bad enough that Sanders had a reputation with the women, but this was an inappropriate and unacceptable reaction from Broadbent. There was no way she could reprimand him at the moment, so she nudged him roughly in an attempt to bring him to his senses and hoped he'd realize he was making a fool of himself. Thankfully he took the hint, reddened slightly and averted his gaze.

With a shake of her head, Jemima walked over and switched off the radio. As the music stopped, Marie's eyes snapped open. A look of embarrassment quickly swept across her.

When questioned, Marie told them she had occasionally walked in the woods, but had never realized a murderer was burying his victims there.

'It makes me realize 'ow vulnerable I 'ave been,' she said, her bottom lip quivering. 'Anything could 'ave 'appened to me. I am lucky to be alive.'

'Didn't you think it was a bit risky going to the wood by yourself?' asked Broadbent.

'Aw, I was not alone,' said Marie. 'I was with Philippe.'

'Philip Davies, the gardener?' asked Broadbent, unable to hide his surprise.

'*Oui*, 'e 'as been teaching me about zee wildflowers. It is very interesting, and 'e is very experienced.'

'And how often have you and Philip Davies gone for walks in the wood?' asked Broadbent, his tone sounding almost disapproving and fatherly.

'Almost every Tuesday for zee last four months,' said Marie. 'We both finish early on zat day, so we 'ave time to go and look for zee flowers.'

'Surely there wouldn't have been many flowers up there in the early part of the year?' said Jemima.

'Sometimes zer were. Sometimes zer were not,' said Marie dismissively.

'Did you ever see anyone else in the wood?' asked Broadbent.

'*Non*. It is always quiet. Zat is why we like it up zer. We can be alone. It is our special place.' Her eyes had a faraway look, as though while she was answering their questions, she was conjuring up images of her encounters in the wood.

'I can't believe she's seeing Philip Davies,' said Broadbent as they made their way outside. 'He's old enough to be her father, and I bet his congregation doesn't know what he's up to when he's not preaching at them from the pulpit. I just don't get it. Marie Frontenac's a beautiful woman. She could have any man she wanted. Why would she go for someone as old as him?'

'You're not jealous are you?' asked Jemima, amused by Broadbent's reaction.

'Of course I'm not. But Philip Davies is a bloody hypocrite. Giving us all that shit about how immoral Tess Williams and Tony Barton were, when all the time he's been having it away with someone young enough to be his daughter. I wonder how he squares that one with God?'

'It's none of our business,' said Jemima. 'As far as we know, Philip Davies hasn't committed any crime. But he has lied to us about not going to the wood, and he does need to tell us whether or not he saw anything suspicious when he was there. I don't blame him for trying to keep his affair secret. He's got a lot to lose if it comes out, and it may very well destroy his family. Let's face it — he's hardly likely to be open about it. He probably hoped we wouldn't find out.'

When they got outside, they saw Philip Davies had turned his attention to the grass. He was moving slowly across the main lawn on a ride-on mower. Despite the hot, dry weather, the grass looked in remarkably good condition. There were no brown patches or obvious weeds. As far as the eye could see, the blades were a soothing shade of green. There was no hint of the wilted browns and yellows you would expect to find growing on all moisture-starved ground.

Before they had a chance to approach Philip Davies, Alistair Williams intercepted them, causing them both to have to stop abruptly.

'I thought you two were coming to talk to my family yesterday?' said Williams. His body language said far more than the words he spoke, as although both hands were at his sides, they were bunched into fists. And Jemima also noticed that the man's accent had coarsened as he struggled to control his emotions.

'We were,' said Jemima.

'Well, what happened then? I took time off work, and you didn't show up. Do you realize how inconvenient that was? I'm a busy man. I can't just drop everything on a whim.'

'I'm sorry about that,' said Jemima. 'We had every intention of speaking to your wife and daughter, but something came up. We'll get around to interviewing them soon enough, but I'm not sure when it'll be.'

'That's not good enough,' snapped Williams. 'I'm getting the distinct impression you're trying to prevent me from being there when you speak to them.'

'I can assure you that isn't the case. Now if you don't mind, we need to speak to someone else,' said Jemima, and she turned to walk away.

'You have to treat people with respect, Inspector. Especially if you expect them to cooperate with you,' shouted Williams, his face reddening with anger.

Jemima spun around so quickly that the gravel beneath her feet puffed up a small cloud of dust. 'Let me make this clear to you, Mr Williams: this is a murder inquiry, and we will speak to whoever we need to, whenever we need to, and if you refuse to cooperate I will charge you with obstruction. Do you understand?'

'Yes,' hissed Williams, his hands balled into fists.

Chapter 22

'Williams has got a temper on him,' said Broadbent, as they walked towards Philip Davies.

'And he'll keep it under control, if he knows what's good for him,' muttered Jemima.

Philip Davies couldn't see them heading towards him, as the mower was moving away, but as it reached the verge and he changed direction, it was clear from the expression on his face that he wasn't going to be as keen to talk to them this time.

'Can't you see I'm busy?' he shouted, then sighed loudly in frustration.

'You haven't exactly been truthful with us, have you, Mr Davies?' asked Jemima as he brought the mower to a halt.

'I don't know what you're talking about,' he snapped.

'You've kept information from us. You failed to tell us you're a regular visitor to the wood. Marie Frontenac told us about your Tuesday visits,' said Jemima.

'Now you just be careful what you say. I don't want anyone spreading rumours about me. I've done nothing wrong,' said Davies as he switched off the engine and stepped down from the machine.

'Apart from having an affair with a girl young enough to be your daughter,' said Broadbent. 'I wonder what your family and your congregation would have to say if they knew what you've been up to?'

'Don't you threaten me, lad! And don't you judge me either. You've no idea what my life is like; I kept my marriage vows until I met Marie. I got married twenty-six years ago, and of those, only seven of them were happy ones. Apart from our belief in God, and the three children we've created together, my wife and I have nothing in common. We hardly speak to each other these days. We keep up the pretence of being man and wife, for the outside world, but we don't sleep in the same bed. The kids are not happy about the situation, but they know we don't believe in divorce. My wife can't even bear me touching her. She insists you should only have sex to create life. The last time we were intimate was when our youngest, David, was conceived, and he's fifteen years old now!

'Well, I can't live like that. I need more from a relationship. I'm grateful Marie came into my life. She's a lovely woman, and I'm lucky to have her. I thank God for her every day. I know I shouldn't have got involved with her, but she makes me feel alive, and that's what I want. I need a life, not just an existence. We've been discreet. We meet once a week, and no one else knows about it. We're not hurting anyone, so don't let any of this get out, or it'll finish me and upset my children.'

'We're not interested in spreading gossip about you, Mr Davies. We've got more important things to worry about; I just need to know if you've seen or heard anything unusual when you've been in the wood. Whatever you and Marie choose to do is none of our concern. Now, do you usually go to the same spot?' asked Jemima.

'Yes, but if the weather's bad, we stay in the car. There's a bit of a pull-in up there.'

'I need you to show us the route you take,' said Jemima.

'What, now?' asked Davies.

'Yes, you can show us on a map,' said Jemima.

Broadbent headed back to the car to retrieve an Ordnance Survey map from the glove compartment. As he returned, Broadbent could see Jemima and Davies were talking to each other, but they had already finished their conversation by the time he rejoined them. Thinking no more about it, he opened the map to reveal the wooded area.

'That's where I park the car,' said Davies, pointing to the area where the police vehicles had parked. 'We walk along this path for a few hundred yards, and then there's a bit of a clearing where we usually go. It must be about there.' His finger traced the route they took.

'That's very close to where the bodies were found,' said Jemima. 'Are you sure you've never seen or heard anything while you've been there?'

'We're not exactly interested in anyone else, Inspector. We don't get to spend much time alone, so we make the most of it. I've heard the occasional animal, but that's only to be expected, as there are foxes and badgers up there. I've noticed the ground was disturbed in a few places.'

'Where, exactly?' asked Jemima.

'Well, not far off the path. Probably around that sort of area,' said Davies, making a circling motion on the map. 'But that's down to animals, isn't it?'

Jemima and Broadbent returned to the house to speak to Marie, who confirmed everything Davies had said. She also told them she was in love with Philip Davies and begged them not to tell anyone about their affair.

'Where next?' asked Broadbent.

'I want another word with Helen Tremaine. She seems to be determined to keep things from us,' said Jemima.

'Like what?' asked Broadbent.

'The fact they have a son and daughter.'

'Really? They never mentioned it, and I don't recall seeing any photographs of them around the house.'

'Exactly, and that's not normal. So what're they hiding?' asked Jemima. 'According to Davies, the daughter must be about thirty, and the son's a couple of years younger. Apparently, they lived here until about five years ago and then moved out. Davies said he's never seen them visit their parents. But he did say that a couple of weeks ago he thought he saw them driving a car along the lane between Lisvane and Pontprennau.'

Footsteps could be heard coming down the stairs, and Helen Tremaine appeared in the hallway, closely followed by her husband.

'Still here, Inspector?' asked David Tremaine.

'I've just had a phone call from Vanessa Bolton,' said Helen Tremaine in an unnaturally high-pitched voice that failed to mask her distress and barely controlled anger. 'I thought you'd have had the courtesy to tell me about Tara.'

'As you know, when we spoke this morning we hadn't identified the body, and since then we've been busy with our inquiries,' said Jemima dismissively. 'But there are a few questions I'd like answers to.'

'Might I suggest we go into the drawing room?' said David Tremaine. 'My wife needs to sit down.'

Chapter 23

As they followed the Tremaines into the room, Jemima said, 'I explained yesterday that we need to know of any friends or family who visit you at home, and I'd like to have their names now please.'

'There's only Sylvia,' said Helen Tremaine.

'That'd be your sister-in-law, Sylvia Shackleton?' asked Jemima.

'Yes, that's right,' said David Tremaine. 'We don't socialize much at home.'

'And what about your children, Adam and Martha, do they ever visit you?'

Jemima saw what little colour there was drain from Helen Tremaine's cheeks. 'Our children? They've, they've…'

'We don't see our children anymore,' interrupted David Tremaine rather brusquely, as he reached for his wife's hand and squeezed it tenderly. 'I'm afraid it's a rather complicated situation: family stuff, nothing pertinent to your investigation. We fell out some years ago. They let us down, and we had a terrible argument. You know what it's like when tempers flare. Things get said which you can't take back. Well anyway, they left. Adam and Martha moved out, and we've had nothing to do with them since. It broke our hearts, but there's no way we'll ever be reconciled again. And before you ask, I'm not prepared to go into what happened, because quite frankly it's none of your business. Adam and Martha haven't set foot in this house for a number of years. Though I assure you, despite any differences we have with our children, I'm confident they have nothing to do with these murders. Now can we leave it at that? As you can see, this is having an adverse effect on my wife.'

'Just a few more questions,' said Jemima, unperturbed by David Tremaine's dismissive outburst. 'Do you have forwarding addresses for your children?'

'No!' bellowed David Tremaine. 'We don't know where they are, and we have no intention of ever contacting them again.'

'Why doesn't your brother visit you, Mrs. Tremaine?' asked Jemima.

'Oh really, this is getting ridiculous!' shouted David Tremaine. 'Our family life has no bearing on this investigation. We've cooperated with you every step of the way, but your questions are bordering on the impertinent. If you persist with this line of questioning, then I'll have no option but to lodge a complaint.'

'Your wife knew one of the murdered women,' said Jemima. 'The women's refuge is linked to one of the victims, as is your home. That gives me the right to find out everything I can about you, your family, your employees and anyone else you know. And until I'm satisfied that I have all the information I require, I will continue to ask questions, whether they make you feel uncomfortable or not. Now, I'd like to know why Bernard Shackleton doesn't visit you.'

'I... I don't approve of the way he treated Sylvia,' said Helen Tremaine. 'She's been a close friend of mine for many years, and I can't bring myself to forgive him.'

'What did he do?' asked Jemima.

'He was unfaithful to her,' whispered Helen Tremaine, and as she spoke Jemima noticed how David Tremaine's grip tightened on his wife's hand.

'How often does Sylvia Shackleton visit you?' asked Jemima.

'A couple of times a week. She's calling around tomorrow morning,' said Helen Tremaine.

'What did you make of that?' asked Broadbent as they walked to the car.

'They're hiding something from us,' said Jemima. 'It seems pretty extreme to cut your children and your brother out of your life. Of course, it doesn't mean it's linked to these murders, but we have to check it out.'

Chapter 24

Jemima and Broadbent arrived at Alistair Williams' cottage. As there was no doorbell, they knocked and waited. Moments later the door creaked open, and the sharp sound made Jemima wince. The hinges needed oiling, and up close it was evident the building was rundown and in need of maintenance.

Melanie Williams stared blankly at them. Satisfied they were no threat to her, she relaxed and leaned casually against the doorframe. Her eyes seemed glazed, her skin sallow and flaky. Jemima knew the woman had either been drinking or was stoned. She was so unlike her husband that it was hard to imagine them as a couple, as Alistair's neat appearance was such a contrast to this woman's almost sluttish look.

Melanie was at least forty, yet she was desperately trying to look ten years younger. It was barely 4:30 in the afternoon, yet she looked as though she was ready to go out clubbing. In contrast to her husband's crisp shirt, silk tie, and expensive suit, Melanie's clothes were gaudy and cheap. The strap of a purple lacy push-up bra was visible on her left shoulder. The remainder of the garment was on display beneath a cerise low-cut Lycra top.

Jemima found herself wondering how uncomfortable the woman must feel, given the position into which her heavy breasts were forced. A thick black plastic belt with an oversized buckle strained around her midriff, and a short purple pencil skirt moulded itself over a stomach and buttocks that lacked the firmness of youth. Her black patent sandals glittered with a variety of fake gemstones, and the heels added at least two inches to her height, which without shoes would have been about five foot nine.

'Detective Inspector Huxley and Detective Sergeant Broadbent,' said Jemima as they held out their warrant cards for inspection. 'We're investigating the recent murders, and we'd like to talk to you and your daughter. May we come in?'

'Yes,' said Melanie Williams, pouting in a similar way to Marie Frontenac. She lacked the natural beauty and grace of the cook, and as she suggestively licked her glossed lips, Jemima couldn't help but grimace.

'Nice house,' Broadbent said. It was obvious to both women that he was staring at Melanie's breasts. Jemima shot him a disapproving look, and Broadbent blushed like an unsophisticated teenager caught in the act of doing something wrong.

From a distance, the outside of the house had seemed in good repair. On closer inspection, the black gloss of the front door was peeling away to reveal a previous coat of red paint. The base of the nearest window frame was rotting and would need replacing soon. The inside of the house was far from nice. If anything, it was shabby and grim. The green carpet in the hallway was grubby and almost threadbare in places, whilst finger-marks were visible on the woodchip wallpaper.

Melanie led them into a grimy kitchen, where a stack of dirty dishes was piled in the sink. Soiled laundry was heaped on the floor, and the room smelled of stale cabbage and cigarettes.

'Sorry about the mess. You know how it is, not enough hours in the day. Can't take you into the lounge, my daughter's in there; she's doing her homework. Can I get you a drink?' she asked as she picked up a half-empty bottle of red wine and began to top up her glass.

'No, we're fine,' said Jemima. 'As I've already…'

'No surprise there, you stuck up cow,' muttered Melanie under her breath.

'This isn't a social call. We're here on official business, Mrs. Williams,' said Broadbent. 'We're trying to establish whether you or your daughter noticed anything unusual on the estate in the last few months. Any strangers hanging around, people acting oddly, or any abnormal activity up in the wood? Even a seemingly insignificant detail could be relevant to the inquiry.'

'I'm an insignificant detail,' slurred Melanie.

'I don't understand,' said Broadbent, looking puzzled.

'I'm an insignificant detail,' repeated Melanie, raising the glass to her lips and taking a large gulp of wine. 'Or at least that's what they all think. If you want to investigate a crime then look no further, 'cos I've been stabbed in the back by so many of the bastards, it's a wonder I'm still alive. They don't care about me; no one does. Thing is, I'm not a bad looking woman for my age, nothing a bit of Botox wouldn't fix. Great tits, that's what they all say about me. I saw you looking at them just now. Great fucking tits! Of course, they're always keen at first. Gis a suck and a feel, Mel, they say, and when they've sampled what's on offer, it's always the same story. It's bye-bye, Mel; your tits are great, but you're not as young as you used to be. They prefer the younger girls. Got tighter pussies see, makes them a better fuck. As for you Mel, you could get a double-decker bus up yours. But never mind eh, great tits.

'I used to be a good wife and mother. Seventeen years I've given that unfaithful bastard. Seventeen years only to find out he's been screwing around behind my back. And do you want to know how I found out? Well, I'll tell you. The bastard gave me a present. Not the usual box of chocolates or bunch of flowers. Oh no, Alistair's original, I'll say that about him. Only went and gave me Chla-fucking-mydia! Been screwing some stinking whore behind my back! Handing over our money so he could stick his dick inside her and get some disgusting disease! And when I find out, he says it proves he loves me, because he'd gone with a prostitute, and wasn't having an affair with anyone. He said it was just sex, like I should be grateful.

'So I thought, OK, two can play at that game. I'll get myself a man who appreciates me. Someone younger. Someone with a bit more stamina. Someone who's keen to please me for a change. So I had a couple of flings, and then I ended up with Tony Barton. In all the years I'd known him, he could never take his eyes off my tits. I knew he fancied me. It was obvious from just looking at his trousers. When I gave him the come-on, he couldn't believe his luck. We couldn't get enough of each other. It made me realize just what a pathetic little man Alistair is, and I mean little! So I started taking better care of myself, you know, jogging and that, to keep in shape. Well, I finally had something to look forward to, something that was just for me. It's like I was young all over again. Someone wanted me. I had a man who made me feel sexy and desirable.

'But how wrong was I? It lasted less than two months. I was out jogging when I saw them together up in the woods. Tony Barton was only fucking my bitch of a daughter as well as me. She'd just had her fifteenth birthday. Only stopped playing with Barbie dolls a couple of years ago, and there's him sticking his prick inside her. Probably feeding her the same lines he fed me. I should've been enough for him... I should've been enough,' she sobbed, slamming her wine glass down on the work surface.

'Did you confront them?' asked Jemima, touching Melanie's shoulder.

'Gerroff me, bitch! I don't need your sympathy,' she snapped, shrugging Jemima's hand away. 'No, I didn't confront them. I was too shocked. I couldn't believe what I was seeing. It was like my insides were being ripped out. I threw up. I just puked, stood there for a while and watched them fuck. I couldn't stop myself. It was like I was rooted to the spot or something. Of course, they never saw me. They were enjoying themselves too much. It was as if I didn't exist.'

'Did you confront Barton afterwards?' asked Broadbent.

'No, I never saw him again. I went and found Alistair. Told him what was going on, and he went racing up there. Well, he had to protect his little girl, didn't he? When he came back, his knuckles were bruised and bleeding. His shirt was ripped, and his suit was wrecked. Tess hasn't spoken to him since. I can't bring myself to look at either of them,' she spluttered. 'I don't have a family anymore. I've been through hell, and no one gives a damn,' and with that, Melanie picked up her almost empty wine glass, threw it at the wall then lay her head on the work surface and sobbed inconsolably.

With the noise Melanie was making, no one heard the front door open.

'What's going on?' demanded Alistair Williams as he stormed into the kitchen. His eyes narrowed as he saw Jemima and Broadbent with his wife. 'I told you not to speak to my family without me being here,' he snapped. 'You've no right to go upsetting my wife like this.'

'You hypocrite!' spat Melanie, as she jerked her head up and glared at her husband. 'They haven't upset me. You're the one who did that, by going with that stinking whore and giving me chlamydia. You're to blame for all this!'

'I'd like you to leave,' ordered Williams as he glowered at Jemima and Broadbent. 'Go on, get out!'

'What's going on?' asked a frightened voice as Tess Williams appeared in the kitchen. She was a tall, willowy girl, with many of her mother's features, though she looked older than her fifteen years. 'Have you been fighting again?' Tess asked her mother.

'Go to your room, Tess,' ordered Williams.

'You can't tell me what to do. You're nothing but a bully,' Tess countered, her chin tilted defiantly.

'I said, go to your room!' bellowed Williams.

'What're you going to do if I don't? You going to kill me, too?'

'Enough!' shouted Williams as he raised his arm to backhand his daughter.

'Oh no you don't!' shouted Broadbent. He leaped forward to grab Williams, but the older man was too quick. He swiped his daughter across the face, while simultaneously using his other arm to elbow Broadbent in the gut.

Jemima was shocked at how quickly things had gotten out of hand. Broadbent let out a low moan as he doubled over, and there was blood trickling from Tess Williams' lip. She screamed obscenities at her father, who quickly raised his arm to strike her again. Jemima kicked at Williams' left leg, and he fell to the floor, screaming in pain as she took out a set of handcuffs to restrain him.

'He's a fucking animal!' yelled Tess Williams. 'He killed Tony. I saw him do it! And I bet he killed those women too.'

Chapter 25

It took a long time for Tess Williams to calm down. After recovering from the initial shock of her father hitting her, she raved hysterically about wanting justice for Tony and was adamant her father had killed him. She screamed, shouted and stamped her feet in a full-blown temper tantrum, refusing to believe that after the confrontation she'd witnessed between her father and her lover, Barton had been hospitalized, treated and had returned home a few days later. There was no reasoning with her. She hated her father and wanted to make him suffer.

It was evident that Tess Williams desperately needed her mother's support. She was a child playing at being an adult, floundering and unable to cope with the surge of emotions. Anyone could see that she was confused, frightened and angry. Every adult in her life had let her down in one way or another, and there was no one to turn to for the support she so desperately needed.

Every so often she pleaded with her mother, but Melanie resolutely refused to acknowledge her daughter or even meet her gaze. They sat a few feet apart, but may as well have been on different continents. There was a heartbreaking moment when Tess reached out to touch her mother's arm, only for Melanie to swat her daughter's hand away in a sharp, dismissive action without even glancing at her.

Throughout the entire interview, Melanie sat with her back to Tess, looking disinterested, picking at ragged bits of skin around her fingernails. She was immune to her daughter's distress and didn't want to be there. She refused to interact with anyone in the room. The family was close to breaking point, and there was no quick fix in sight.

When Tess eventually regained her composure and was shown the underwear recovered from the wood, she confirmed they belonged to her. She explained that she'd removed her knickers to have sex with Tony Barton, and had been too traumatized by her father's violent attack on her lover to think of retrieving them at the time. She also explained she had been too scared to return to the wood, as she believed Tony's body was still up there.

They arrested Alistair Williams for assaulting his daughter and Broadbent, but instead of coming quietly he was still in a belligerent mood. It had taken two officers to wrestle him into the back of a police car. When he arrived at the station, he refused to answer any questions until a duty solicitor was present, and only spoke to say that Barton had had unlawful sex with Tess.

'Has anyone managed to locate Barton yet?' asked Kennedy.

'Peters was dealing with it this morning, but he and Sanders have gone to speak to Rachel Hawley's family. I'll try and get hold of him to find out the latest. One of Barton's neighbours said they thought he'd gone to stay with his brother in Uttoxeter.'

'We need to know if Barton is prepared to press charges against Williams,' said Kennedy. 'It's unlikely he will, as he'd have to admit to having sex with a minor. Williams is obviously a man who lets his emotions get the better of him, but I doubt he's stupid. It's odds on he'll withdraw his allegation about Barton. If he doesn't, then Barton will probably land him with an assault charge. From what you've told me, there'd be no shortage of witnesses to corroborate the extent of Barton's injuries. He was hospitalized, so Williams could be looking at

ABH at the very least. But I don't think I could predict which way the daughter will go on this.'

'She's furious,' said Jemima. 'As far as I can make out, she's refusing to believe Barton's alive. Seeing her father attack her lover like that has obviously scared her. It's probably easier for her to think her father's killed him than accept that Barton's just taken off without her. But she must have heard her mother telling us about how Barton was having an affair with her while he was seeing Tess. Surely that would put a different spin on things.'

'We'll keep Alistair Williams in a cell until the duty solicitor arrives,' said Kennedy. 'Give him time to cool down, and reflect on what he's done. Let me know the outcome when Staffordshire manage to speak to Barton. Do you think Williams could have killed those women and buried them in the wood?'

'I don't know,' said Jemima. 'I don't think we can simply rule him out. He's violent. His wife told us that he'd used prostitutes. He could have found out about Helen Tremaine's involvement with the women's refuge and seen those women as being available to use and abuse. But why risk disposing of the bodies so close to home? And how does the MO fit with him? The pomegranate seeds in the mouth? The very specific method of violence? I don't think it's his style. He's prone to violent outbursts, but he's a scrapper, not a planner. He uses his fists when his temper gets the better of him. I'd say he's too emotional to have carried out premeditated attacks.'

'What time's the briefing session?' asked Kennedy.

'Six o'clock.'

'Well don't start without me,' he ordered.

Jemima returned to the incident room to discover that Ashton was taking a statement from Tess Williams about her father's recent assault. Broadbent was busy typing up his version of events. There was no sign of Sanders or Peters. Sally Trent was engrossed in the contents of the various files that were piled on her desk.

'How'd the Terence Lane interview go?' asked Jemima.

'I'm certain he's not involved with these deaths,' said Trent. 'To tell you the truth, it was a complete waste of time bringing him in. We sent some uniforms out to pull in Peter Jacobs, and he only went and attacked one of them. Turns out he's a user, a heavy one at that. He was too off his face to recognize it was the police at his door. Thought someone was there to steal his stash. They've got him down in the cells now, charged him with assault, but his head's so messed-up I'd say he's not capable of doing anything like this.

'Simon Quinn's a no-go, as well. Only went and got himself smashed up in a car crash a couple of years ago. Both legs amputated at the knee. I bet there were a lot of women celebrating the day that happened.'

'Good work, Sally. At least we can cross those three off the list. Any update on Dwayne Richardson?'

'No, he's still missing.'

'OK. Do me a favour, and see what you can find out about a Bernard Shackleton. He's Helen Tremaine's brother. They had a falling out some years back, and the Tremaines ostracized him. It may be something and nothing, but take a look to see if he's got a record. And while you're at it, see if you can dredge anything up on Adam and Martha Tremaine. Turns out they're the estranged son and daughter that no one seems keen to talk about.'

Chapter 26

With barely an hour until the briefing session, Jemima set about writing her witness statement. She never liked this part of the job, even though it was an easy enough task. With twenty minutes to go, she signed the statement, opened the internet browser on her computer and typed in 'pomegranate'.

Within seconds, more than thirty million results became available. Jemima was amazed to find that half the planet seemed to have connections with the fruit: Afghanistan, Armenia, Bangladesh, Burma, China, Egypt, Israel, and so the list went on. Pomegranates were used in cocktails, Ayurvedic medicines, and there were even claims its juice may help prevent heart disease. The fruit also had strong symbolic connotations, and this interested Jemima more than anything else. In some cultures, the pomegranate represented fertility. To the Ancient Egyptians, it was a symbol of ambition and prosperity and was also used in the treatment of tapeworm. In Ancient Greece, Persephone, Hades, Zeus, Side, Rhea, and Hera were all linked to the pomegranate. It was also associated with Judaism, Christianity, Islam, and Hinduism.

It was pot luck as to whether any of this information was going to prove useful to the investigation. And as she didn't have any clear line of thought to follow, Jemima decided to begin with the link to Ancient Egypt, but the search didn't yield much of interest. Apart from a few names she'd never heard of, the only thing she established was that a silver vase in the shape of a pomegranate was discovered in the tomb of Tutankhamen.

Jemima changed her focus to Ancient Greece and began to research Persephone, the goddess of the harvest, queen of the underworld, daughter of Zeus and Demeter. Jemima's interest was aroused when she discovered Persephone was also known as the goddess of death, as she married her uncle, Hades. When Zeus allowed his daughter to be dragged down to the underworld by Hades, the crops failed and people became hungry as the goddess of the harvest was gone. As a result of this, Zeus ordered Hermes to bring Persephone back from the underworld. However, the Fates commanded that whoever ate or drank while they were in the underworld were forced to spend eternity there. Hades did not want to lose Persephone, so he tricked her into eating pomegranate seeds, which compelled her to return to the underworld for part of each year.

Jemima began to feel a glimmer of excitement. She knew it was far-fetched but thought she might be on to something. Was there someone out there who believed he was the reincarnation of Hades? Was he selecting vulnerable women to play the role of Persephone? It didn't explain everything, especially the use of an asymmetric blade, but at least it was a reasonable starting point. She made a note to ask Ashton to undertake a search for men with the surname Hades. She was a bit reluctant to follow up on the theory, as it seemed like a ridiculous idea, but she knew that significant breaks sometimes came from the most bizarre hypotheses.

Sanders and Peters arrived back at the station just as the six o'clock briefing session was due to begin.

'How did it go with Rachel's family?' asked Jemima.

'I hate that part of the job,' said Peters, shaking his head. 'The mother was in bits, and her youngest daughter, Karen was only just holding it together. They've had a tough time recently. Rachel's father died about six months ago, and Rachel went missing a few weeks after that. She'd got married about two years earlier to someone called Damon Hawley, and they got a place of their own.

'Rachel's mother swore Hawley was a good bloke, but it was obvious that Karen didn't think so. Not that she said anything in front of her mother. Karen offered to get us a photograph of Rachel and Damon, so I went with her. That's when she told me she knew Damon had been giving Rachel a hard time. She said Hawley was two-faced. Laid on the charm whenever he saw them, but it was a different story behind closed doors. She'd seen bruises across Rachel's back and stomach but said Rachel never actually admitted that Hawley beat her. Karen begged Rachel to leave him and come back home, but she got the impression Rachel was scared about what Hawley would do to her if she just walked out on him. She said everyone liked her sister, and that the only person who was a threat to her was Damon Hawley.'

'The mother gave us Hawley's address and told us where he works,' said Sanders as he took up the story. 'He lives on the Parklands up in Thornhill. We called around there: great looking house, decent area. Not the sort of place you'd expect to find one of the neighbours abusing his wife. We took a look at the outside of the property. It was all locked up, no one home. We tried to talk to the neighbours. Most of them were out, but we managed to speak to one elderly couple who said they'd spotted Hawley leaving home a couple of weeks ago carrying a suitcase. They thought he was probably going on holiday.'

'Have you checked with his employer?' asked Jemima.

'His boss confirmed it. The holiday was booked about a year ago, which is way before Rachel went missing. They reckon he's gone to Benidorm. Even had a postcard from him yesterday, but nothing of interest on there, just the standard "having a great time, see you soon", sort of thing. Everyone agreed it was his handwriting. We checked it against samples from paperwork at the office. It certainly looked the same. He's expected back at work the day after tomorrow. They were fairly sure he was flying to Cardiff, so we're going to check the flight manifests to establish when he's due back. We'll arrange for him to be picked up at the airport.

'Hawley works for a small firm in Caerphilly. They make ergonomically designed office furniture. He's one of two sales reps — been with the company since he left school. No one had a bad word to say about him. All male employees, so no chance to get a woman's take on him. The consensus was he's a hard worker, brings in the business, seems as if he's an ideal employee. The manager said Hawley was always well-turned-out, punctual and meticulous, possibly bordering on obsessive. They take the piss out of him when he's not there. Said he's not the sort of bloke who can take a joke. Apparently, he always has to have things just so, doesn't like anyone using his desk.

'He also said Hawley didn't tend to socialize much after work, likes to get home to his wife. No one there had ever met Rachel, but Hawley gave the impression they were a devoted couple. They didn't know she'd gone missing. It came as a complete surprise when we explained why we were there, so it seems as though Damon Hawley is good at keeping up a front.'

'I want you both to go back to the Parklands by 6:30 tomorrow morning. I'll meet you there, so don't think of being late,' said Jemima. 'It's not going to make us popular, but you need to talk to the rest of the neighbours before they go to work. See if you can gather more background information on Hawley. Someone may have seen or heard something. We've got enough grounds for a search warrant, so I want forensics to give the house a thorough going-over, and I'll supervise that. These women might have been killed there. Has Prothero given us anything on the other victims?' she asked, turning her attention to Ashton.

'He's just sent through the report on Bethany, along with her dental x-rays. The bad news is they don't match the records we've received for Victoria Larkin or Kylie Trinket. There are no distinguishing marks on the body, but it's the same MO. He's made a start on Carla. He's hopeful about letting us have his findings by lunchtime tomorrow.'

'Where are we with Amy Wright's dental records?' asked Jemima.

'Still haven't been able to contact her dentist. I sent someone around there, but the building had been demolished. I haven't been able to contact her family either. I've spoken to someone at the Health Authority, and they confirmed the dental practice shut down about eighteen months ago when the dentist retired. The majority of patients registered with other practices, but they've got no record of Amy having done so. I also asked uniform to speak to the neighbours to establish if anyone knew where Amy's family were, but there was no luck there either. They got back to me saying the house looked deserted and none of the neighbours were talking.'

'We need to extend the search area on the missing persons. So far, we've got a link to the women's refuge. If any of the other victims spent time there, they might not necessarily have lived locally. If I wanted to disappear, I know I wouldn't want to hide out close to home. I'd only do that if I didn't have a choice in the matter, otherwise I'd want to put as much distance between myself and whoever I was trying to get away from.'

'I'm already on it,' said Ashton. 'I've been thinking along the same lines myself, so I expanded the search criteria and came up with another six missing women. Holly Vetch was twenty-two when she went missing from her home in Abergavenny about eighteen months ago. Her sister alerted the police and insisted her disappearance had something to do with Holly's husband, Sean Vetch. She claimed Vetch was violent towards his wife. Holly still hasn't been found, and there was nothing to link him to his wife's disappearance. There was also a note on file to say Vetch died in a motorcycle accident five weeks after his wife was reported missing.

'Annabel Jackson was twenty-eight when she disappeared from her home in Tredegar nine months ago. She had three kids, all in primary school. Dropped them off there one day, and never picked them up. Her partner Ciaran Murphy confirmed they lived together at the family home, and he swore blind he didn't know what had happened to Annabel. Said she had no reason to take off like that. As far as he was concerned, they had a happy relationship. He was adamant Annabel would never leave the kids. Friends and family all backed up his story.

'I haven't had time to look at the information on the others. They're Jasmine Young, aged twenty, missing from Bristol. Kym Grant, aged twenty-one, from Swansea. Lara Knight, aged twenty-five, from Pontardawe, and Abbie Hope, aged seventeen, from Bridgend.'

'Have you got photographs of each of them?' asked Jemima.

'Yes, but they're not printed out yet,' said Ashton.

'Well, sort it out immediately after the briefing session, and I'll show them to Harriet Breen when I go to the refuge this evening. Oh, and good work, Ashton,' Jemima added. Ashton was proving himself to be someone she could work with, and Jemima was thinking of asking Kennedy to offer him a permanent posting on the team. 'Another thing we need to take account of is that Rachel Hawley was lucky enough to have a family, but some of these women didn't have people who cared about them,' she continued. 'If that's the case, it's unlikely their abuser will have reported them missing. These men aren't the sort of people who want to draw attention to whatever's been going on behind closed doors. They've got a lot to lose if their secret gets out, so they'd probably choose to track down the women themselves. If the victims fall into this category, then there's not a lot we can do unless we're able to identify them through dental records or we already have their DNA on file. Did you turn up anything on Bernard Shackleton?'

'He served eight years for rape — targeted single women through a dating agency, where he registered under the alias Adam Tremaine,' said Trent.

'That's his nephew's name,' said Jemima.

'Exactly,' said Trent. 'Explains why Helen Tremaine disowned him.'

'What's his MO?'

'Well, it's not straightforward rape,' said Trent. 'He selected women in our victims' age range and had a particular method of foreplay. Dressed them in some funny looking nightshirt, tied them up, put a rope around their necks. Pulled the nightshirt up, posed them so he could take photographs. When he was happy with the souvenir shots, he'd go ahead and rape them. He served time at Parkhurst without incident. Was let out on early release five years ago and spent the next two years attending sessions with his parole officer, who didn't have a bad word to say about him. Reckons Shackleton's one of her success stories. Convinced he's a reformed character and no danger to anyone.

'Shackleton's kept himself busy since he got out. It seems he learned how to cook when he was inside. When he was released, he used an inheritance to open up a restaurant down on the Gower. He's doing very well for himself by all accounts. Got awarded a Michelin Star about a year ago, and can't keep up with the demand. He's taken on three full-time staff, and people are booking tables a few months in advance.'

'He could easily get over here from the Gower,' said Jemima. 'Given his history, previous MO and knowledge of the dump site, we need to question him. Arrange for Swansea to pick him up. Broadbent and I'll go and interview him in the morning. I'd like you to come to the women's refuge with me, straight after the briefing,' she said to Trent.

'Did Staffordshire get in contact with Barton?' asked Kennedy.

'I haven't heard back from them yet, but we've been out for most of the day,' said Peters.

'Well, check your answering machine,' said Kennedy, 'and give them another call if they haven't left a message. We've got Alistair Williams in custody. He attacked both his daughter and Broadbent this afternoon. It seems as though Williams gave Barton a pasting when he discovered him having sex with Williams' underage daughter. Sanders, I want you to sit in on the interview with me. I want to find out if Williams has anything to do with these murders.'

Chapter 27

Jemima arrived at the women's refuge for the second time that day. She pressed the buzzer as they held their ID's up to the monitor, and once the woman inside the refuge was satisfied, she operated the mechanism to open the gates. Jemima and Trent walked towards the house and, eventually, the front door opened.

Harriet Breen was a squat, muscular looking woman with short grey hair and thin lips. She looked harassed and didn't seem particularly pleased to see them.

'I've been expecting you. Hurry up and get inside so I can lock the door. You've called at a bad time. One of the women's a bit spooked. Reckons she saw her ex in town this afternoon. Now she's afraid he may have spotted her, and everyone's waiting for something to kick off.'

'Has there been any sign of someone hanging around outside?' asked Jemima.

'No, but most of these women have spent so much time being scared that they jump when they see their reflection in a mirror. They're safe enough here, though. Not that they'll take my word for it. I keep telling them, no one's going to get in, especially on my watch,' said Harriet.

'Let's hope your confidence isn't misplaced,' said Jemima. 'I take it you know that the woman who went by the name of Tara Fenton was murdered about a fortnight ago and buried in Helen Tremaine's wood?'

'Yes, Vanessa told me when she did the handover. I can't believe it. It's awful. I'll help in any way I can. I liked Tara, but unless you've proof someone's targeting these women, then I don't want you scaring them further by making them think they're more at risk than they are. They've got enough on their plates as it is. Some of them may put on a bit of a front, but believe me it's just their way of getting through the day. Most of them are fragile. Something like this could send them over the edge. So I'm asking you to think about what you say to them. Just show some sensitivity, that's all.'

'We've no intention of scaring anyone,' Jemima assured her, 'but we need to find out as much as we can about Tara. We'll need to speak with Tania Stockbridge, Faith Jones and any of the other women who knew her.'

'You can't talk to Faith tonight,' said Harriet. 'She's the one who thought she saw her husband. You'll not get any sense out of her at the moment, but Tania will probably talk to you. She and Tara were friends. Well, as close as any of them get to friendship in here, though I doubt they'd have shared much personal information. Conversations around here tend to be quite superficial. Everyone's scared of revealing something that could lead to them being forced to return home. They all want new lives and have too much to lose if something goes wrong. Everyone's wrapped up in their own problems. It's an unwritten rule that no one pries into someone else's business. If anyone chooses to reveal something about themselves then it's fair enough, but no one pushes for personal details. As you can imagine, there's no such thing as real trust in a place like this.'

'So what do you know about Tara?' asked Jemima.

'Not a lot. She was in her early twenties. I got the impression she was either married or engaged. She never said, but I noticed tan lines on her ring finger. She was quiet, and a bit more together than some of the others. She'd taken some severe beatings. I saw some nasty looking scars on her back, but they weren't fresh ones. I never heard her say anything about who she was running from. Oh, and she had a thing about dolphins, not that it'd be relevant to your investigation. Only we've got some jigsaw puzzles, and one of them is of dolphins. She loved that puzzle. For some reason, she seemed to know an awful lot about the creatures. Couldn't shut her up once she started talking about them.

'She was due to leave us soon after she disappeared. Vanessa had sorted out a place for her. Somewhere up in Scotland. I was surprised when Tara didn't turn up the night she went missing. It wasn't like her. I always thought she had her head screwed on. She seemed determined to make a fresh start. There was no hint she was planning to go off by herself. She was counting down the days to her move. You worry about some of them, you know, how they're going to cope after they leave here. But I didn't worry about her. I just thought she'd do all right for herself.'

'Did she ever mention that she thought her husband had tracked her down?' asked Trent.

'Not to my knowledge,' said Harriet, shaking her head. 'I hadn't heard her speak about anyone from her past.

'Hey Tania, these are the police officers I was telling you about,' said Harriet as a woman walked into the room.

Tania Stockbridge had the appearance of a woman who had suffered a lot of hardship during her life. She was overly thin, to the point of looking emaciated. Her skin was preternaturally pale, and her eyes looked too big for her face. Her black hair was cut in a ragged bob and hung limply over sunken cheeks.

As she walked cautiously towards them, a small girl of probably no more than three years of age trailed closely behind her. The child had a healthier complexion than the mother, but her rheumy eyes, snotty nose, and food-stained mouth made the girl an unappealing sight. Even Jemima didn't feel the usual lurch in her stomach that she seemed to experience whenever she was near a young child. One of the girl's chubby arms clung tightly to a grubby-looking pink teddy bear, which was missing an eye. The child looked tired as she sucked fervently on two of the fingers of her free hand.

'Harriet told me about Tara,' said Tania, perching herself on the arm of a chair. She pulled her daughter protectively towards her and absentmindedly began to twirl strands of the child's hair around her fingers as she continued to speak. 'Tara was sound. She used to tell my Daisy stories about the dolphins. I told her she'd make a great mum. Was it her bloke who got to her?'

'We don't know,' said Jemima. 'We're trying to find out as much about her last days as we can. Was she worried her husband would find her?'

'No more than the rest of us, but she never got spooked though. She was just excited about startin' over again,' said Tania.

'Where did she go on her last day here?'

'Just out for a walk, as far as I know,' said Tania. 'She always went out at least once a day — said she couldn't stand being cooped up all the time. She was careful though. Stuck to places where there were lots of people, regularly changed her route and the time she went out.'

'Wasn't she worried someone would recognize her?' asked Trent.

'Nah, if you saw her when she was out, you'd most likely think she was a boy. She wore real baggy clothes, dark glasses, and put her hair up under a baseball cap.'

'Did Tara get along with everyone here?' asked Jemima.

'Yeah, but she used to spend more time with me and my Daisy. She used to play with her when I'd go and have a bath. Daisy took a right shine to her. And Tara always seemed to get on well with Katie, but she only helps out on Fridays.'

'Katie who?' asked Jemima.

'I don't know her other name. I think she's a friend of Vanessa's. I've never really had much to do with her. Think she's a bit up herself. I got the impression she don't think much of me and my Daisy.'

'Was Katie here the day Tara went missing?' asked Jemima.

'Don't think so. Like I said, she's only here once a week. Look, I'd better get this one to bed. She can be a right little cow when she gets overtired,' she said, gently ruffling her daughter's hair. When Tania got up to leave, Daisy began to grizzle, and in a matter of seconds, the child's moans had escalated into full-blown screams of protest.

'I knew this would happen,' sighed Harriet as she strode back into the room. 'There's always hell to pay when that kid gets overtired.'

'Who's Katie?' asked Jemima.

'Can't say I know anyone called Katie,' said Harriet, shaking her head.

'Tania just told us someone named Katie helps out here on Fridays.'

'That's news to me. I've never seen her,' said Harriet.

'She said she's a friend of Vanessa's,' prompted Jemima.

'Well, you'd better ask Vanessa, then. As I said, I've never seen any Katie,' said Harriet.

'One more thing: have any of these women ever stayed here?' asked Jemima, as she spread out the photographs Ashton had recently printed off.

'Kirsty,' croaked Harriet as she picked up the photo of Lara Knight. 'Kirsty Ward, she just upped and went about six months ago. She's not dead as well?'

'Not as far as we know, but she was reported as missing,' said Jemima.

Chapter 28

After leaving the women's refuge, Jemima dropped Trent off and went back to the station. It was almost eight o'clock, but there was still a chance Kennedy wouldn't have left for the night. As she walked past his door, she noticed the light was on, so she knocked and entered his office. Paperwork covered his desk. He looked up from his keyboard and stopped typing.

'Could do with a secretary,' he said, gesturing at the chaotic state of his office. 'How'd it go at the refuge?'

'It seems Rachel Hawley was due to leave. They'd found her a place in Scotland, and she was keen to go. On the day Rachel went missing, she'd gone out for a walk and never came back. One of the other women said that whenever Rachel ventured outside, you'd be hard-pushed to know whether she was male or female. She always wore baggy clothes, dark glasses, and had her hair up under a baseball cap. So it makes me think she was taken by someone she knew.

'I was given the name of another volunteer, someone named Katie. As far as I can make out, she's probably a friend of Vanessa Bolton. She helps out at the refuge on Fridays. Harriet Breen's one of the night staff and she'd never heard of her. Helen Tremaine hasn't mentioned her either. So I'll follow it up with Vanessa when I get back from Swansea tomorrow. How did Williams' interview go?'

'Quite a transformation: it seems that spending time in the holding cell mellowed him. He answered all the questions we put to him and offered to apologize to Broadbent. He's scared of being prosecuted, afraid he'll lose his job,' said Kennedy.

'So he should be. But you're still taking it to the CPS?' asked Jemima.

Kennedy nodded. 'He can't go around assaulting people whenever he feels like it, and his daughter's adamant she wants him prosecuted. It'll be their call as to whether they think there's a case. Staffordshire came back and said they'd spoken with Tony Barton. He insists no assault took place. So we won't be bringing a case against Williams on that score. When we informed Williams he wouldn't be charged with the assault on Barton, he indicated on a map where he found him with his daughter. It tallies with what the wife and daughter told us. Williams said he hadn't seen or heard from Barton since that night, and he was certain his daughter hadn't either, as they've virtually got the girl under house arrest. He and his wife are escorting her to and from school. They've confiscated her mobile phone and are only allowing her supervised internet access. It's no wonder that the girl hates her father.'

'Do you think he's responsible for these murders?' asked Jemima.

'I wouldn't have thought so. Apart from having easy access to the burial site, there's nothing to link him to the deaths. They were planned. Ritualistic. As you've already said, he's more fists first, think later, and he's got enough problems at home. He may have hit out today, but he's a victim himself.'

'What do you mean?' asked Jemima.

'You've seen for yourself that his wife likes a drink. Well, apparently it's become more of a problem since Alistair gave her chlamydia. He told us that lately he often returns home from work to find her drunk, and she sometimes becomes physically abusive towards him. He showed us his torso. It's a patchwork of bruises. Apparently, she attacked him with a frying pan last week, though he doesn't want to make a complaint against her. I think he still loves her and knows he's to blame for her current state of mind.

'I spoke to Melanie Williams after I'd finished with her husband, and she admitted to attacking him. She showed no sign of remorse. Reckons he deserved it and said he's responsible for destroying their family. I've told them they need to think about the effect their behaviour is having on their daughter. I suggested that if they want to stay together, they attend counselling sessions to try to get their relationship back on track, and both enrol on anger management courses. But as far as the law's concerned, there's nothing more we can do. We'll just have to hope they sort themselves out before things escalate further and we're called in to pick up the pieces.'

'What a mess,' said Jemima, shaking her head in disbelief. 'Do you think Melanie Williams could have killed those women?'

'It did cross my mind, but I don't think she'd be capable. She's off her face most of the time.'

'You'll probably say this is ridiculous, but I think it's possible these deaths might be rooted in Greek mythology.'

'How so?' asked Kennedy, his face showing no sign of surprise.

'Well, I haven't had a chance to do much research, but pomegranates are linked with Persephone. She was the goddess of the harvest, and also the goddess of death, as she married her uncle, Hades. He ruled the underworld where the dead went, but Persephone didn't want to remain in the underworld, so Hades tricked her into eating pomegranate seeds, which made her return there for part of each year.'

'So what you're saying is that whoever's killing these women thinks he's Hades and is condemning these women to spend time with him in the underworld?' asked Kennedy.

'Possibly,' said Jemima. 'Like I said, I need to do some more research first.'

'It's worth a shot as we've got fuck all to go on at the moment,' said Kennedy.

Chapter 29

Jemima pulled up directly behind Peters' and Sanders' unmarked police car, cut the engine and got out of the car. They had parked in front of Damon Hawley's property. It was an early morning start, and Jemima could see the two men gazing idly out of the windscreen at a black and white cat that was running across an open-plan lawn. The feline had been hunting and was proudly taking home its prize, mouth open to accommodate a small bird, whose head was lolling at the end of a broken neck. Another life ended before its time.

'So, why aren't you knocking on doors and speaking to the neighbours?' asked Jemima, as Sanders opened the car window.

'Thought we'd better wait for you,' Sanders replied.

'I'm not going to hold your hand, Sanders. Stop being so bloody lazy and go and do your job,' she snapped. 'I'll wait here for the forensics team.'

Before Jemima had a chance to open the car door, a van rounded the corner and stopped behind her vehicle. The forensics team had arrived.

'Hey! Looking good there, Brackley!' called Sanders, as two forensics officers got out.

'Down boy. Can anyone smell cat pee?' asked Carys Brackley as she wrinkled her nose and started sniffing the air. 'I think there's a tomcat around here that needs to be neutered.'

'Sorry about him,' said Jemima as she introduced herself as the officer in charge. 'Sanders, you can question the neighbours by yourself. Go on, get on with it! Peters, you can help me search Hawley's house.'

Sanders' face darkened, as he was clearly annoyed at the slight. His lips parted slightly, as though he was about to say something. But whatever it was, he thought better of it, and turned away and headed in the direction of the nearest neighbouring property.

'It's almost a shame to have to force the door,' Jemima observed. 'It looks like a show home. I mean look at it: the windows are clean, and there aren't even cobwebs on the woodwork. By all accounts, Hawley's been living alone. I wish my husband was this domesticated. And look at the garden; there's not a blade of grass out of place, and the borders don't have any weeds.'

'It fits with his boss's observation of Hawley being OCD,' said Peters. 'I bet it'll be spotless inside.'

There was a low side gate, with no padlock, making it easy for anyone to get into the back garden.

'Not security conscious,' Jemima noted. 'And just look at that. He's only gone and left a key in the lock.' She gestured to the glass panelled back door. 'Stand back. I'll have this opened in no time.' She broke one of the small panes, knocked out the glass so that there were no jagged edges, then reached through and turned the key. 'You'd think people would have more sense than to make it this easy.'

'So what're we looking for?' asked Carys as she stepped into her overalls.

'Evidence to suggest a murder or attack having taken place inside,' Jemima replied. 'His wife's body was one of those discovered up in the woods. It's possible he's our killer. We know he was knocking her about before she ran out on him. She was staying at a refuge in Cyncoed, so he could have found her, brought her back and killed her here. He may have done the other victims as well. Your lot told us those women didn't die at the dump site, and we haven't got anyone else in the frame at the moment, so this is as good a place to start looking as any.'

Once inside, it was evident no one had been in the house for a while. A selection of mail lay on the mat inside the front door. The oldest was date stamped nine days earlier. The atmosphere was clean but stuffy, which suggested the windows hadn't been opened recently, and there were no perishable food items in the refrigerator or kitchen cupboards.

The decor was minimalistic. White, clean edges, no artwork, no personality. Nothing to offend. Nothing to invite. Apart from a selection of neatly arranged tinned goods and cereal packets in the kitchen cupboards, it was as if no one lived there.

'We'll sweep through with the ultraviolet,' said Carys, referring to the type of light used to detect latent fingerprints, spilled bodily fluids, and just about any evidence of a violent crime that the naked eye would be unable to detect. 'It'll take a while, but if there's anything here, I'll find it.'

As there was nothing of interest in the downstairs rooms, Jemima and Peters made their way to the bedrooms, which were as bland and uninviting as the rest of the house. The wardrobes were full of men's clothing. Shirts and suits hung in an orderly display of colour and shade. Underwear and socks were rolled neatly away in drawers. A smaller cupboard turned out to be a purpose-built shoe rack, where several pairs of highly polished shoes were displayed as though they were ready to go on sale.

There was nothing to suggest a woman had ever lived in the house. There were no photographs, clothes or personal items that may have once belonged to Rachel Hawley. It seemed

Damon Hawley had eradicated any trace of his wife from his life.

'We've found something in the kitchen. It looks as though they could have had a fight down here,' shouted Carys from the bottom of the stairs. 'Someone did their best to clean up in here, but it's next to impossible to get rid of every trace,' she continued, as Jemima and Peters walked into the kitchen. 'You can see splashes of blood on this wall. From the height and the pattern, it suggests someone received a blow, possibly to the head, which would have connected with the wall. The dragging pattern is consistent with them sliding to the ground, and if you take a look at the floor, you can make out a smallish area where the blood pooled.'

'Are you saying this could be the murder site?' asked Peters.

'No, there's not enough blood for that,' Carys replied. 'This would have been a relatively minor injury, but consistent with your theory of domestic abuse. We've still got to go through the rest of the house, so who knows what we'll find.'

Chapter 30

At 10:30 that morning, after Jemima had picked up Broadbent, the traffic on the westbound carriageway of the M4 was already heavy.

'Are you wearing aftershave? You're not on the pull, are you?' asked Jemima as the air-conditioning system wafted the pleasant citrusy smell of Broadbent's skin.

'Nah, those days have long gone. Wouldn't have the energy now. Just bought some new deodorant, and splashed on a bit of aftershave, that's all. Wanted to feel a bit more human. What d'ya think?'

'Not bad,' smiled Jemima. 'It's definitely an improvement on the last few weeks. At least now I don't feel like puking when I'm sitting next to you.'

'Was I that bad?' asked Broadbent, his cheeks burning with embarrassment.

'Put it this way: it's a toss-up whether you or the chicken shit smelled worse, and the jury's still out on that one,' laughed Jemima.

'Has anyone ever complimented you on your people skills?' asked Broadbent.

'All the time; it's one of my greatest strengths.'

The further west they travelled, the more ominous the sky became. A bank of cloud was building, grey and foreboding. They were leaving the sunshine behind and heading into more unsettled atmospheric conditions. The weather forecast had mentioned the possibility of showers in the west of the country, and as they approached the stark openness of Briton Ferry, a flash of lightning streaked across the sky.

Orange windsocks that in recent weeks had draped limply against their poles were now horizontal, warning drivers of the danger of crosswinds on this exposed section of motorway. Jemima gripped the steering wheel a little tighter as a gust hit the side of the car, taking her by surprise. Thunder rumbled threateningly in the distance, like a prolonged roll on a bass drum adding depth and texture to an unseen symphony orchestra. Even though the storm was still some distance away, the rain began to fall.

Large water droplets hit the windscreen, increasing in regularity until it was impossible to notice individual spots. The moisture spread a grimy residue over the glass, reducing visibility as the rain steadily washed away weeks of dust and encrusted dirt. Jemima squirted the windscreen washer in frustration, which helped to clear away the grime, and for a minute or so the air smelled of detergent. It was still raining when they reached the police station.

There turned out to be no family resemblance between Bernard Shackleton and Helen Tremaine. He was the younger sibling by almost three years but looked significantly older than his sister. His hair was predominantly grey and thinning on the crown. He was an unattractive man whose shoulders were bulky and rounded. His lips were full, teeth slightly yellowed, and nose too red and bulbous. He possessed a flabby midriff, the curse of many a chef. His hands were large and meaty, while his fingernails were short and scrupulously clean.

Shackleton had been brought to the station almost an hour earlier, and he was in a belligerent mood. 'This is police harassment. I've done nothing wrong. I'm a law-abiding citizen with a business to run,' he complained as officers escorted him into the small interview room.

'You're also a registered sex offender, Mr. Shackleton. A convicted rapist, so drop the act,' said Jemima sharply. 'Now sit down. We want to talk to you. I take it you've waived your right to have a solicitor present?'

'I don't need one. I haven't done anything wrong. You've no right to treat me like this,' said Shackleton, glaring defiantly at both Huxley and Broadbent. 'I've paid for what I did. That's all behind me. It's forgotten, and I've moved on. I've got a new life now.'

'I wonder if the women you raped have managed to forget about what you did to them?' asked Jemima with an uncharacteristically hard edge to her voice. 'You see, it's not so easy to move on with your life when you've been the victim of sexual assault. As I recall it, you tied those women up for hours, while you terrified, humiliated, and raped them. Some of your victims said they thought they were going to die. And you can bet your life that most, if not all, of them still wake screaming in the middle of the night because they can't forget about what you did to them.'

'To us, you'll always be the sick fucker who raped those women, and now we're wondering if you've returned to your old ways,' said Broadbent.

'I'm not that sort of man anymore. I was in a bad place back then. Things were happening in my life. I wasn't in my right mind.'

'Spare us the excuses. We're not interested in them. Don't you think everyone tries to justify things they shouldn't have done? Whatever your reasons, it doesn't make it right,' said Broadbent.

'I'm not trying to make excuses. I've already accepted that what I did was wrong, and I can assure you I haven't raped anyone else,' said Shackleton. 'I can't even remember the last time I had sex. I spend up to eighteen hours a day at my restaurant. I barely have time to sleep. My work is my life. By the time I close up the restaurant, I'm knackered. I work, I eat, and I sleep. That's my life in a nutshell.'

'You must have time off?' said Jemima.

'Two mornings a week,' Shackleton replied. 'I live above the restaurant to maximize the amount of time I can spend in the kitchen. But during those mornings I have to clean my flat and do the shopping.'

'You've turned into a right little housewife, haven't you?' sneered Broadbent.

'I don't have to put up with your sarcasm. I've worked hard to build up my business. People like what I do and pay a lot of money to eat at my restaurant. They want food prepared by me, or at the very least food prepared under my supervision. My life's a treadmill. I've become a living cliché, a victim of my success.'

'You employ staff?' asked Broadbent.

'Of course I do. I have a full-time sous-chef, maître d', kitchen hand, and three part-time waiters. I couldn't run the restaurant by myself. It's too much for one person. You've only got to look at my diary and accounts to see how popular the restaurant's become. I don't know which rape you're investigating, but presumably, you've still got my DNA on file? Check it against anything you like; you won't get a match, and if you haven't kept my DNA, then I'm happy to provide you with another sample. I've got nothing to hide. I'm telling you the truth. I haven't raped anyone.'

'What's the name of your restaurant?' asked Jemima.

'Why, you thinking of eating there? It's a bit pricey for a police officer,' said Shackleton cockily. When he got no reaction from either Jemima or Broadbent, Shackleton sighed and continued, 'It's "The Stone Sickle," near Port Eynon. It's got a Michelin star. People travel quite a distance just to eat there.'

'When's the last time you visited your sister?' asked Jemima, failing to look impressed by Shackleton's boast.

'My sister?' asked Shackleton, raising his eyebrows in surprise. 'What's this got to do with her? I haven't had any contact with Helen since before the trial. She never forgave me for using Adam's name. Why are you asking? Is she all right? She's not the victim?'

'No,' replied Jemima in an offhand manner. 'Just answer the question. When were you last in Cardiff?'

'I haven't been there since the trial. I've no need to go there. I upset a lot of my family back then, and if you knew anything about my family, you'd realize they're not the forgiving type. They made it clear to me that as far as they're concerned, I don't exist anymore, and to be honest, it suits me fine. I've put the past behind me.'

'And your ex-wife?' asked Broadbent.

'Sylvia? No,' said Shackleton, shaking his head. 'I haven't seen her since the day of my arrest. She never came to the trial or even visited me in prison. She filed for divorce less than a week after the arrest, and I didn't contest it. Well, I couldn't, could I? Our marriage was no great shakes anyway. I should never have married her in the first place. She wasn't the woman for me. I've only ever loved one woman, but when it came down to it, she didn't feel the same way about me. We had children together, not that my name is on their birth certificates. Then one day she told me it was over. There was no warning, no second chance. That's when everything in my life started to go wrong. I'd have done anything for her and the kids, but it wasn't to be. She used me and then turned her back on me.

'One of my biggest regrets is not being a good husband to Sylvia. She deserved better. Prison gave me a chance to reflect and repent. I'm ashamed of the way I used to live my life, but I've got things back on track, and I'm proud of who I've become. I'm a changed person now. I've built up a successful business, and I've beaten the odds. I wouldn't risk what I have now for anything.'

'Have you had any contact with your niece or nephew?' asked Jemima.

'No. I never saw much of the children after they started school. Martha was a spoilt brat who always got whatever she wanted. No doubt she's still a bloodsucking leech. She's probably living up at the big house with my sister and that lame husband of hers. I bet they're giving her a substantial allowance for doing sod all, while the servants get to spoon-feed her and wipe her overprivileged arse. And as for Adam, if he had any sense he'd have walked out on them as soon as he could. I've seen dogs shown more affection than that kid ever got when he was growing up.'

'Your sister and brother-in-law seem to have fallen out with their children. They claim not to have been in contact with them for years,' said Jemima.

'Must've been something serious then,' said Shackleton. 'As I said, I'm not surprised they don't see Adam. They never had much time for him. He was always a bit of an embarrassment to them. If Adam had any sense, he'd have told them where to stick their pathetic attempts at parenthood. As for Martha, they always used to let her get away with murder. I can't think of anything good to say about her. She always was a little bitch.'

'We'll need verification of your movements over the last six months,' said Jemima.

'Well, you can look at my diary and speak to my team. I've been open about my past. Everyone on my payroll knows I've been to prison. But I'd like you to tell me what you think I've done,' said Shackleton.

'We're not accusing you of anything at the moment. We're investigating some murders. Bodies have been found buried in the grounds of Llys Faen Hall,' said Jemima. 'All of them were female, and there was a sexual element to the crime.'

'Murder! You think I'm capable of murder?' asked Shackleton, his eyes wide with surprise.

'I don't think anything at the moment, Mr. Shackleton. The only thing I know for sure is that you're a convicted rapist who's familiar with Llys Faen Hall. Now if you don't mind, I'll take the DNA sample you offered to give us, and we'll leave it at that,' said Jemima. 'Once you've given us the sample, you're free to go, and a local officer will come to your restaurant to examine your diary and interview your staff.'

Chapter 31

'Shackleton's not responsible for these deaths,' said Jemima as she and Broadbent headed to the women's refuge.

'How can you be so sure?' asked Broadbent.

'He runs a busy restaurant. Like he said, it's going to be easy enough to check his whereabouts. He spends most of his time surrounded by people. If he's telling the truth, he only has two mornings a week to himself. We know Rachel Hawley went missing during the day. Shackleton would have to get over to Cardiff. That's going to take the best part of an hour without any traffic hold-ups. Then he's got to travel back. How would he have found the time to abduct, kill and dispose of the bodies? It doesn't add up.'

'He could have an accomplice,' said Broadbent.

'He could, but I doubt it. He'd want to be in control, and because of his commitment to the restaurant, he'd either have to relinquish some of his responsibilities to another member of staff, which will be easy enough to check, or he'd have to rely on someone else to abduct the women. Either way, he wouldn't be fully in control of things. I just can't see it.'

When they reached the women's refuge, Jemima asked to speak to Vanessa Bolton.

'Last night, one of your residents mentioned someone named Katie,' Jemima said when Vanessa appeared. 'I've already talked to Harriet Breen, but she claims not to have heard of her, yet I've been told Katie helps out once a week.'

'Yes, that's right,' Vanessa confirmed. 'Katie Walker, but Harriet wouldn't know her. Katie comes in on a Friday. She's a friend of mine. Well, when I say she's a friend, she's just someone I know. I met her at Hermione's Holistic Medicine Centre. It's in Penarth. Katie runs it with her husband, Chris. She's an acupuncturist, and she's been treating me for a problem with my knee.

'I don't usually mention the refuge to anyone, but during one of my treatment sessions, Katie happened to be talking about a documentary she'd seen on a woman who killed her husband after suffering years of physical abuse. Katie was angry that any man could treat his wife like that and said it was a shame more women didn't find the courage to walk out on abusive partners. One thing led to another, and that's when I told her about this place.

'She came for a look around, and I have to say I was quite surprised when she asked if she could come and help out. To be honest, I can't see how she manages to find the time. Hermione's is such a popular place, and their waiting lists are unbelievably long. For some of the treatments, especially acupuncture, you've got to wait weeks just to get an initial consultation, and the sessions aren't cheap.'

'Why didn't you mention her before?' asked Jemima.

'Well, as I said, she only helps out once a week, and she doesn't even do a full day. It's only four hours at most. I didn't think it was important, as she won't be with us much longer. You see, Katie told me last week that she and her husband have just had confirmation they'll be adopting a baby in a few weeks time.

'We're going to end up short-staffed. I'll have to stop working here soon, at least for six months or so, and when I come back, I'll probably only do two mornings a week. I won't want to be separated from this little one for too long,' she said, smiling as she patted her stomach. 'And Helen seems to be dragging her heels finding extra cover. So I'm afraid the refuge is going to suffer. We're going to lose two volunteers in the space of a couple of weeks.'

Vanessa Bolton certainly hadn't exaggerated the popularity of Hermione's if the number of cars in the car park were anything to go by. There were spaces for up to twenty vehicles, and all of them were full. Most of the cars looked expensive. There were Mercedes, Jaguars, BMWs, a Lexus, a couple of sports cars, as well as the usual quota of Land Rovers. Having failed to find a parking space, Broadbent ended up having to park two streets away as the roads immediately surrounding Hermione's were a 'residents only' parking zone.

Hermione's Holistic Medicine Centre was located on Harcourt Street. It was a large impressive looking building. Clever marketing and unabashed courting of local celebrities and key members of the media had turned Hermione's into a place to be seen.

As soon as Jemima and Broadbent walked through the door, they realized that no expense had been spared. Everything said quality, from the thick, luxurious carpets to the soothing array of pastel shades on the walls. Comfortable bespoke furniture put clients at ease, moulding around the body whatever your shape or size. It was more like a lounge area in a luxury hotel than a waiting room at a treatment centre. Everything was designed to create a sense of wellbeing. It reinforced the idea that Hermione's was about quality, and clients could be assured of getting the best possible service.

An elaborate arrangement of lilies and orchids brought life and colour to an ornately carved beech reception desk. Water gurgled and trickled over an array of well-worn pebbles arranged in an indoor water feature located in the waiting room. It was relaxing, both to watch and listen to, especially when it was so warm outside. Slow, soothing music was piped throughout the building and played unobtrusively in the background. Jemima thought it was probably panpipes. She loved the haunting, hypnotic sound, as it was very restful. A leaflet at the reception desk explained there were fifteen treatment rooms where therapies such as acupuncture, aromatherapy, naturopathy, and reflexology were administered, and it seemed as though there was no shortage of people who were more than happy to pay for the services on offer.

'May I help you?' asked the receptionist, whose name badge told them she was called Candice. She was a petite redhead whose large green eyes were enhanced by immaculately arched eyebrows that made it seem as though she were perpetually startled. Her hair was cut in a modern asymmetric style that Jemima knew would require a large amount of effort to keep it looking just right. Her unnaturally white teeth were slightly out of alignment but not so much that you'd notice, as your eyes were drawn to her collagen-enhanced lips, which were a vivid shade of plum and so highly glossed that they looked as though they were coated in plastic.

Flashing their warrant cards, they asked to speak to Katie Walker.

'She's with a client at the moment,' said Candice. 'She should be free in about ten minutes or so. Her next appointment's just been cancelled. Take a seat in the waiting room, and I'll let her know you're here.'

Katie Walker was exactly as Vanessa Bolton had described her. Unlike the receptionist, Katie's skin was barely covered with a layer of foundation, and apart from the slightest hint of mascara, she wore no other make-up. Her light-brown hair was pulled back off her face and held in place with a no-nonsense bobble. There was nothing fancy about her, and for a co-owner of such a successful business, she displayed no airs or graces. She had the traditional 'girl next door' look, and her mannerisms conveyed sincerity. She spoke without any definable accent. Her voice was gentle and soothing, and her body language open. Jemima imagined Katie Walker would fit in well at the refuge, as she seemed calm and caring. She was someone it would be easy to trust.

Katie's eyes brimmed with tears as Jemima told her about Tara Fenton's death.

'I knew her,' she said. 'She was such a lovely person. You don't think Helen Tremaine had anything to do with it, do you, what with the body turning up on her land? Oh, take no notice of me, I'm just not thinking straight. Of course, Helen wouldn't have anything to do with it. Not that I've ever met her, but she must be a decent person. After all, she set up the refuge.'

'We're looking at every possibility at this stage,' said Jemima. 'Have you ever noticed anything suspicious while you've been at the refuge?'

'Like what?'

'Anything. Have you ever seen anyone hanging around outside or any of the women being hassled? Did any of them ever mention being approached by strangers?'

'Not really. Most of them spend their lives being spooked. It's only natural, I suppose, if you've lived with a violent thug. I'd say they're all careful not to put themselves at risk again. Most of them keep to themselves. No one seems to open up much. Everyone's too scared they'll be found and forced to go back to their old life. It could be their only chance of starting over, so they've got a lot to lose if it goes wrong.

'You must have spotted the security cameras and panic alarms? They're everywhere. I'd be amazed if anyone could get to those women while they're inside the refuge. It's all wired up to the police station. It couldn't be more secure. Whoever did this must have abducted Tara while she was outside the refuge. Perhaps her partner discovered where she was staying? I just wish I could help in some way; I'm afraid I haven't been able to tell you anything useful.'

'Does your husband know you volunteer at the refuge?' asked Broadbent.

'Not exactly,' said Katie, looking slightly embarrassed. 'He knows I do some voluntary work on a Friday, but I haven't told him what it is. They like to keep things quiet at the refuge, and they certainly don't like having men involved with the centre. Chris and I are quite trusting of each other. He's never asked where I go or what I do, and I haven't volunteered the information.'

'One last question: what's your impression of the women who help out at the refuge?' asked Jemima.

'I've only ever met Vanessa,' said Katie. 'She's great. Everyone gets on well with her. I couldn't imagine she'd be involved with these murders, and I think the others must be OK too, because I've never heard anyone complain about them. It's a reasonably happy place.'

'Thanks for your time,' said Jemima as she stood up to leave.

'No problem. I just wish I could have helped,' said Katie. 'Look, I know you're rushed, but while you're here would you like a quick tour of the place? It's the business woman in me coming out. I know you're both here on official business, but you're also potential clients, and I'm sure we could offer you great rates.'

'Yeah, I'd like to have a quick look round,' said Jemima, thinking how good it would be to book a massage once the investigation was over.

'Great. Of course, I can't take you into every room. There are clients in most of them. We use the basement for storage, and have five treatment rooms on the ground floor and ten on the first floor.'

'What about the second floor?' asked Jemima.

'That's where Chris and I live,' said Katie. 'It's large enough for the two of us, and at least we don't have to sit in traffic while we're on our way to work.'

Chapter 32

'What do you make of Katie?' asked Jemima as she and Broadbent walked back to the car.

'Seemed nice enough,' said Broadbent.

'Didn't you think it was a bit odd she should ask about Helen Tremaine's involvement? Surely an abusive partner would be the first person you'd suspect?'

'Yeah, now you come to mention it, it probably was a bit odd. But she'd only just found out about the murder, so as she said, she probably wasn't thinking straight.'

As they walked into the incident room, it became apparent something had happened. Kennedy was in the thick of it, holding court with his newly acquired entourage. His mood seemed upbeat, and his body more animated than in recent days. His voice had a new energy and eagerness, and the rest of the team were hanging on his every word.

'You're just in time,' he said, indicating that they should join the others. His face flushed with a glow that took years off his recently jaded appearance. 'We've had a breakthrough thanks to the wonders of forensic science. Prothero's report on Debbie just came through. It turns out she's Victoria Larkin from Brecon, aka Charlie Jones, a former resident at the refuge. It looks like everything's pointing to Helen Tremaine.

'The forensic science team has confirmed there's no evidence to suggest that Damon Hawley's house was the murder site. So I've asked Sanders to arrange with the forensics team for a coordinated search of Llys Faen Hall. Given the size of the place, it'll require all of you to participate. The victims could easily have been killed there. Its remoteness makes it an ideal spot, and it's hardly any distance to the burial site.

'And, Huxley, I want Trent and a WPC to go back to the refuge. No point upsetting those women further by having male officers tramping around. I want the place searched thoroughly from top to bottom, belt and braces stuff. They're to look for evidence of a struggle or anything to suggest something untoward happened there. I know it's a long shot, but I want us to cover all the bases. If Helen Tremaine is involved, then it might just be where she's hidden the weapon.'

Jemima was furious. She'd been out of the office for a few hours, and suddenly Kennedy seemed to have taken over the investigation. He was putting her in her place, ready to take the glory for himself. How did that make her look to the rest of the team?

It was suddenly clear to Jemima that Kennedy didn't trust her to run this case. But she didn't understand why he had come to that decision. She was good at her job, and this was insulting. He was treating her like a junior officer.

Jemima also didn't think Helen Tremaine was a murderer, and she wanted her thoughts out there so that when Kennedy drew a blank with this line of inquiry, everyone would know that she'd done her best to stop him wasting everyone's time by focussing on the wrong person. There was a chance he'd get annoyed if she voiced her doubts in such a public way, but if he reacted badly, she'd have to front it out. She just wasn't prepared to let him narrow the focus of the investigation at this stage without challenging him.

Even as she spoke, Jemima could hear herself sounding like a petulant child, and it wasn't as if she had any better ideas to offer at the moment. It was just a feeling she had. She was sure he was wrong.

'If Helen Tremaine killed those women and buried them in the wood, then why did she take a walk there with her husband and the dog? It would've been too big a risk. They live on a large estate. There must be hundreds of routes for a morning stroll. We know the bodies were buried in shallow graves, so there was a good chance of them being discovered by someone or dug up by an animal. It was just a matter of time.

'I'm the first to admit Helen Tremaine hasn't been straight with us. She hid the fact that her brother's a convicted rapist, and she was very cagey about why they don't have any contact with their son and daughter, but I don't think she's responsible for these murders. She doesn't even look capable of lugging those bodies up there, let alone digging holes big enough to bury them. Also what about the sexual element to the murders? I'd be surprised if a woman did that. It's too brutal. I think you're way off the mark on this one, sir.'

'I'm not suggesting Helen Tremaine's responsible,' said Kennedy, his voice suddenly low and dangerous. Jemima could tell by his eyes that he was annoyed at her voicing doubts in front of the team, but he had the good grace not to admonish her in front of the others. Instead, he shot her a warning look, letting her know she had overstepped the mark. She refused to avert her eyes and glared at him defiantly as he continued to speak. 'All I'm saying is that she's the one person who links the victims to the location. And let's not forget she could have had an accomplice. I'm going into this with an open mind, Huxley. I'm just asking you to do the same.'

'I always keep an open mind, sir,' she replied, in as steady a voice as she could muster. 'I just think it's possible someone could be trying to set Helen Tremaine up.' In all the years she'd known him, Kennedy had never admonished her for offering a differing opinion, and she was shocked at his reaction. It never occurred to her that she could have voiced her doubts in a more tactful way.

Even without looking round, she was certain that Sanders was smirking. He wasn't in her line of vision, but she knew he would be relishing her unexpected humiliation in front of the team. It was just the sort of thing a man like him would enjoy. It would encourage him to think he could treat her like shit too. There were a few seconds when she had an overwhelming urge to walk over and punch him in the face. She knew it would make her feel better for all of a minute, but then she'd be suspended and possibly lose her job and her pension. It wasn't worth it. Her only option was to suck it up. The men in this force were all sexist bastards. She wouldn't give any of them the satisfaction of knowing they'd got to her. She was better than that.

'By the way, how did it go with Shackleton?' asked Kennedy in a tone which made the question seem like an afterthought.

'I'd be surprised if he's involved,' Jemima replied. 'He claims not to have had any contact with the Tremaines since his arrest. He volunteered a sample of his DNA — in fact, he practically insisted on it. It's not the actions of someone who's got something to hide, and if what he's told us is true, then he hardly spends any time away from his restaurant. I've asked the locals to check things out at their end.'

'Well, her brother may be in the clear, but at the moment Helen Tremaine's in it up to her neck,' said Kennedy. 'I've sent a car over to bring her in. It's time we made the woman realize she's our prime suspect. She had the means and opportunity, but we still haven't got a motive yet. She needs a wake-up call. Living in a big posh house doesn't mean she gets special treatment from us. Huxley, I want you to sit in on the interview with me.

'Where are you on your enquires, Trent? What do we know about Victoria Larkin?' pressed Kennedy.

As Trent started to reply, Sanders' phone rang, and he walked away from the group to go and answer it.

'Victoria Larkin was one of the women identified in the first trawl,' Trent explained. 'She lived in Brecon with her partner Kai Bletchley. Filed complaints against him on numerous occasions, but it was the usual story: she withdrew the allegations as soon as it looked as though the CPS would proceed. The local police said it was like banging their heads against the wall, as she refused to testify against him.

'She was reported missing about eighteen months ago by her friend, Sasha Tallis. Given the history, the local police thought they might be looking for a body and not a missing person. They put a lot of resources into finding her. They pulled Bletchley in, but he denied killing her. But when it came down to it, there was no evidence to prove she was dead, so they had to let him go.

'It seems Bletchley wasn't too upset about Victoria going missing, as a few weeks later he hooked up with a woman named Catriona Lomas. He must have laid on the charm, because she moved in with him. Pretty soon Bletchley was up to his old tricks again, but Catriona wasn't such a pushover. During one of his attacks, she went for him with a kitchen knife. He ended up having to have an emergency splenectomy. Kai Bletchley finally met his match.'

Sanders rejoined the group. 'Just organized the rest of the search team. They'll meet us up there in two hours,' he said to Kennedy.

'Excellent. Come on people, let's get moving. You know what you've got to do. I don't want us to waste any more time,' barked Kennedy.

'Sir, can I speak to you in your office?' asked Jemima. She was determined to confront him and ask him why he had suddenly felt the need to take over the investigation.

'Not now, Huxley. Whatever it is, it will have to wait. For now, I need you with me in the interview room,' he ordered, as he marched off.

Chapter 33

Helen Tremaine was in a belligerent mood. Her eyes had narrowed to a malevolent squint, and she looked ready for a fight. Her voice betrayed the anger she felt. She spoke more rapidly than usual, each word quivering with suppressed emotion. It had a detrimental impact on an otherwise polished accent and suggested that perhaps Helen Tremaine hadn't been born with a silver spoon in her mouth.

'Where do you people get off, dragging me in here like a common criminal?' she snapped. 'We've given you access to our home, and your presence has been disruptive and upsetting. I want this matter cleared up as much as you do. Do you realize how frightening it is for me to find out a madman has been murdering women and burying their bodies on our land? I knew one of those women. She was someone I was doing my best to protect. I feel as if I've let her down, and I'm scared you're going to tell me the other women were also people I knew. I'm even terrified I'll become one of the victims myself. I feel as if someone's targeting me, and I don't know why!'

'Helen Tremaine, I am going to ask you some questions. You are not obliged to say anything in response to the questions, but if you do say anything it will be taken down in writing and may be used in evidence,' said Kennedy, unmoved by the woman's impassioned monologue. 'I have a warrant here to search your home, and another to search the women's refuge in Cyncoed.' Kennedy slid the documents across the table. 'My officers have been instructed to search both premises in connection with these murders, and if you or anyone else tries to prevent them from carrying out those duties, we will be forced to make an arrest.'

Helen Tremaine's eyes widened in surprise, and her jaw dropped. 'Why are you searching our home? We haven't done anything. I keep telling you these murders aren't anything to do with us. This is turning into a complete farce. I don't think you're doing enough to find whoever's responsible. You don't seem to have a lot to go on, and you're wasting time asking irrelevant questions about my family, yet they've got nothing to do with these murders. You're persecuting us, and I'm not prepared to answer any of your questions until my solicitor arrives. It's not that I've got anything to hide, it's just that I want you to stop treating me like this.'

'Persecution's a strong word, Mrs. Tremaine, and I can assure you we're doing nothing of the sort. We intend to find the person or persons responsible for these crimes, and at the moment you're the only link we have to two of the victims and the murder site.'

'I keep telling you it's a horrible coincidence, but that's all it is. It has nothing to do with — two, you just said two of the victims?' said Helen Tremaine, as the heightened colour in her cheeks drained from her skin. 'What do you mean two — who was the other one?'

'Victoria Larkin, but you would have known her as Charlie Jones,' said Jemima.

'Oh, my word!' exclaimed Helen Tremaine, as her hands flew to her mouth and she began to cry and shake uncontrollably. 'This can't be real — this can't be real,' she muttered over and over again, as she wrapped her arms tightly around her chest and rocked backwards and forwards.

'Can I get you a glass of water, Mrs. Tremaine?' asked Jemima, concerned that the woman was losing it.

'Pl-please,' she stammered as she struggled to compose herself.

Jemima was almost at the door when she heard a commotion in the corridor. There was the sound of heavy footsteps, and as Jemima reached for the door handle, there was a knock on the other side of the door as a young, red-faced PC pushed it open and announced the arrival of Helen Tremaine's solicitor.

Prudence Dwight was a short, thickset, bullish type of woman, who had been at the back of the queue when beauty was handed out. She had no sense of style, no sense of humour, and her view of the world was as black and white as her clothes.

'Dresses like a Dalmatian, but nowhere near as friendly as one. Think of a Rottweiler in a suit, and you won't go far wrong,' was how Kennedy first described her to Jemima.

Dwight more than compensated for her lack of physical appeal with her intelligence, tenacity, and fearlessness, and it was these attributes that made her a very successful lawyer. She was always in demand, as there were plenty of clients willing to pay her exorbitant fees. Prudence Dwight was the legal profession's version of Marmite: clients loved her, police officers hated her. There was no middle ground. But whichever side you were on, only a fool would make the mistake of underestimating the woman.

Jemima returned with the glass of water, and before she'd even had time to sit down, Dwight was on the attack.

'Why have you brought my client in for questioning?' she demanded, glaring at Kennedy as she heaved her overstuffed leather briefcase onto the table, swinging it wide like a hammer thrower. Like its owner, the bag had seen better days. Its leather was scuffed, creased and stained. The metal clasp had long since broken, leaving the multitude of files she carried around at the mercy of the elements.

Kennedy flinched as the base of the bag narrowly missed his hand and thudded ominously on the table. Dwight's self-satisfied grunt showed she was aware that she had already unsettled him.

Kennedy recovered quickly and said, 'Your client knew two of the victims whose bodies were buried on her land. My officers have found her to be evasive, and she has withheld information about members of her own family. Information we believe may have a bearing on the case. We have not arrested your client, but she has been cautioned, and we need her to answer questions about herself and her family to help us eliminate them from our inquiry. If she fails to cooperate, I will have no choice but to charge her with wasting police time. Due to the serious nature of the case, we need answers, and we need them now.'

'I'd like a few moments to confer with my client,' said Dwight in a very matter-of-fact tone.

When Kennedy and Jemima returned to the interview room, Dwight explained that Helen Tremaine was prepared to answer any questions put to her. Kennedy reminded them she was still under caution.

'I know, but I've already told you my family has nothing to do with any of this,' pleaded Helen Tremaine.

'That is a matter for us to determine,' said Kennedy.

'You failed to tell us your brother is a convicted rapist,' said Jemima.

'I haven't seen or spoken to my brother in fifteen years,' said Helen Tremaine. 'I don't even know whether he's still alive, and if he is, he knows he wouldn't be made welcome in our home. He used our son's name to commit his crimes. He implicated Adam! We won't ever be able to forget what he did, and we'll certainly never forgive him. But whatever feelings I have for my brother, I'm sure he doesn't know about the refuge. So how could he possibly have killed Tara or Charlie? It's a ludicrous suggestion.'

'You've also been evasive about the whereabouts of your son and daughter,' said Kennedy.

'That's because I don't know where they are,' said Helen Tremaine. 'I've already explained that David and I fell out with our children about five years ago. We told them they were no longer welcome at the Hall, and neither of us has had any contact with them since. I don't want to go into detail about it. It was a family matter which has no bearing whatsoever on what has just happened. Surely we can't be the only parents to fall out with their children?'

'Are your children aware of your involvement with the women's refuge?' asked Kennedy.

'No, it came about after they left home. I had a lot of time on my hands, and I just wanted to do something to help people. I get lonely. David's out all day, and this was something I could do. I wanted to feel useful. I don't need to go out to earn money. I'm in the fortunate position of being able to give my time for free, and I desperately want to help these women.'

'Very commendable, I'm sure,' said Kennedy.

'So there's no way your son or daughter would have been able to tell your brother about the refuge?' asked Jemima.

'Of course not, I've already told you they don't know about my charity work either. And apart from that, they'd never want to have anything to do with Bernard ever again. We were all furious at what he'd done.'

Chapter 34

The search of Llys Faen Hall was an unenviable task. Due to the size of the estate and the number of outbuildings, extra officers had been drafted in to help. Jemima and the others were to search the main house, while a dog team began to comb the land and outbuildings. The victims' wounds suggested there would have been significant amounts of blood loss at the murder site. It would have been virtually impossible to eradicate all traces of it. Forensic officers had been instructed to examine the washing machines and hoses, together with all sinks, baths, showers and drains on the estate.

There was the sound of hurried footsteps from inside the house, and Janet Bleasdale soon appeared at the door.

'We've got a warrant to search these premises,' said Jemima, holding out the document. 'Mrs Tremaine is already aware of this.'

'But the Tremaines aren't here at the moment,' said the housekeeper, looking flustered. 'You'd better come in, but I can't imagine what you're hoping to find. No one here's responsible for the deaths of those women. You'll just be wasting your time.'

'Is there anyone else in the house?' asked Jemima.

'Only Marie — she's in the kitchen preparing dinner,' said Janet.

'I'll have to ask you both to stop whatever it is you're doing and remain in the hallway until our search is complete.'

'You can tell her yourself. I'm calling Mr Tremaine,' said Janet Bleasdale. 'This isn't right. You shouldn't be treating us like this.'

Jemima and the others began their search upstairs, while forensics officers went to work in the kitchen and bathrooms.

'I've never seen such a fantastic house,' said Peters, running his hand up the highly polished oak banister as he ascended the wide staircase. 'They gotta be minted to afford a place like this. I mean, who has servants these days? They've got a housekeeper, cook, gardener, gamekeeper and estate manager. It's like stepping into one of those old-fashioned BBC dramas.'

'There's plenty of money around, but not for the likes of us, unless you're on the take, that is,' said Sanders. 'Come on. Let's see if we can find anything to tie them to these deaths. We'll search the rooms together. Don't want to be accused of planting evidence if we find anything. And don't forget to examine their clothes.'

'Haven't you seen enough women's underwear?' asked Peters.

'Cheeky git!' laughed Sanders. 'I'm not into grannies. Anyway, you'd probably be able to camp out in a pair of her knickers. It's a well-known fact, the older the woman, the bigger her knickers.'

'And even now he's contemplating sticking his pole in another tent,' said Ashton as he high-fived Peters.

'I'm not going to respond to that. Anyway, I thought all you Hooray Henry types were above gutter humour,' said Sanders with a smirk.

'I'm afraid you've misjudged us, but it's a common misconception amongst the lower classes. To set the record straight, we enjoy gutter humour as much as you plebs. We merely deliver it with better grammar and superior diction,' said Ashton, doing his best to keep a straight face.

'That's enough of the schoolboy humour. There's work to do, and I want everyone focussed on the job,' ordered Jemima.

On either side of the galleried landing was a corridor. A plush cream carpet ran the length of each walkway, and the walls were covered in a bespoke peach and cream brocade paper. There were seven bedrooms on this floor: four on one side and three on the other. Each heavy oak door was closed, and the wood seemed to absorb the natural light.

The first two bedrooms were large and immaculately decorated with silk wallpaper in pale pastel shades. A small crystal chandelier hung from an ornate moulding in each ceiling. As the sun shone through the large sash windows, the crystals acted like prisms, causing shimmering rays of different coloured light to dance across the walls. The effect was mesmerizing. The windows stood open about six inches, allowing what little breeze there was to cool the otherwise oppressive atmosphere. It also had the effect of gently moving the crystals, which tinkled whenever they happened to collide with each other.

The bedrooms were mirror images of each other, with the same furniture, colour scheme, and accessories. It seemed as though no expense had been spared in the decoration and dressing of these rooms, but the newness of everything showed just how infrequently they were used. The pale carpets still retained the springiness of pile that had hardly been walked upon. The beds were made up, dressed with an array of plump cushions in an assortment of materials in differing shades of pink. Burgundy silk throws provided a further touch of luxury to the lower section of the cream bedding. Both guest rooms had a dressing room and en-suite wet room, though each was devoid of clothes or personal belongings.

The master suite was even more luxurious. It was vast and modern with two dressing rooms leading off the sleeping area.

Unlike the guest rooms, this suite was filled with personal paraphernalia.

They say you can tell a lot about a woman from the contents of her wardrobe, and Jemima could see Helen Tremaine was a woman who liked to shop. Her dressing room resembled a stockroom of an upmarket boutique, as designer labels vied for space on four hefty rails extending the length of the room. She had eclectic tastes ranging from casual to ultra chic, and many of the items looked as though they'd hardly been worn. Trousers and dresses filled the bottom two rails, while jackets and tops were draped from the upper ones. Ten ball gowns and an array of cocktail dresses of all colours and shades hung elegantly next to three fur stoles. At the far end of the room was a bespoke shoe cupboard, with an individual compartment for each pair. There must have been room for a hundred pairs, yet every compartment was full, while a further sixteen boxes were stacked in two neat piles on the floor.

It was immediately apparent that David Tremaine did not share his wife's passion for clothes, though his dressing room still contained more garments than the average man would possess. There was a rail on which hung numerous suits in various shades of black and grey, along with various immaculately pressed shirts, silk ties, cravats, and bow ties. This dressing room contained a smaller shoe cupboard, in which there were twenty-three pairs of rather conservative-looking footwear, along with two pairs of training shoes and a rather worn set of bedroom slippers.

Searching through the clothes was a slow and mundane task, as they had to check pockets and examine the fabric for evidence of bloodstains. They were still working their way through the dressing room when the man himself appeared.

'Is this necessary?' he asked. 'You're treating us like common criminals. Do you honestly think we've got anything to do with those women's deaths?'

'It doesn't matter what we think, sir,' said Jemima, as she carefully replaced one of David Tremaine's suits on the rail. 'We're just doing our job. We have to be thorough. Somebody killed those women, and their bodies were found on your land. Your wife has a direct link with two of the victims. So we have to consider the possibility of your involvement. If you've done nothing wrong, then we should be able to rule you out of our inquiries. This isn't personal; it's just procedure.'

'Janet's told me you'd removed our washing machine,' said David Tremaine.

'Not us specifically, sir,' said Sanders. 'That'll be the forensics team. They'll be examining all the laundry facilities.'

'You actually think we did it, don't you?' asked David Tremaine, shaking his head in incredulity. 'You've got this so wrong, and while you're wasting time on us, the killer's still out there. Just hurry up and do whatever it is you feel you have to do, because I'd like to have my home back.'

The following three bedrooms turned out to be much like the first two guest rooms. So much so that when Jemima opened the door to the last bedroom, she was surprised at what she saw. This room was far larger than the guest rooms but looked smaller because of the way it was decorated. Peacock tail feathers were painted on almost every inch of the walls. It was a highly personalized work of art, overpowering, yet surprisingly beautiful. Someone had clearly spent hours decorating this room. The intensity of the pattern and the vibrancy of the colours were overwhelming.

Jemima stood there, staring at the walls. She thought they were horrible but had a feeling that there was something obvious that she was missing. Though, for the life of her, she couldn't think what it was. Her train of thought was broken as Sanders entered the room.

'Whoa! This is fucking creepy,' he said.

'Whoever's responsible for this is either an arty type or just some complete nutter,' said Broadbent. 'Often the same thing, I suppose. Those creative types are all a bit strange. I couldn't put up with this. I find it too oppressive.'

'It'd put me off my stroke, and that's for sure,' said Sanders. 'Parts of those feathers look like eyes. They'd always be watching you. It'd give me nightmares if I had to sleep in a room like this.'

A search of the cupboards showed them to be devoid of any personal items, and when they asked him later, David Tremaine grudgingly admitted the room had been his daughter's. He explained she had an obsession with peacocks since her early teens, and it was at her insistence his wife had acquired the birds that now lived in the grounds.

'Personally, I think the room's hideous, but my wife won't let anyone redecorate it. She designed it with our daughter. I made a concession with that room, but she's not going to have a free rein on the rest of the house. If my wife had her way, she'd have the place filled with all sorts of dubious artwork.'

'And where's your daughter now, sir?' asked Jemima.

'Oh, not that old chestnut again,' sighed David Tremaine. 'As I've said on numerous occasions, we haven't seen her for a long time. We're not what you'd call a close family.'

'And what about your son?' asked Jemima.

'No, we have nothing to do with him either.'

'Do they live locally?' pressed Jemima.

'I don't know!' snapped David Tremaine. 'Why can't you people seem to understand that we haven't been in contact with either of them for a very long time? I have no idea where they are. They could be anywhere.'

The search of Llys Faen Hall was a slow process, and when the Tremaines were informed that they weren't allowed to remain at their home overnight, David Tremaine had threatened them with a lawsuit. It was all bluster, as when it came down to it, there was nothing he could do.

Helen Tremaine took the news calmly, her earlier indignation a thing of the past. Discovering that Charlie Jones was one of the victims had hit her hard. For the moment, all the fight had gone out of her. She had the bewildered look of the recently bereaved, and was either a good actress or was genuinely shocked, confused and frightened. She sat on the stairs, staring blankly at the wall, while Ashton accompanied David Tremaine as he went around the house collecting personal items for an overnight stay.

Chapter 35

Back at the station, the evening's briefing session had been uneventful. They were no closer to finding the murder site or the weapon, and still had nothing to tie Helen Tremaine to the murders. As yet, they had no other suspect. The mood was flat. Everyone was tired, and Jemima was still resentful towards Kennedy.

It was while she was driving home that Jemima realized just how hungry she was. She'd been on the go all day and hadn't eaten anything since breakfast. By now it was almost nine o'clock, fifteen hours since she'd last had any food. She was exhausted, frustrated and hoped Nick had thought to save her something to eat.

When she arrived home, there was no sign of Nick's car on the drive. The house was in darkness, and every window closed. As she opened the door, the heat hit her. It was stuffy, stale, and oppressive but at least the awful smell from the fields had finally gone.

Jemima switched on the kitchen light to find dirty dishes strewn across the table. It had been Nick's turn to do the washing up, but apparently, he'd found better things to do. She opened the oven to see if he'd left her any dinner, but there was nothing apart from a greasy tray with the cold burnt remains of some oven chips. The fridge was just as bare, with only a few unappetizing lettuce leaves, their edges already turning brown. Jemima grunted in frustration and threw the lettuce in the bin. She slammed the fridge door and tried the freezer, but it was just as empty. Nick had promised to go shopping. He'd let her down again.

It was the final straw. She'd kept her temper in check all day. It had taken a considerable amount of effort, and as far as she could see it hadn't done her any good. Keeping her thoughts and feelings to herself just seemed to encourage people to mistreat her. But she hadn't expected to come home and find that Nick was just as bad as everyone else.

The feeling of anger rose too quickly for her to realize it was a disproportionate response. She stormed upstairs feeling let down and betrayed. She couldn't understand why Nick was so thoughtless and unreasonable. He knew she was working on the biggest case of her career, and he couldn't expect her to pick up the slack at home. She was under pressure and wanted out. If Nick had walked in at that moment, she'd have had a go at him. She deserved better than this. She was his wife, and he wasn't showing her any respect or consideration. What exactly was it that she was getting out of this marriage?

Jemima changed out of her work clothes, ran downstairs, grabbed her bag and keys and set off to the supermarket. The tyres squealed as she drove erratically, taking bends far too quickly. When she reached the car park, the vehicle jolted as she stopped it abruptly with the handbrake. She ended up parking diagonally across two bays. It was something she never condoned. She was always quick to criticize other drivers for their sloppy parking, but at that moment she didn't care. If anything, it gave her a perverse sense of satisfaction.

Inside the shop, she whizzed up and down the aisles. Within ten minutes her trolley was full. Fortunately, there were hardly any other customers around, as Jemima was in no mood to slow down. She'd be capable of trolley rage if anyone dared get in her way. She hated shopping at the best of times and certainly didn't want to be in a supermarket at this time of night, but she needed to eat something as she was beginning to feel quite shaky. She grabbed a microwaveable prawn makhani and some naan bread then headed for the checkout.

When Jemima arrived home, there was still no sign of Nick. She pierced the lid on the makhani, put it in the microwave, and opened a few windows before unpacking the groceries.

As she moved the dirty dishes from the table, a tumbler slipped through her fingers and shattered as it hit the tiled floor. Splinters of glass flew everywhere.

'Fuck it!' she shouted, bending down hastily to pick up the pieces, cutting her index finger in the process. She cursed again. Nothing in her life was going right at the moment.

The microwave pinged to say the food was ready, but she needed to clean and dress her wound. Everything was conspiring against her.

Having dealt with the cut, she found a dustpan and brush and cleared away the broken glass. By the time she opened the microwave door, she was trembling. The smell of food made her mouth water, and she greedily spooned everything onto a plate, poured herself a glass of wine and sat down at the table to eat. As she was finishing her last mouthful, she heard the front door open.

'I'm back!' called Nick in a cheerful voice. His cheeks had a rosy glow, and the smell of alcohol was noticeable on his breath.

'Where've you been?' demanded Jemima.

'They wanted me to do a feature on a new Devils signing, and it took a lot longer than I thought.'

'Oh, and I suppose you had to go to the pub as well?' snapped Jemima, feeling churlish as the words spilled out of her mouth. The last thing she needed after the day she'd just had was for things to kick off at home, but she just couldn't help herself.

'Look, I don't wanna argue with you. I popped into the Vaults after work. Not that I should have to explain myself to you. It was Bethan Ford's leaving do. I only stayed for the one, so don't make a big deal out of it.'

'I'm not making a big deal out of anything,' said Jemima, annoyed that Nick seemed to think he was making such a plausible excuse for what was really his thoughtless behaviour. She wasn't going to allow him to wrong-foot her, and she certainly wasn't going to forgive him that easily. 'I just didn't expect to come home and find no food in the house. You know how tough things are at the moment. I'm working all hours and getting nowhere. I haven't had time to go off on a jolly. I'm bloody knackered, and I've still had to sort out the shopping, and now I've got to clean up the kitchen. I just want you to show me some consideration, for fuck's sake.'

'Show you some consideration! How about you show me some consideration for a change? I don't know what's up with you lately. You've changed. You're the self-centred one, Jemima. We've both got careers, and mine is just as important as yours. So how about you cut me some slack?' shouted Nick, his features hardening as he slammed his fist on the table.

'That's so unfair, and you know it,' said Jemima as she stormed from the kitchen like a petulant teenager, taking pleasure in slamming the door behind her as she went. Her heels ground into the carpet as she thudded up the stairs, making far more noise than was necessary. Suddenly every aspect of her life seemed unbearable. She knew she was going to snap if she didn't calm down. Right now she was tired and angry. Nothing was going the way she expected it to. All she wanted to do was fall asleep and never wake up again, so she undressed and got into bed.

As she turned off the bedside light, Nick started to play his music downstairs. She could feel the bassline of Iron Maiden's 'Run to the Hills' sending shock waves through the mattress. She felt like screaming. It was another uncalled-for, insensitive attack on her. How much more was she expected to take? She began to cry. She wanted Nick to turn the music down, but couldn't face another confrontation. So she wrapped the pillow around her head and pressed it firmly to her ears.

Jemima struggled to sleep. It always happened when she was angry. She couldn't switch off, and her muscles refused to relax. Ever since she was a child, she'd had a habit of replaying confrontational moments in her head. She couldn't seem to let things go. Always needed to analyse situations and think of ways she could have handled things better. She'd never once come up with the perfect put-down when it mattered. Others seemed to manage it, yet the ideal words only came to her after events had moved on and she was left smarting and humiliated.

It didn't help that Nick had chosen to listen to a selection of Aerosmith, Guns N' Roses, and The Clash at full blast. She needed something to soothe her, but this music was not conducive to sleep. She couldn't relax despite being exhausted, and the music blared out relentlessly until almost one o'clock in the morning. It was another reason to resent her husband.

When Nick eventually switched the music off, Jemima heard him head up the stairs. Even then he made no attempt to be quiet. She fully expected him to switch on the light when he came into their bedroom, but he went into the spare room instead. His absence unsettled her more than she thought possible. She'd expected him to get into bed with her and had steeled herself for a final act of defiance, having worked out exactly what she was going to say. But Nick had stolen the moment from her, and she felt cheated by his display of indifference.

She needed him to apologize, feel him lying next to her, hear his steady breathing, and know that she could reach out and touch him if she wanted to. But Nick had decided this wasn't going to happen. It seemed she had no say in anything anymore. The whole world had turned against her.

Chapter 36

Jemima decided to have an early start in the morning. Be up and out before Nick woke up. Let him stew for a while. She needed to focus on the case and couldn't do that if she started the day off with an argument with Nick. She wanted to put yesterday behind her and was determined not to allow anyone to undermine her again.

When she arrived at the station at a little after 6:30 a.m., there were a few members of the night shift winding down in readiness to go home and get some sleep. She knew it would be a while before any of her team would arrive, so it was an ideal opportunity to continue her research into Greek mythology. Her confidence had taken a knock yesterday, and she didn't want to make a fool of herself if this idea of hers proved to be wrong. The best way forward was to do some research first. At least that way she minimized the risk of looking like an idiot in front of the team.

She knew pomegranate seeds were an important element in these murders. They held some significance for the murderer, and if she could establish what that was it may help identify the killer. Jemima decided to find out as much as she could about Hades. An internet search told her he was the eldest of Cronus and Rhea's male offspring. His siblings were Zeus, Poseidon, Demeter, Hestia, and Hera. There was a plethora of information available on the internet. Greek mythology had been something that had never interested Jemima, and she wondered why it held such a fascination for so many people.

As she scanned the information, she discovered the Titans had ruled the world during the Golden Age, and Hades, Zeus, and Poseidon, known collectively as the Olympians had plotted to overthrow them. The three brothers had received help from the Cyclops, who gave each of them a weapon. Hades had the Helm of Darkness, a helmet that allowed him to become invisible. He used this to enter the Titans' camp without being seen, and once inside he destroyed their weapons. Zeus received a thunderbolt, which he used to attack the Titans, and Poseidon was given a trident to raise the level of the seas and so drown them.

With the Titans overthrown, the three brothers became the new rulers of the world. Hades ruled the underworld, where he guarded the souls of the dead, and whenever anyone entered his realm, he would not allow them to leave. He terrified the living, and they regularly offered him blood sacrifices in the hope it would appease him.

The more Jemima discovered about Hades, the less convinced she became of his relevance to the case, so she turned her attention to Zeus. Jemima already knew he was considered to be the Father of the Gods, but as she continued her research, she established he was also the god of the sky and thunder. There were various symbols associated with him, such as the bull, and the thunderbolt. When she clicked on the word 'thunderbolt,' she saw what could easily pass for the weapon used to mutilate the corpses.

'I don't believe it!' she cried in astonishment.

'Don't believe what?' asked Kennedy as he strode into the room and dragged up a chair.

'I think I may have found the murder weapon,' said Jemima, all thoughts of yesterday's issues with Kennedy now forgotten. 'Someone's made a metal thunderbolt. Look at it. It's the right shape.'

'It's possible, but you'll need to check with Prothero to see what he thinks,' said Kennedy. 'Let's face it; there're plenty of nutjobs out there. But I still don't understand what the pomegranate seeds have to do with this. Wasn't Persephone Zeus's daughter?'

'That's what everything seems to suggest,' said Jemima.

'You told me that Hades made her eat those seeds. So are we looking at two male killers working together?'

'I dunno,' said Jemima. 'The only thing I'm sure about is that we need to continue researching the link with Greek mythology. I think we should also search for references to Zeus, Hades, or Persephone with links to Cardiff, just in case it throws something up. There's got to be some connection to the refuge. Those women aren't going to trust men. They'd never go off willingly with a stranger, yet three of them have ended up dead. Do you think a woman could be luring them from there? Someone they know and trust, one of the staff, maybe?'

'That could be where Persephone comes into it,' said Kennedy. 'Are you certain the murders are not being carried out at the refuge?'

'As sure as I can be,' said Jemima. 'Trent did a thorough search and didn't come up with anything. It's a busy place. There're always people around. Someone would have seen or heard something if the murders had been committed there, and there's no easy way to smuggle a body out. I just don't think it's possible.'

'Then it's time you visited the staff at their homes,' said Kennedy. 'Get Sanders, Peters, and Ashton to finish off at Llys Faen Hall, while you and Broadbent do all the legwork. Have Trent continue with the internet trawl. And Huxley, are you feeling OK? It's just that you didn't seem quite yourself yesterday.'

'I'm fine,' she replied, thinking she'd have felt a lot better yesterday if he hadn't treated her like shit.

Chapter 37

Harriet Breen lived alone in a small neat bungalow in Rhiwbina, a pleasant suburb to the north of the city. Like its neighbouring properties, Harriet's bungalow was set back off the road. A low brick wall separated a small front garden from the pavement. Metal gates urgently in need of some restorative paintwork opened directly onto a driveway, where a red Ford Fiesta was parked. The bungalow itself looked appealing. The windows were clean and bright, while pristine white lace curtains prevented passers-by from having a view directly into the property.

The lawn was in good condition, while four hanging baskets brightened up the otherwise drab rendered walls at the front of the bungalow. Each basket overflowed with flowers as red, orange, white, pink, and yellow petals competed for space.

As Jemima and Broadbent walked up the driveway, a large ginger tomcat lazily opened its eyes. The animal was overweight, contented and clearly enjoying the sunshine as it stretched out to absorb as much heat from the sun's rays as it could. The cat wasn't unnerved by their arrival and rolled onto his back, exposing matted fur on his white belly. He confidently stretched out his legs and opened his mouth in a lazy yowling yawn. As Broadbent crouched down to tickle the animal, the feline rewarded him by purring loudly. There were a few scars on the animal's ears, suggesting it had either been involved in a fight or had injured itself some other way. And as Broadbent straightened up, he was immediately forgotten as the cat looked away and began to lick at one of its front legs.

Jemima ignored the animal, walked up to the front door and rang the bell.

Harriet Breen held a bundle of crumpled clothes in her arms as she answered the door.

'Oh, it's you,' she said, arching her eyebrows in surprise. 'What do you want?'

'We're checking on anyone with links to the refuge,' said Jemima.

'I suppose you'd better come in then. I'm just about to stick these in the washing machine. Have there been any developments?' she asked as she walked to the kitchen.

'Not as such, but as two of the victims spent time at the refuge, we're doing background checks on everyone working there, and that includes home visits,' said Jemima.

'You don't seriously think I've got anything to do with it?' asked Harriet, shaking her head in disbelief.

'We're just being thorough,' said Jemima. 'We need to stop this person before they kill again.'

'I know,' sighed Harriet. 'Those women need to feel safe. They've seen too much violence already. My niece, Dervla, was only twenty-two when her husband killed her. She's the reason I got involved with the refuge in the first place. She was my sister's youngest and had a bright future ahead of her. We always thought of ourselves as a close family, but none of us knew that her husband was hurting her. Three years she suffered at his hands, and we didn't have a clue what was going on. He always seemed so nice. He was an accountant. You'd think the worst he'd have done is bore her to death. When I think back, it's easy to see we were all too trusting. None of us saw past his smart suits and insincere platitudes. We didn't know he had it in him.

'During the court case, we discovered he used to stub out his cigarettes on Dervla's back. She had forty-seven separate burn marks on her body. The poor girl must have been in agony, yet she never asked for help. He got away with it because he was always smart enough never to do anything that showed. And the tragic thing is she found the strength to fight back on the night she died. She stabbed him in the shoulder with a pair of scissors, but it didn't stop him. He strangled her with his bare hands.

'I decided to help out at the refuge because I wasn't there for our Dervla, and I'll never be able to forgive myself for that. I know I can't bring her back, but I'm doing this for her. So you go ahead and search every inch of this place if you have to. I'll even give you the keys to my car if it helps. But just get on and do it, so you can eliminate me and go out and find the man responsible.'

The bungalow was easy to search. It was cluttered with tacky ornaments, decorated in a chintzy style, and was spotlessly clean. Broadbent even searched the attic, which looked as though no one had ventured in there for years. Nothing incriminating was found in Harriet's car, and the property didn't have a garage.

While they were searching, Harriet got out a collection of press cuttings related to the death of her niece, and Jemima realized that Harriet was genuinely concerned for the welfare of the women she helped. This woman hadn't murdered anyone.

As they were about to leave, Jemima's phone rang.

'Where are you?' asked Kennedy.

'Just leaving Harriet Breen's,' said Jemima.

'Bernard Shackleton was murdered last night. They found his body this morning. I've been told that he was the victim of a frenzied attack. There were multiple stab wounds with what they believe to be an asymmetric blade. It has to be linked to our case.'

'Do you want us to head over there?' asked Jemima.

'No, that's not why I've called you. Vanessa Bolton's missing. She hasn't been seen since leaving the refuge yesterday evening. Her husband says he's spoken to all of their friends, but no one knows where she is, and I don't need to tell you she's eight months pregnant.'

'Do we know what time she left the refuge?' asked Jemima.

'About six o'clock,' said Kennedy.

'If we get details of her vehicle, perhaps we can use CCTV cameras to try to locate her,' said Jemima.

'I've already got officers on it,' said Kennedy. 'We've got to do everything we can to find her. We're talking about two lives here. If that sick bastard's taken her, then I doubt he'd spare the child.'

'Vanessa Bolton didn't return home last night. Did you see her leave the refuge?' Jemima asked Harriet, once she'd hung up.

'Yes,' said Harriet. 'I was about five minutes late getting there. We spoke for a few moments. It must've been around 6:15 when she left.'

'When you arrived at the refuge, did you notice any strangers hanging about outside?'

'No. There was nothing unusual. It was quiet,' said Harriet.

'Did Vanessa say if she was going straight home?' asked Jemima.

'We didn't make small talk. Vanessa just gave me an update on what was happening.'

'Who took over from you this morning?'

'Helen Tremaine,' said Harriet. 'It's Vanessa's day off.'

Chapter 38

Jemima and Broadbent returned to the station, where Kennedy was coordinating the search for Vanessa Bolton. Officers had already been deployed to question residents living in the vicinity of the refuge. Others were working their way through CCTV footage to try to establish the route Vanessa Bolton had taken.

Trent was keen to join a search team, but Kennedy insisted that she continue trawling the internet for information on Zeus, as he thought Huxley might be on to something. Trent was not happy.

'I've found another link between Zeus and the pomegranate seeds,' said Trent as she glanced up from the screen. 'Zeus married his sister, Hera, and one of her symbols was the pomegranate.'

'So was Persephone their daughter?' asked Jemima.

'No, Persephone was the daughter of Zeus and Demeter. Demeter was another of Zeus's sisters.'

'So this is all about incest,' said Jemima as Trent and Broadbent looked at her blankly. 'Have the Tremaines returned to Llys Faen Hall?'

'Yeah, they were given the all clear about an hour ago. Forensics didn't find anything at the house, but officers are still searching the grounds,' said Trent.

'Come on, we're going back up there,' said Jemima as she started to run out of the room.

Janet Bleasdale opened the main door to Llys Faen Hall, and her welcoming smile faded as soon as she realized it was them.

She made no attempt at politeness, shook her head in disbelief and sighed disapprovingly. 'Haven't you caused enough upset?' she demanded.

'Are the Tremaines inside?' asked Jemima.

'They're having lunch, and they're not to be disturbed,' Janet replied forcefully.

Jemima ignored the housekeeper and walked through the open door, marching briskly toward the dining room. Broadbent strode along behind her while Janet rushed along in their wake, protesting against their presence in the house.

The Tremaines were dining with Sylvia Shackleton, and all three were sat around a table set with an array of silver tureens and crystal glasses when Jemima and Broadbent clattered into the room. No one seemed particularly happy. David Tremaine's face had an unhealthy pallor. Helen Tremaine also looked the worse for wear, with substantial dark patches beneath her bloodshot eyes.

'I'm sorry. I couldn't stop them,' cried Janet. 'I tried to tell them…'

'What the hell do you want this time?' demanded David Tremaine. 'You can't just walk into my house any time you feel like it!'

'Are you and your wife Zeus and Hera?' asked Jemima.

'What are you talking about?' demanded David Tremaine, staring at Jemima as though she were mad. 'Haven't you got better things to do than disturb us while we're having lunch? Your officers didn't find anything when they searched this house yesterday, so you've no reason to be here. After that debacle, I'd have thought you'd have finally accepted we have nothing to do with these deaths. This is police harassment, and I've had enough. I'm going to contact my solicitor and make an official complaint. Now just get out and leave us in peace!'

'Answer the question,' demanded Jemima. 'I asked if you and your wife are Zeus and Hera?'

'Oh for God's sake!' said David Tremaine, rolling his eyes in despair. 'What planet are you people from? I know you're probably not the brightest, but I would have thought even you would have realized this is the 21st century, not ancient bloody Greece.'

'They're not Zeus and Hera,' laughed Sylvia Shackleton, amused at David's lack of understanding. 'She's Rhea, so I guess that must make him Cronus.'

'Shut up Sylvia, you're drunk,' snapped Helen Tremaine. 'Can't you see we're in the middle of lunch?' she added, giving Jemima the most withering of looks.

'You're a bit defensive aren't you?' asked Sylvia. 'I was only telling them the truth. After all, Rhea's your middle name. Helen Rhea Tremaine. Didn't you ever wonder about the stone lions, Inspector? But then I suppose you wouldn't have received a classical education at whichever state school you attended.'

'What have the lions got to do with anything?' asked David Tremaine.

'Oh, you were always a bit dim, David,' sighed Sylvia. 'Utterly clueless on anything that isn't business-related. You're just so focused on making money. Didn't you ever wonder why Helen wanted those lions in the first place?'

'Helen?' he said, looking questioningly at his wife.

'I don't know what she's talking about. Just ignore her, David. She's drunk. Sylvia, it's time you went home.'

'You haven't told him, have you? All the years you've been together, and you haven't told him,' sneered Sylvia.

'Told me what?' snapped David Tremaine.

'Her middle name's Rhea…'

'I know that,' said David Tremaine.

'Let me finish,' said Sylvia. 'I was going to say that Rhea was a Greek goddess, and the lions used to pull her chariot. That's why she wanted the stone lions. She told me that when they were teenagers, Bernard used to joke about her being the reincarnation of the goddess Rhea. It's all a bit sick really, because Rhea was married to Cronus, only she shouldn't have been because they were brother and sister. They had an incestuous relationship. It's just as well Helen married you. Otherwise, I'd have had my suspicions about Martha and Adam being Bernard's kids.' She laughed.

'Oh God, tell me you didn't!' bellowed David Tremaine, the colour draining from his cheeks.

'Can we talk about this later?' asked Helen Tremaine in a shaky voice.

'They're his kids!' bellowed David. 'You lied about the sperm donor. They're his bloody kids! How could I not have seen it? And it's going to happen again.'

'Shut up, David!' ordered his wife. 'Now isn't the time to speak about this.'

'Sperm donor?' said Sylvia Shackleton. 'Does that mean you're not their biological father?'

'I'm sterile,' said David without taking his eyes off his wife. 'Helen knew that when she married me. You stupid bitch, Helen, what've you done?'

'Are you saying Bernard is Cronus, and he's their father?' asked Sylvia incredulously. 'Is this true, Helen?'

'Go home, Sylvia!' ordered Helen Tremaine.

'I asked you a question, and I expect you to tell me the truth!' screamed Sylvia as she jumped up and sent her chair crashing to the floor. 'Bernard was my husband. Now tell me, is he their father?'

'Yes,' whispered Helen Tremaine, failing to meet anyone's eyes.

'You bitch! How could you? You were my best friend. How could you do that to me? It's no wonder Bernard didn't want me. He was in love with you all the time. That's why he dressed those women up the way he did when he raped them. He wanted them to look like women from Ancient Greece. He was pretending to be Cronus.'

'Cronus and Rhea were the parents of Zeus and Hera, weren't they?' asked Jemima, realizing the importance of what she'd just heard.

'That's right,' said Sylvia. 'Cronus was murdered by his sons.'

'Where are Adam and Martha now?' asked Jemima.

'We don't know,' said Helen Tremaine.

'Are they having an incestuous relationship?' asked Jemima.

'How dare you!' screamed Helen Tremaine, as she leaped to her feet and raised a hand to strike Jemima.

'That's enough, Helen,' ordered her husband, grabbing one of her arms roughly. There was a moment of silence as the chair teetered precariously on its back legs before Helen Tremaine slumped heavily onto it. 'Yes, yes they are,' murmured David Tremaine, unable to look at anyone as he spoke.

'How could you?' sobbed his wife. 'It's family business. It's got nothing to do with these murders. They'll arrest them now, and everyone will know what's happened. The tabloids will love it. We'll never be able to face anyone again. How could you do this to us, David? How could you?'

'Well, it appears they're not my family after all!' shouted David. 'You've been living a lie for long enough. It's time you faced up to what you've done. I thought I knew you. I trusted you, and you deceived me in the worst possible way. You disgust me, Helen! You've had two children with your brother, and now they've gone on to have an incestuous relationship with each other. My God, when will this depravity end? I'll tell you what happened,' he said, turning back to face Jemima. 'We came back early one day and found them having sex in the hall. I went to pull them apart, and Adam attacked me. You've no idea how repellent I find all of this. It was hard enough having to accept that our children are having a sexual relationship with each other. But now, to discover my brother-in-law is actually their father…'

'Have you got a photograph of your son and daughter?' asked Jemima.

'No,' said Helen Tremaine. 'David burned every photograph we had of them.'

'Enough lies, Helen! Yes, we have a photograph. There's the one you hid beneath the carpet in Martha's room,' said David Tremaine. 'You thought I didn't know about it, but I did.'

'Shut up, just shut up!' screamed Helen Tremaine. 'They're our children. You're supposed to protect them.'

'They're not my children, Helen. Anyway, they don't have anything to do with these murders. We haven't seen them for years,' said David.

'I'm going to your daughter's room. It's the one with the peacock feathers,' said Broadbent.

'That's right. Pull up the carpet to the left of the door, and you'll find an envelope. The photograph's inside,' said David.

'Have you seen your niece and nephew recently?' asked Jemima, turning her attention to Sylvia Shackleton.

'No, I haven't seen them for many years,' replied Sylvia. 'I didn't know they were in a relationship until now, and I certainly didn't know they were my ex-husband's children! Believe me; this has all come as quite a shock.'

'I've found it,' said Broadbent as he rushed back into the room.

'Let me see,' said Jemima, holding out her hand impatiently. And as she removed the photograph from the envelope, she was shocked to see the face of Katie Walker smiling up at her. 'You've lied to us!' she shouted at Helen Tremaine. 'You said you hadn't seen your daughter recently, but she helps out at the refuge.'

'She does not!' said Helen Tremaine.

'She's using a different name. She calls herself Katie Walker,' said Jemima.

'Vanessa's friend, Katie? But I've never seen her. She's never been there when I'm at the refuge.'

'Whether you knew your daughter helped out there or not is irrelevant at the moment. We've just had a report that Vanessa's gone missing, and you'd better hope we find her in time.'

'I don't understand,' said David Tremaine. 'Are you implying Martha has something to do with these deaths?'

'That's exactly what I'm saying,' said Jemima.

Chapter 39

'Sir, it's Huxley,' Jemima shouted breathlessly into the mobile phone as she ran towards the car. 'I think Vanessa Bolton's at Hermione's Holistic Medicine Centre, located in Harcourt Street, Penarth.'

'That fits with what I've just heard,' said Kennedy. 'A camera spotted her car heading out of Cardiff on Penarth Road at about 6:30 last night.'

'You need to get an armed response unit there immediately,' said Jemima. 'Chris and Katie Walker own the property. They're the Tremaines' son and daughter. I believe they're our killers, and I think they've got Vanessa Bolton lined up as their next victim if they haven't already killed her. They're after her baby.'

'Are you sure about this?' asked Kennedy.

'As sure as I can be. I just hope we're not too late. You've got to trust me on this. Broadbent and I are on our way there now. You're closer than us. We're just leaving Llys Faen Hall, but we'll have to negotiate the city traffic. We need that armed response unit!'

Jemima and Broadbent arrived at the scene just after Kennedy had deployed officers to seal off the immediate area and evacuate neighbouring properties. The car lurched to a halt, and they jumped out, flashing their IDs as they ducked under the police tape and ran towards Kennedy.

From their vantage point on the street, it looked as though it was business as usual at Hermione's. The patients' car park was full, and the door to the reception area was open.

'Are you sure this is the right place?' asked Kennedy.

'It's got to be,' said Jemima, sounding more confident than she felt. 'They're the killers. They pass themselves off as a married couple, but they're brother and sister. It was the Greek mythology link which led me to them. As far-fetched as it sounds, Helen Tremaine's middle name is Rhea. In Greek mythology, Cronus and Rhea were the parents of Zeus and Hera. David Tremaine isn't their father. He told us he's sterile, and until now he believed his wife had used a sperm donor to get pregnant, but it turns out she'd been having an affair with her brother. So Bernard Shackleton was their father.

'David Tremaine didn't know about his wife's incestuous relationship with her brother, but he knew about Adam and Martha's relationship. It's the reason the Tremaines disowned them. Adam Tremaine changed his name to Chris Walker. He's Zeus, and his lightning bolt is the blade used to mutilate the victims. Martha Tremaine calls herself Katie Walker, and she's Hera. That's why pomegranate seeds were in the victims' mouths.

'These murders are some twisted revenge on their mother. That's why everything links back to the women's refuge, and why the bodies were buried out at Llys Faen Hall. They wanted those bodies found. It also explains why they killed Bernard Shackleton with the thunderbolt. They must have discovered he was their birth father.

'And now I think they're going to kill Vanessa Bolton for her baby. Vanessa told me that Katie and Chris Walker are about to adopt a baby. They lied to her. They'd never be allowed to adopt a child. They're planning on taking Vanessa's baby, and the only way they can do that is to kill her. We've got to get in there before it's too late.'

'Where's the bloody ARU?' shouted Kennedy as he looked over his shoulder.

'They'll be here in ten,' replied one of the uniformed officers.

'We've got to get those people out of there,' said Jemima, nodding towards Hermione's.

'We don't know if the Walkers are on the premises,' said Kennedy.

'Let me go in,' said Jemima. 'I've already been inside, so I know the layout.'

'No, it's too dangerous. We wait until the ARU arrives,' said Kennedy.

'We don't have time,' countered Jemima. 'If Vanessa Bolton's still alive in there, then every second counts.'

'OK, but I don't want you taking any unnecessary risks,' said Kennedy, despite being uncomfortable with the situation. 'Evacuate the building and find out if the Walkers are inside, but no heroics. Enough people have died already.'

Jemima's feet were leaden as she walked purposefully across the car park, and her fear intensified with every step she took. Every cell in her body was screaming at her to walk away, but she battled to retain control of her senses. She tried to calm herself by concentrating on moving her legs, first one then the other. It should have been easy. She'd been doing it since she was a child. Just keep moving. She knew she needed to act as normally as possible, and not give the game away by showing she realized something was probably very wrong inside the building.

It was the first time she'd ever done anything like this. It was one thing insisting on being the first officer to go in. It was quite another thing walking in alone and unarmed, unsure of what you were about to face. A shiver shot down her spine.

The sun was intense, yet she had goosebumps. It was as though someone had poured a bucket of iced water over her.

Jemima coughed nervously, her throat suddenly dry. She held a hand over her eyes to block out the sun and noticed a slight tremor in her fingertips. Background sounds faded until she could only hear the whoosh of blood as it travelled at breakneck speed through her veins.

Everything seemed so peaceful, yet the apparent ordinariness of the scene made it all the more terrifying.

As she reached the main entrance, she could see Candice sitting at the reception desk. Jemima quickly glanced around, but everything seemed normal. Candice was speaking to a client over the telephone.

'Won't be a second,' she said to Huxley as she covered the mouthpiece. Then, glancing down, she removed her hand and said, 'Sorry about that, Mrs. Frampton. Yes, I've confirmed it for two o'clock on the 23rd.'

Everything was as it had been on Jemima's previous visit. Fresh flowers adorned the desk, water gurgled over pebbles in the water feature, and the sound of panpipes played in the background. Candice looked as aesthetically perfect as ever, all high-gloss, capped teeth, and collagen enhancements. Jemima smiled as she realized that even at such a moment, she was still capable of having petty thoughts.

'You were here yesterday, weren't you?' asked Candice as she put the phone down.

'That's right,' said Jemima. 'Are Mr. and Mrs. Walker around?'

'No, and I probably shouldn't tell you this, but it's a big day for them,' she said in a conspiratorial whisper. 'They've been waiting to adopt a baby, and it all went through last night. They've got a little boy. I don't think they've decided on a name yet. At least, they haven't told me what it is. Mrs. Walker's upstairs with him now, but Mr. Walker had to go out somewhere. I haven't seen him at all today. They've probably got so much to do at the moment. They're going to be wonderful parents. It's so exciting.'

Jemima jabbed a button on her mobile and speed-dialled Kennedy, who answered almost immediately. 'They've got the baby,' she said in a low voice, moving away from Candice as she spoke. But she needn't have worried about being overheard, as the receptionist had seemingly lost interest in Jemima, and was now flicking through a glossy magazine.

'The ARU have just arrived,' said Kennedy.

'I've just been told Katie Walker's upstairs with the baby. Chris Walker's gone out somewhere. It's business as usual inside. The waiting room is full of clients, and presumably the treatment rooms are already in use.'

As she ended the call, Jemima turned her attention back to the receptionist.

'I'm a police officer, Candice,' she said, showing the woman her warrant card. 'In a few moments, armed officers are going to enter the building. We need to evacuate the centre as quickly and as quietly as we can. You're in no immediate danger. Just follow the officers' instructions, and they'll get you out of here safely. Are all of the treatment rooms in use?'

Candice nodded in the affirmative, her jaw slack and her eyes wider than ever. At that moment, an armed officer appeared at the entrance.

'Move forward and follow his directions,' ordered Jemima, as she walked into the waiting room and addressed the people inside.

The evacuation was underway, and within ten minutes Hermione's was clear of staff and clients.

Chapter 40

The external door to the double garage was locked, and there was no sign of the key for the internal door either. Someone brought a battering ram from one of the vans, and a single blow was sufficient for the door and frame to splinter, though not to separate. A second strike saw the door give way, and the smell of death rushed out to meet them.

The Walkers had obviously been too busy to clear up after themselves, and the area was awash with blood. It looked and smelled like an abattoir. Plastic sheeting covered the floor and every other surface, making the scene look staged and surreal. Filthy pools of blood had formed along the creases, and a mass of bloody footprints was clearly visible.

There was no doubting the fact that Vanessa Bolton had been alive when they cut into her flesh. The evidence was all around. Blood had sprayed over the wallcoverings, staining the protective surface in messy brownish arcs. It looked like the artwork of the insane. A scene none present would ever forget and made all the more disturbing by the knowledge that until moments ago, it had been business as usual in this very building.

It seemed the Walkers were a resourceful couple. What looked to have originally been a table tennis table was set in the middle of the room. It had been strengthened to bear additional weight, and its surface was crudely modified to incorporate restraints to secure the victims. Anyone strapped to the table would have been unable to move. A plastic sheet covered much of the surface, with holes allowing the restraints to poke through. Beneath the table was the largest pool of blood.

No one entered the garage, as it was evident from the state of the room that Vanessa Bolton was no longer alive. No one could have lost that amount of blood and survived. A trail led to a large chest freezer located against the right-hand wall. It was where the SOCOs eventually found Vanessa's body, but for now, there was the more pressing matter of rescuing the baby, if it was still alive.

Armed officers were already in position outside the entrance to the living quarters. When they received the order to enter the apartment, they burst through the door to find Katie Walker standing in the kitchen cradling an agitated baby with one arm while holding a knife to its throat.

'Stay back!' Katie ordered. Her face was pale and gaunt. There were dark smudges under her eyes, and her hair was unbrushed. Her loose cotton shirt was stained and buttoned incorrectly.

The atmosphere in the apartment felt overly hot and stale. It would have benefitted from a flow of air, but the windows were closed. There was a smell of soiled nappies, and an array of baby paraphernalia littered every conceivable surface.

Pressing the child closer to her chest, Katie repeated her warning. 'Stay back, or I'll kill him.' Her hand trembled slightly. 'Lower your weapons. If you want to keep the child alive, then you're gonna have to let me walk out of here with it.'

The baby seemed to pick up on Katie's distress. Its chest rose and fell in rapid movements as it emitted a succession of pitifully weak cries.

'I haven't hurt him. I just can't get him to feed,' said Katie, looking around wildly. 'I think there's something wrong with him. I've done my best, but I don't know what he wants.'

'The baby can probably sense you're uptight,' said Jemima as she entered the room looking and sounding far more composed than she felt. She ordered the armed officers to step back. 'You look tired, Katie. Did the baby keep you up all night?' Katie didn't respond, so Jemima continued, 'Babies pick up on things. They know when their mother's stressed. Can I take a look?' There was still no response, but Jemima knew she had to keep trying. She needed to make a connection with this woman. 'Is it a girl or a boy?'

'A boy,' said Katie, gripping the baby even tighter. 'He's my little boy.'

'And he's lovely. Have you thought of a name for him?'

'No.'

'Have you let a doctor check him out?' asked Jemima.

'No, I don't want him to see a doctor.'

'He's so small, Katie. Your baby may be ill. Surely it's better to let a doctor take a look at him? Just give him a quick once over. It'll give you peace of mind.'

'I've told you, he's not seeing a doctor!' snapped Katie.

'Well, can I take a look at him then?' Jemima persisted, struggling to keep her voice soft and neutral.

'No, no one touches my baby!'

'I think I know what's upsetting him,' said Jemima. 'It's the knife. Look at it; the light's reflecting off the blade and its shining in his eyes. They're so sensitive, Katie. Bright light will hurt them. Just move the knife away from him. You don't want to damage his sight. Come on now; you're his mother, I know you want what's best for him.'

Katie glanced at the baby's face and realized Jemima was right. The blade was reflecting light into his eyes, so she pulled her arm back slightly and repositioned it, but continued to grip the knife tightly. Her knuckles were white with tension, and the way her hand trembled caused the reflection to dance across the ceiling.

'Why don't you…' began Jemima.

'All clear!' called an officer from one of the other rooms.

Startled at the sound of another voice, Katie spun round, and after that everything happened so quickly. In a jerky movement, she went to reposition the blade, and it looked as though she was about to slash the baby's throat. As the knife moved, an officer standing outside of Katie's field of vision fired a single shot. The bullet shattered her skull and knocked her off her feet. In a reflexive movement, Jemima dived to grab the baby, only just managing to get her hands under the tiny body moments before it would have hit the floor.

Chapter 41

In the hours following Katie Walker's death, all available police officers were pulled from other duties to search for Chris Walker. But with no real background information on him, it was like trying to find a needle in a haystack.

In the meantime, Jemima and Broadbent remained at Hermione's Holistic Medicine Centre, in the hope that they would find something that would help them locate Chris Walker. When the search of the Penarth property proved futile, Jemima decided to speak to Sylvia Shackleton.

'I've not been inside a police station before,' said Sylvia, as Jemima escorted her from the reception desk to a nearby interview room. 'I don't understand why you need to speak to me. It's not as if I can tell you anything. After all, Martha is dead, and Adam has done a disappearing act.'

'I'm just after some background information. Let's get the formalities out of the way before we begin,' said Jemima, as she began to record the conversation. 'I've asked you to come in today, as you have a unique insight into the dynamics of the Tremaine family. You were once married to Helen Tremaine's brother, and even after the breakdown of your marriage, you remained a close family friend. I want to have a better understanding of Chris and Katie Walker, and you're best placed to give me an unbiased account. Don't hold back, by feeling a misguided sense of loyalty. I need to know everything about that family, warts and all.'

'Believe me, I don't have any loyalty, misguided or not towards Helen or her brats. My eyes have been well and truly opened. I never thought I'd say this, but Helen Tremaine, the woman I stupidly thought of as my best friend, is rotten to the core. She's nothing but a duplicitous cow. She's turned Martha and Adam into monsters. And I hope they all rot in hell!'

'For the purposes of this conversation, I'd ask you to refer to your niece and nephew as Katie and Chris Walker, as their names were legally changed,' said Jemima.

'Well, it's all such a mess. They changed their names to hide their identities. But are they really my niece and nephew? We've established they're Bernard's children. If I was still married to him, I suppose it would make them my step-children, but as I'm not … they're nothing to me,' said Sylvia.

'Tell me about the Tremaines,' said Jemima, doing her best to hide her exasperation. It was evident that Sylvia Shackleton was emotional and still smarting from recent revelations. Jemima had no time for bruised egos. She needed cold hard facts. With any luck, they would contain the odd nugget or two of information, which could lead them to Chris Walker.

'David is the most driven man I've ever met,' Sylvia began. 'He's also generous, and one of the nicest people I know. But business always comes first with him. It's the reason he's so successful. But it's obviously had a detrimental effect on his personal life. I've known Helen the longest. Or, at least, I thought I knew her. In her younger days, she was quite the beauty. She turned David's head. He was smitten from the moment he met her. She couldn't believe her luck. He was a gold-digger's dream.

'When they married, Helen hoped to persuade David to delegate some of his responsibilities and spend more time with her. But he'd laughed at that suggestion and said he had no intention of easing up. David had worked ever so hard to grow the company. It was a massive part of who he was, and he enjoyed the challenges it posed.

'Helen was devastated. She claimed that she wanted their relationship to work, but David didn't give her the attention she craved. She was just so needy and self-centred. That's when Bernard started spending more time with her. He told me that he was just looking out for his sister, as she was going through a rough patch. But now I know that he lied to me. The pair of them must have been at it like rabbits. The very thought of what they've done makes me feel sick and ashamed.'

'I appreciate that this is difficult for you, but please try to stick to the facts,' Jemima said. 'Chris Walker is still out there, and I'm trying to get a better understanding of his formative years. I need to know everything I can about him, as it may help us to find him.'

'Yes … I'm sorry. I'll do my best, but it's far from easy,' said Sylvia.

'I understand. Please continue,' said Jemima.

'David and I were kept in the dark. We both thought our marriages were tickety-boo. I guess that makes us stupid and complacent. Until recently, I didn't realise that David was infertile. Helen told me years ago that he was keen on them starting a family. She had her misgivings. Helen enjoyed her independence and was far too selfish to be a parent. It was no secret that she didn't take to motherhood. The nurturing instinct never really kicked in.

'I know for a fact that David disapproved of Helen employing a nanny. He wanted his children to be brought up in a family environment, but then he wasn't the one stuck at home with them. David always wanted a son, and he didn't hide the fact that he was disappointed when Ma— Katie was born. Throughout the pregnancy, he'd often fantasised about spending his leisure time with a son he could groom to become his successor. He planned to teach their unborn son to shoot and fish. The two of them would spend weekends hiking and camping, getting away from it all.

'We all knew it was an idealised fantasy, as David wouldn't have the time or the inclination to do any of those things. Ever since I've known him, he's struggled to delegate. He was proud of the fact that hundreds of people relied on him for their livelihoods, and insisted that staying ahead of the competition took up most of his waking time. His business dealings required a twenty-four-seven commitment.

'Katie was a nightmare child. She was odious. I blame Helen. That woman refused to set boundaries. She gave in to the girl's every whim. Helen just wouldn't say no to her, and by the time Katie started school, the girl was used to calling the shots. Right from the start, Helen was determined that Katie would have the best of everything.

'The child wasn't even a week old when they put her name down to attend an expensive day school for girls. It had an excellent reputation, but Katie was a brat. She rebelled against any form of authority and refused to follow their rules. She was forever getting excluded from classes and activities. It was the same story throughout her time at school. Each teacher claimed Katie was disruptive and disrespectful, and Helen didn't take it well.

'I never thought the girl was exceptional in any way. She just seemed average. Though it was noticeable that she didn't appear to have friends. She had a low boredom threshold, craved an inordinate amount of praise, and reacted very badly if she wasn't the centre of attention.

'Helen's answer to every problem was to throw money at it. And Katie was one hell of a problem. Helen showered her with gifts. Whatever Katie wanted, Katie got, from designer clothes and expensive spa treatments to singing lessons and a grand piano. I used to despair at the amount of money Helen lavished on that child. And it wasn't as if Katie appreciated it. She was a child who wanted something right up until the moment she got it. Then she'd decide that it wasn't good enough and she wanted something completely different.

'There's one afternoon I'll never forget. I was at the Hall with Helen. We'd just sat down when Katie came marching into the room and suddenly declared that she wanted to have a horse. Helen looked at me, then turned to Katie and told her that she wasn't going to have one. As far as I'm aware, it was the first time she'd denied her daughter anything.

'The look on Katie's face was priceless. She clearly hadn't anticipated her mother's refusal. I thought there was going to be an argument, but I was wrong. It was a far more extreme reaction. Katie stormed upstairs and set about breaking toys and wrecking her bedroom. I told Helen to go up there and sort her daughter out. But she didn't. Helen just sat on the sofa and covered her ears.

'I was horrified. For almost half an hour, the only sounds I could hear were objects being hurled against the wall, as Katie destroyed her room. I've never known anyone, child or adult, to have such a vile temper. The girl was out of control. Helen asked me to go upstairs with her, as she was too afraid to go alone. And when we reached the bedroom, the place resembled a war zone. Katie had moved on to the master suite. Helen got there just as Katie hurled a bottle of her mother's perfume at the mirror.

'It was the perfect moment for Helen to assert her authority and bring the girl in line. Instead, Helen went ahead and bought Katie a horse. What's more, she also arranged for a stable block and ménage to be constructed on the estate.

'In my opinion, that girl was born a psychopath. She was incapable of connecting with anyone on an emotional level and certainly didn't care about anyone else's feelings. I haven't come across anyone as cold and calculating as Katie. She took pleasure in manipulating people and manoeuvring situations to her own advantage. She'd lie convincingly at the drop of a hat, had no conscience, and ruthlessly exploited people's weaknesses. But she could also be charming and delightful when she wanted to be. Though if things didn't go her way, there'd be no reasoning with her, and on the few occasions Helen saw fit to punish her, Katie showed no remorse. Life was so much easier for everyone when Katie got her own way.'

The interview room was a comfortable temperature, yet Jemima had broken out in a cold sweat. Her clothes clung uncomfortably, making her skin feel damp and itchy. Worse still, as Jemima moved her arms, she could smell her own body odour. She desperately wanted to get out of this small room, as it suddenly felt cramped and claustrophobic.

Jemima had listened attentively to what Sylvia had to say about Helen Tremaine's relationship with her daughter, but as the words tumbled out of Sylvia's mouth, Jemima's thoughts had darkened. Unfettered resentment and a wave of anger had quickly built up to tsunami proportions, which Jemima had no chance of controlling. The ferocity of her feelings had taken her by surprise. She realised that she had to get out of there. Having to listen to Helen's Tremaine's life story made Jemima want to hurt herself.

Sylvia continued to speak, utterly oblivious to the sudden change in Jemima's mood.

Jemima's chair almost toppled backwards as she stood up abruptly. 'I need to take a comfort break. I'll be back soon,' she gabbled as she headed for the door. Her vision was blurred by tears, which had formed but not yet fallen. She clumsily felt for the door handle, quickly patting the surface until she managed to locate it. Once she'd made it outside, Jemima raced along the corridor as she headed towards her desk. And the tears began to fall.

Chapter 42

This was a new low for her. Jemima had never experienced a full-blown meltdown in work before. But right now, she needed to cut herself. Her emotionally messed up state of mind had affected her ability to do the job. The desire to cut into her flesh was so strong that it was useless to try to fight it. Jemima needed to mutilate herself every bit as much as she needed air to continue breathing. The release it provided would allow her to regain control of her emotions — hopefully before anyone realised that she was acting strangely.

As she had sat and listened to Sylvia describe Helen's relationship with Katie, Jemima's mind had gravitated towards her own fertility issues. That particular demon had long since waged war on her. It was a war of attrition that she was losing.

In the beginning, it had been easier to shut these dark thoughts out. Get on with life until she was slapped in the face by the next monthly disappointment. But with time came the knowledge that other women, many of whom in Jemima's opinion were far less deserving, had been granted the gift that she was denied. It seemed that everywhere she looked, the evidence was being thrown in her face. And Jemima began to realise that she would never be one of the fortunate ones.

The operations room was empty apart from Broadbent, who was talking to someone on the phone. Jemima walked past him quickly, keeping her head down as she scuttled up to her desk, opened the drawer of the pedestal and removed her shoulder bag.

'Are you all right?' asked Broadbent, placing his hand over the mouthpiece, so that whoever he'd been talking to would be unable to hear.

At first, Jemima ignored him, and headed back towards the door.

'Jemima! Gov! Are you all right?' he called.

'Yeah, I'm fine,' she muttered, as she kept on walking.

Jemima knew that Broadbent didn't believe a word of it. He'd obviously sussed that something was up with her. And she'd eventually have to come up with some lame excuse to shut him down when he asked her about it. But that was an issue she'd address later. Right now there was a far more pressing matter to deal with.

Jemima breathed a sigh of relief as she opened the main door to the female toilets and realised that she was alone. She rushed to the furthest cubicle, locked the door behind her and opened the inner zipped compartment of her bag, where she'd hidden the razor blade. It was wrapped in tissue paper and placed inside a small plastic container.

As she closed the lid of the toilet, it slipped through her fingers, crashing loudly on the seat. Jemima jumped and cursed herself for being so clumsy. There was no time to lose, as she needed to get back to Sylvia. She placed the container on the lid of the toilet, then ripped a substantial amount of paper off the roll fixed to the side of the cubicle and crumpled it into a wad. She undid her trousers and they slipped towards her ankles.

Jemima picked up the container, popped the lid, and dropped the blade onto the palm of her free hand. There was no time to drag things out to experience the maximum benefit from the cut. This occasion had to be purely functional, a way of ridding herself of unwanted distractions, freeing her mind to concentrate on the here and now.

She stretched out a section of skin near the top of her inner thigh, selecting a place that was already scarred. Because of the circumstances, Jemima couldn't afford to go too deep or too long. This cut would only be superficial, yet effective nonetheless.

As the blade sunk into her skin, Jemima gasped, and threw her head back. Pain caused lights to dance in front of her eyes. The breath caught in her throat as blood began to flow, and Jemima swallowed hard. She leant heavily against the wall of the cubicle, momentarily unable to independently support her own weight.

Within the space of a few seconds, Jemima could sense the darkness fade away. It was as though self-harming had become her narcotic of choice. The release it gave would give her the strength to deal with Sylvia Shackelton. Jemima's mind was already beginning to clear.

She removed the blade, wiped it clean and dropped it back into the container. Pressing hard on the cut with the wad of tissue, she used her other hand to rummage through her bag until she found a suitable dressing to cover the wound.

Jemima headed back to the interview room in a better frame of mind. She took a deep breath to steel herself as she reached out to open the door to the interview room. And as she stepped inside, she was surprised to find Broadbent chatting away with Sylvia Shackleton.

'Your sergeant is very considerate,' said Sylvia, indicating the cup of coffee that Broadbent must have brought for her. The tone of her voice left Jemima in no doubt of the implied criticism of her.

'Mind if I sit in on this?' asked Broadbent.

'Be my guest,' said Jemima.

Sylvia continued with her narrative.

'Chris was born shortly after Katie's second birthday, and during those last few months of pregnancy, Helen resembled a whale. People had often asked her if she was carrying twins, but there was only one child. Helen had difficulty eating and sleeping. She hated being pregnant. She told me that she couldn't wait to get the child out of her.

'All through the pregnancy, she'd been hoping for a girl. She'd expected the birth to go smoothly, but it hadn't. The labour was difficult. She'd wanted a natural birth, but the baby had been distressed, so they'd performed an emergency caesarean section. Helen hadn't wanted to give her consent, but David had insisted.

'Helen was livid, as she didn't want to have a scar. She'd had the birth planned out. Yet at the last minute, the decision was taken out of her hands. She hated it when things didn't go her way. Chris was a large baby. He weighed almost ten pounds at birth, and Helen was devastated when they told her it was a boy.

'Helen toyed with the idea of breastfeeding. But for some reason, Chris had difficulty latching on, and she actually blamed him for it. After those first few days, her nipples were cracked and raw. They must have hurt like hell. But Helen never seemed to produce enough milk to satisfy him, and within minutes of feeding and changing him, Chris would cry again. I remember that his body would go rigid, and his skin turned almost purple as he screamed in protest. Helen just wasn't able to satisfy him, and after those first few exhausting weeks, she decided baby formula was a better option. And it appeared that Chris preferred it too. He quickly settled into a routine and began to thrive. Instead of feeling relieved at her new-found freedom, Helen persuaded herself that her son had rejected her. So she gave up on him.

'Chris always loved his food, and no one was surprised that he became overweight. Everyone thought he was a lazy boy, as he never wanted to run around or kick a ball. Helen disliked the boy and did everything she could to avoid spending time with him. I know that I usually sing David's praises, but even I have to admit that David was a useless parent. There was a time when he tried to bully Chris into taking part in activities which other boys seemed to enjoy. But Chris hated all team sports and refused to join in. The boy was a loner.

'I felt quite sorry for Chris. David was embarrassed by him, and Helen despised him. They packed him off to boarding school as soon as they could. I had a close relationship with Chris when he was younger. He was devastated when he realised they were sending him away. He wanted to live at home and attend a day school like his sister, but his parents were having none of it. David was an alumnus of the boarding school Chris attended. He was well aware of the pitfalls of sending such a young child away to school but maintained it was a character-building opportunity, which would make a man of their son.

'It's awful when I reflect on it. I should have stood up to them. But it really wasn't anything to do with me. The boy was five years old and terrified of being sent to live amongst strangers. But David insisted it was for the best. I'm sure that even at that age, Chris understood that they were using their wealth to buy their freedom. His parents didn't love him. They never showed him affection or spent any time with him.

'Throughout his early years at school, Chris took every available opportunity to try and get his parents to change their minds about keeping him there. Whenever he returned home for the holidays, he told them how much he hated it at the school. He even begged me to speak to his parents. But nothing would change their minds.

'I used to visit Chris at school. David knew about it, though I don't think Helen did. Chris looked forward to my visits. He despised his parents for making him stay there, as he was bullied at every opportunity. The persecution by the other boys was relentless. It was part of the school culture, almost a rite of passage. The masters knew what went on, but viewed it as acceptable behaviour. As far as they were concerned, it was just part of growing up, and as long as there was no extreme violence, it wasn't considered to be harmful.

'Chris was an easy target, as back then, he was quite a sweet boy. The boys had a pack mentality, encouraged by stories shared with older friends and siblings. Everyone knew it was survival of the fittest. They selected victims by spotting weakness and went all out to make their lives hell.'

'Chris's experiences as a child would have shaped the man he became,' said Jemima.

'He was terrified in those early years,' said Sylvia. 'He was overweight and had no self-confidence. Chris was always going to be the victim. He told me that the bullying started the moment he arrived at the school. It was relentless and cruel. The other boys called him Piggy, and they set out to make his life hell.

'Chris was almost ten years old when the school arranged for him to have an eye test. His poor eyesight was noticed by a teacher when Chris had been unable to read something written on the board. The optician was appalled that no one had thought to get the boy's sight tested sooner. Chris was prescribed glasses. It transformed his life. He gained confidence, became more aware of his body and began to realise he could change the way he looked.

'In a remarkable display of willpower, he stopped comfort eating and accepted that he could turn his life around. He decided to lose weight. It took almost two years. He changed his diet, worked hard, jogged every morning and sweated it out in the school gym three times a week. For the first time in his life, Chris began to like the way he looked. By the time he was sixteen years old, he was six foot tall, muscular and lean.

'Chris stayed on at school until he was eighteen, and during his final years was hailed as being the best athlete the school had ever produced. He specialised in middle-distance running, and represented the county on numerous occasions, always coming in ahead of the competition. He told me that the boys who had once made his life a misery were now in awe of him. But Chris held a grudge. He was determined not to forgive them for the way they'd treated him throughout those early years.

'David was finally proud of his son, but it meant nothing to Chris. He'd accepted his father's rejection long ago. He didn't need anyone's approval or admiration. When Chris finished school, his father offered to take him into the family business and train him up so that one day he would run the company. I know for a fact that Chris told him that he could go to hell.

'David couldn't believe it. It hit him hard, as he wasn't used to rejection. He'd grown to admire his son. Primarily because Chris had achieved so much during his final years at the school. The walls of David's office were crammed full of photographs of Chris being presented with medals and trophies for all the races he'd won. It had always been David's dream to work alongside Chris, to keep the Tremaine legacy alive. I don't believe he'd ever considered the possibility that Chris wouldn't feel the same way.

'There had never been any question of Katie having a role in the business, even as an office junior. David didn't like or trust her. He always said she was lazy and thoroughly objectionable. He particularly disliked her knack of winding people up, as it would be detrimental to staff and customer relations. At least David got that right. I wouldn't have put it past her to run the company into the ground, just for the sheer hell of it.'

Chapter 43

The post-mortem established that Vanessa Bolton had died from severe haemorrhaging caused by the caesarean section the Walkers had carried out. There was no sign of any damage to her vagina, nor were there any pomegranate seeds in her mouth. It seemed that unlike the other victims, the Walkers had simply killed Vanessa for her baby.

The child was taken to the special care baby unit. Despite his early, unorthodox birth, he was a healthy weight, though slightly dehydrated, and after suffering a few setbacks, he began to do well.

Liam Bolton was distraught when he discovered what had happened to his wife and child, but after the initial shock had passed, he coped remarkably well considering his life had been turned upside down. He refused all offers of help in organizing Vanessa's funeral, as he wanted to do it himself. And in the early days, most of his time was spent at the hospital with his son.

Although the Walkers had done their best to clean up after each of the other murders, the SOCOs found traces of blood that eventually linked them to six of the eight corpses buried in the wood at Llys Faen Hall.

As Bernard Shackleton was killed with the same weapon used on the eight women, it seemed logical to assume Chris Walker had murdered him, just as Zeus had killed Cronus; though why he waited until he did remained a mystery to Jemima.

A photograph of Chris Walker featured on national television and many newspapers. The public was advised that he was dangerous and told not to approach him. Despite the high-profile media coverage and hundreds of calls received from concerned people, there had been no confirmed sightings of him.

The Walkers' bank accounts were frozen, and it was soon established that over a six month period, substantial amounts of money had been transferred from their UK accounts into various accounts abroad. They also discovered fake passports in the names of Kyle and Samantha Smith. It seemed the Walkers had planned to leave the country with the baby, and the police were still trying to establish the final destination for the money.

In the days following Katie Walker's death, Jemima continued to research Greek mythology and discovered that peacock feathers were associated with the goddess Hera. It explained why Katie Walker had been so obsessed with the birds. Everything in the lives they'd created for themselves linked back to Greek mythology. They'd chosen the name Hermione for their business because Ermioni, a small Greek town that looks out at the island of Hydra, was also the location of an ancient temple dedicated to Hera.

Jemima also discovered that some Greek dialects refer to pomegranates as *rhoa*, a name associated with the goddess Rhea. It seemed that Chris and Katie Walker had done their best to implicate their mother in the murders of the women. Jemima also established that the sickle was associated with Cronus, as it was the weapon he used to castrate his father, Uranus, and was most likely the reason why Bernard Shackleton had named his restaurant The Stone Sickle.

Once the story broke, the Tremaines received unwanted attention from the press and the public. Everyone seemed to voice opinions on their lives, and none of it was good. Hardly a day went by where they didn't receive anonymous letters containing threats and vile comments. The most disturbing of all was a package containing faeces. The postmarks were varied and spread across the country, and Jemima advised them that little could be done to find the people responsible. David Tremaine had been forced to hire a private security firm to patrol the grounds of Llys Faen Hall, and his business interests were also beginning to suffer.

Helen Tremaine cut her ties with the women's refuge. Reporters had seen to it that everyone knew of its existence, and as all of the identified victims had links with the refuge, the remaining residents no longer felt safe there. Ten days after her daughter's death, Helen Tremaine attempted to take her own life.

'She blames herself for everything that's happened,' David Tremaine told Jemima. 'I've tried to tell her she's wrong, but she knows I don't mean it. There's part of me which thinks she's almost entirely to blame. I'll never be able to forgive her for what she's done to this family. She wants my support, but I can't even bring myself to look at her, let alone put my arms around her. She's made a mockery of everything I believed we had together.

'I should have noticed something was going on between her and Bernard. But it didn't enter my head. I mean, you look for signs of infidelity with other men, but you don't consider the possibility that your wife is having an affair with her brother. They deceived us all. Sylvia didn't have any inkling about what was going on, either. I'll never forgive Helen for what she and Bernard did. Apparently, it had been going on for years. She told me she ended it a few months before he started raping those women. He probably posed his victims the way he did to send Helen a message.

'It's all such a bloody mess. All of those women died because of my dysfunctional family. I'm thinking of moving away, starting over again without Helen. I know I'm a coward, but I can't take anymore. If I'm honest, I wish she hadn't survived the suicide attempt. It would have been better for everyone if she'd died.

'Llys Faen Hall's been in my family for generations. Until my father's days, it was always seen as a symbol of cruelty and oppression. I thought we'd moved on from all of that, but what have we turned it into, eh? Our children have taken things to a whole new level. I always thought we were hardworking, decent people. It turns out I was wrong. I let Helen take control of the kids because I was too busy making money. I wanted to make my mark. Well, I've certainly done that. I failed to notice my wife was unstable and her kids were rotten.

'I know I'm not their biological father, but I have to take responsibility for the way they turned out. I should have been more hands-on over the years. From the time she was little, I knew Martha was a spoilt brat, but I just went along with whatever Helen wanted. I thought we'd got the money, and we can afford to spend it, so why not? But I never thought Adam would turn out the way he did. Oh dear God, I wish we'd done things differently.' His breath caught in his throat. 'If only I'd spoken out when I found them together that day, then things might have turned out differently. But I was too worried about the family name, and Helen begged me not to tell anyone. Now I can see she was just protecting herself.'

Chapter 44

On the day of Katie Walker's funeral, Jemima and Broadbent joined the rest of the police presence in the cemetery. On arrival, David Tremaine nodded his appreciation for their presence and discretion.

Jemima first noticed the man as the coffin was about to be lowered into the ground. He was standing close to a tree, about ten yards away from the open grave. As the bearers picked up the ropes, he stepped a few paces closer. He was tall, with an athletic physique. His eyes were obscured by dark glasses, making it impossible for Jemima to tell if he had spotted them.

'I'm sure that's Chris Walker standing close to the tree,' whispered Jemima. 'Keep an eye on him. I'm going to walk away and circle behind him. I'll call for backup, but if he makes a move, then get after him. It could be our only chance. But don't take any unnecessary risks. You've seen what he's capable of.'

Jemima walked away without looking back until she sensed she was out of sight, then took the mobile phone out of her pocket and called Kennedy, who was sat in a car a few yards from the entrance to the cemetery. Knowing that backup was on its way, she circled to where she'd seen Walker. He was still standing at the same spot, but had removed his glasses and was dabbing his eyes. Jemima was so focused on moving stealthily, that she failed to notice Walker change his stance.

Jemima hadn't expected Chris Walker to turn around so quickly, and with the element of surprise taken away from her, she had less than a second to make her decision. She could see from the corner of her eye that Broadbent was already on his way, but she knew that if she didn't take the initiative immediately, they would lose Walker. Instinct told her that he was going to feign a dummy.

Walker swung right as Jemima lunged left. She thought it was a good call as she propelled her body into his, but her satisfaction was short-lived. They both tumbled to the ground, landing on tree roots, and Jemima felt a sharp pain shoot up her left arm. She cried out and suddenly felt sick. Walker had taken most of the force of the impact, but he now lay on top of her arm.

Despite her physical disadvantage, Jemima tried to restrain Chris Walker until the others arrived. Under normal circumstances, it wouldn't have been too difficult, but he was stronger than he looked, and up close he looked remarkably powerful.

Walker brought a hand up to Jemima's throat and grabbed her neck. As his fingers tightened and sunk into her flesh, she could feel him crushing her windpipe. Her throat was taking the full force of his assault as he fought to straighten his arm and lift her body off his.

Everything was starting to swim in and out of focus, and Jemima realized there was only a matter of seconds before she'd lose consciousness. She was running out of options, and with what little strength she still had left, she forced her knee into his groin. That was what finally put an end to the struggle.

With Jemima's one simple action, all the fight went out of Walker. He howled in pain. His arm gave way, and Jemima's body flopped limply on top of his. The next thing she knew, she was vaguely aware of movement and sounds as Broadbent, Kennedy, and Ashton arrived. They had finally captured Zeus.

Broadbent grunted and wrinkled his nose in disgust as he hauled Chris Walker off the ground. He cuffed Walker's wrists behind his back, read him his rights and escorted him to the police car. Chris Walker's earlier display of strength had deserted him. He stumbled awkwardly, now seeming barely capable of putting one foot in front of the other.

Once inside the vehicle, he slumped forward in the seat, cowed, defeated, exhausted. Tears streamed down his face as his body shook with emotion. He spoke only to tell them that he had not slept or eaten properly in days. His voice was croaky and slow — as though it were too much effort for his lips to move, or his larynx to produce a sound.

It didn't take a genius to realise that Chris Walker was a broken man. His clothes, undoubtedly expensive garments, were no more than foul-smelling rags, stained and discoloured beyond recognition. They were only fit for incineration.

A doctor examined Walker and confirmed that he was currently unfit to be interviewed. No one was surprised.

Everyone was relieved that the interview would have to wait until the following day. It was as much for their benefit as his. As in his current state, no one wanted to have to sit opposite him in an interview room. Kennedy also wanted to ensure they complied with the Police and Criminal Evidence Act. Chris Walker was in custody now, and they didn't want to risk any information extracted during an interview being classed as inadmissible in court.

Chapter 45

The following day, Chris Walker's physical health seemed much improved. After a brief discussion with his client, the duty solicitor informed them that Walker wished to make a statement and was not prepared to answer any questions put to him until what he had to say formed part of the official record.

'Who the hell does he think he is?' snapped Broadbent.

'Let's just go along with it,' Jemima replied, 'and see what he has to say for himself. We can always question him after he gets whatever it is he wants to say off his chest.'

'Are you up for questioning him?' asked Kennedy.

'What's that supposed to mean?' Jemima snapped. 'A few cuts and bruises don't stop me from interviewing someone. You're either going soft, or that was a sexist comment!'

'Oh, get over yourself, Huxley. It was neither, and you know it,' said Kennedy. 'Go with her, Broadbent, and keep an eye on her.'

Chris Walker and his solicitor were already seated as Jemima and Broadbent entered the interview room. Walker glanced up and stifled a yawn. The grime and foul-smelling detritus acquired when living rough had disappeared, revealing a complexion that was pale and haggard. His face was covered with a patchwork of cuts and scratches, as were his hands. His cheeks had hollowed, and he had the look of a haunted man, with sunken eyes lacking vibrancy. It seemed as though he had given up on life.

'Your client's request to make an uninterrupted statement is unusual, but I will allow it,' said Jemima, after the interview formalities had been observed. She turned to Chris Walker. 'Are you ready to make a statement? If you are, then please speak clearly for the tape.'

'I'll tell you everything,' Walker replied. 'But you need to hear it from the beginning to understand why we did what we did. Katie and I were lovers. Our birth names were Martha and Adam Tremaine, but we changed them so that no one would know we were brother and sister. Society will judge us, but we weren't doing anything wrong. It was consensual. There was no harm in it.'

Jemima fought to keep her face expressionless. Walker was already trying to normalise his relationship with Katie, and she wouldn't be surprised if he attempted to justify the horrendous things they'd done to the women they'd murdered. But she was experienced enough to know that her feelings were irrelevant. For now, it was best to bite her tongue and let him continue.

'Katie was two years older than me,' continued Walker. 'I can't recall a time in my life when I didn't love my sister, but as I reached puberty, then adulthood, my feelings for her became sexual. When we were kids, I adored her. She showed me kindness and always had my back.

'I was obsessed with Katie long before we got together. She was out of my league, but I never gave up hope that one day we'd be together. I knew her better than anyone, but even I didn't know her properly. It was easy to underestimate her. A lot of people did. She was such a complex character, which meant that life was never dull when she was around.

'Our relationship worked because Katie called the shots, and I was generally happy to go along with what she wanted. But in public, Katie was content to let everyone think that I was in charge. It was an arrangement that suited both of us.

'When we first got together, I worried that things would end badly. But Katie had this way of making things seem unimportant. She was one of those women who always got what she wanted. No obstacle was insurmountable. In her world, there were never any half measures. It was all or nothing. There were winners and losers. Katie had always been one of life's winners, and she intended on keeping it that way.

'Back then, we still lived with our parents, and I hated that we were forced to treat our relationship as a dirty little secret. In my opinion, it cheapened everything we had together. It was an impossible situation, having to sneak about, stealing moments alone whenever we could. It was torture when we were apart. I lost count of the number of times I almost said or did something which could have given us away. I wanted our relationship to be out in the open. But Katie insisted it wasn't the right time. She made me promise not to say or do anything which would put us at risk. It was difficult, but somehow, we managed to keep our relationship secret for almost a year.

'Then, about five years ago, our parents found out. Our so-called father attacked me. I fought back. It was payback for all those years when he treated me like shit. I thought Mother was going to have a stroke, but no such luck. Everything changed that morning. Our relationship was out in the open, and there was no going back.

'After they walked in on us, everything happened so fast. There were accusations and threats. We had no choice but to leave the house with nothing more than we could carry, which amounted only to our clothes and a few personal possessions. There was no turning back, no safety net. We only had each other, so we had to make our relationship work.

'Those first few weeks were a struggle. We'd lost everything we'd taken for granted, but fortunately, we had enough money put aside. We stayed in a hotel until we rented a furnished apartment. It was our first place together and gave us six months of breathing space. You've seen the tattoos?' asked Walker, suddenly.

'The peacock and the thunderbolt?' said Jemima.

'Yeah, Katie was insistent. This'll probably sound weird, but we'd had this sibling thing going, pretending we were Zeus and Hera. Katie thought it'd be cool for us to have tattoos. I wasn't keen at first, but she was insistent. So I had the thunderbolt on my arm.' He pulled up his sleeve and held his forearm out for inspection. 'She chose it because it's a symbol of power. Katie designed the peacock herself.

'Katie struggled with the reality of day-to-day life. She'd never wanted to become a full-time housewife. She complained that it lacked glamour and excitement. Before she knew it, she'd become the sort of woman she despised. Going crazy, pottering about the apartment finding tasks to fill her time. It wasn't what she wanted from life.

'I began to realise that Katie resented my freedom. I worked in an office: went out in the morning, interacted with clients, had lunch and came home. That's when she enrolled at the local college and signed up for complementary therapy courses. We drew up a business plan, got a loan and bought the property in Penarth. "Hermione's" went on to become an overnight success. We split the duties between us. Katie dealt with the staff and clients. I worked behind the scenes, on the accounts and developing the business.

'The setup seemed to keep Katie happy for a while, but as time went on, things began to change. Maternal instinct kicked in, and the next thing I knew, she wanted to have a child of her own. I was shocked. I loved Katie to bits, but she would have been a useless mother. After all, it wasn't as if she'd had a decent role model to follow.

'Anyway, we kept trying for the best part of a year, but as time went by I started to notice a change in Katie. Things finally came to a head when we found out that she couldn't have children. She'd known for a while that something was wrong. We both had. But until the doctor confirmed the worst, she still had hope.'

Jemima swallowed hard as she felt a lump in her throat. The last thing she had expected when she walked into the room was to have an epiphany about her relationship with Nick, yet a shocking realisation about the state of her own marriage had just smacked her between the eyes.

Chapter 46

Jemima struggled to remain calm. This murderer sitting before her professed to have noticed a change in the woman he loved. Katie had ridden the emotional rollercoaster that Jemima was still on. Yet Nick, the man who professed to love Jemima, hadn't noticed that anything was wrong, despite the obvious scar tissue littering the battleground of her thighs.

What did that say about the state of their marriage? Did Nick even love her?

Jemima hadn't anticipated this unwelcome departure in Walker's narrative. Neither had she expected the worrying seed of self-doubt about a relationship that meant the world to her. Walker was using his sister's name, but he could just as easily be talking about Jemima's life.

The revelations about Katie's inability to conceive hit home in a way that was far too raw and personal for Jemima to deal with. It was as though Walker was taunting her about her own personal demons. Jemima felt the urge to run out of the room. Or scream at Chris Walker, and order him to shut up. But she had a job to do. It was essential to allow Chris Walker to tell his story in his own way.

Jemima owed it to the victims to let him continue. He could stop talking at any time. Refuse to say any more about his crimes. Despite her inner turmoil, Jemima was controlled enough to accept that she had to remain seated and find a way to listen to what Walker was saying.

'The doctor told us that Katie's fallopian tubes and womb had excessive scarring, most likely caused by a severe infection at some time in her life,' continued Walker. 'It was impossible for her ever to become pregnant.

'I remember looking across at her when she got the news, and I swear it looked as though she was drowning. She was always strong and bloody-minded. She'd never take no for an answer. But she opened her mouth to ask a question, and no words came out, only a pathetic little cry. It was so out of character. She was whimpering, like a puppy. It was one of the few times in her life where she wasn't the one in control.'

Jemima's breath caught in her throat. She was on the verge of making a fool out of herself. It would reveal to everyone that she was unfit to be at work. She felt the blood pumping in her ears and fought the urge to lunge at Walker and make him shut up. But something in her brain warned her to rein in her emotions. Before she knew it, her hand had let go of the seat, and her nails dug into her thigh. She pressed as hard as she could, and got some welcome relief from the mild discomfort it caused. It was nowhere near as effective as cutting herself. But it was the only available option and allowed her distress to go unnoticed.

'I asked about IVF treatment,' continued Walker. 'But the doctor said that given our circumstances, there was no way any health professional in this country would offer the treatment. Katie suggested adoption, but the doctor shut that avenue down too. We were being treated like freaks. Katie was different after that. It had a devastating effect on her. That was the start of her obsession to make our mother pay for everything Katie felt had gone wrong in her life.

'We'd been happy for a while. But Katie couldn't let go of the past. She despised our mother. I did too, but I wasn't going to let her ruin my life. I told Katie to stop dwelling on the past and start thinking of the future instead. But she said that without a baby, there was no future.'

To Jemima's relief, Chris Walker's confession soon moved on from Katie's infertility issues. Just as importantly, no one in the room appeared to have noticed the effect it had had on Jemima.

Walker cleared his throat, then continued to speak. There was a noticeable tremor in his voice as he recalled a painful memory. 'Katie became convinced that her infertility was punishment for our relationship. She was angry that I couldn't legally become her husband, and we couldn't have a family of our own. It was as though she was unable to see beyond the negatives. It all became too much for her. It affected her self-esteem and had a detrimental effect on our relationship.

'Until the pregnancy issue, Katie had had big plans. She'd been a firm believer that life was for the taking, and she could have it all. For as long as I can remember, she'd bulldozed her way through obstacles, and bullied people until she got her way. It pissed a lot of people off, but it was something I loved about her.

'She became quiet and introspective, which was so out of character. I knew she was suffering, but I didn't appreciate just how bad things had got until I walked in on her one evening. Katie was in the bath, scrubbing her skin with a brush. And I mean really scrubbing. She was trying to get rid of the peacock.

'When I found her, her skin was raw and bleeding in places. I had to wrestle the brush from her hands. She fought to keep hold of it, scratching and biting me. There was no reasoning with her. It took a long time to calm her down, and she refused to talk to me for days afterwards.

'I felt so fucking useless, as I couldn't change the things which were making her miserable. The impulsive, determined,

Katie was slipping away from me. Her mood swings worsened. She'd fly off the handle at the smallest of things.

'I was convinced that she was going to leave me, and in a last-ditch attempt to save our relationship, I tried to fill our time with trips and activities. I wanted her close so that I could keep an eye on her. And I hoped that a break in our day-to-day routine would distract Katie, keep her busy and stop her brooding on things she had no control over. But as it turned out, it was the worst thing I could have done. My best intentions ended up lighting the touchpaper, which ultimately led to Katie planning the murders.

'It all came down to our so-called uncle. We hadn't seen or heard from Bernard for years. He'd stopped calling round to the Hall, and Sylvia had divorced him. As usual in our family, no one spoke about what had gone on. But it was evident that there had been some sort of scandal.

'Things came to a head on a trip to the Gower. We'd driven to Port Eynon to have lunch at a restaurant recommended by one of our clients. It's called The Stone Sickle. I almost choked on my food when I looked up and saw Bernard. He came out of the kitchen to speak to a few of the guests. He stopped a few feet away from our table, but he didn't recognise us. He hadn't seen us since we were kids.

'We listened in on the conversation and soon realised that it was Bernard's restaurant. We heard him say that he had two grown-up children named Adam and Martha.

'We already knew that David wasn't our biological father but had been told that our fathers were anonymous sperm donors. So we had spent our entire lives believing that we had different fathers. The realisation of what our mother had done, and the lies she had told sent Katie over the edge. She was suddenly determined to make our mother pay, and I decided that

Bernard wasn't going to get away scot-free. After all, we'd been punished for our relationship, and they certainly had a lot to answer for.

'Over the next few weeks, Katie brooded on ways to hurt our mother until she found out, quite by chance, about her involvement at the women's refuge. It was a complete coincidence that Vanessa Bolton signed up at Hermione's for a series of acupuncture treatments. And during one of those sessions, she mentioned the women's refuge. Katie had asked a few polite questions at first. It was just small talk. But that changed when Vanessa told her the refuge had been set up by someone named Helen Tremaine. Katie was genuinely interested, and Vanessa invited her to visit and eventually help out.

'Katie had found a way back into our mother's life and was determined to make her suffer. The more Vanessa Bolton told her about our mother's charitable work, the more Katie appreciated what these women meant to her. It seemed that since we'd left home, our mother had put her heart and soul into the refuge. The most surprising thing to me was that the stone-faced old cow actually had a heart.'

Jemima and Broadbent shifted in their seats as they sensed things coming to a head. Chris Walker was finally getting to the bit they wanted to hear. The distasteful eulogising about his sister had finally petered out, and with a bit of luck, they would be rewarded with a blow-by-blow account of the couple's murderous spree.

Not that it would be easy to listen to, far from it, but it was necessary, as it may be useful further down the line, to help identify some of the victims. Or to be made aware of other, as yet undiscovered corpses at other burial sites.

'Katie and I were so different,' Walker continued. 'She was an accomplished manipulator. Whereas with me, what you see is what you get.'

Jemima smiled, encouraging him, but she didn't believe a word of what he had just said. Chris Walker was just as guilty as his sister.

'Katie could read people and knew exactly how to play them. She taught me that a smile or a look of embarrassment somehow made people trust you. Whenever she spent time at the refuge, Katie's biggest concern was to ensure that she didn't bump into our mother. After only a few visits, she came up with the plan to murder the women. She knew the risks but was sure that we could get away with it if we planned and executed things carefully.

'I thought she was joking at first, as she'd always had a warped sense of humour. But when I realised that she wasn't, I told her she was out of her mind. Those women had done nothing to us, and I didn't want to have any part of it.

'She was always saying that I should man up, and she was right. I should have stood up to her and made her listen to reason. But when it came down to it, I couldn't. I was afraid I'd lose her. I told her she should leave things alone. She should have walked away from the refuge and left our mother to get on with her life. But Katie was having none of it. She laughed at me for being so weak.

'I told her that I'd prefer to concentrate on the life we'd built together, and make the most of what we had. But Katie said she was going to kill the women whether I helped her or not. That's when I told her she'd have to do it without me. I hoped it would make her think again, but it didn't. It just seemed to make her all the more determined.

'I suggested we should go up to the Hall and have it out with our mother, but Katie didn't want to do that. She said she wasn't interested in talking about things. She wanted the ultimate revenge. She was intent on destroying our mother and her carefully crafted fake reputation.

'Katie said that I was either with her or against her. If I let her down on this, then our relationship was over. She hated our mother and Bernard and said she wouldn't be surprised if we'd inherited all sorts of genetic abnormalities. By then, she'd convinced herself that our parentage was the reason why she couldn't have children.

'I told her that she needed to get a grip. What Mother and Bernard had done was no different to what we were doing, except they didn't have the guts to live together as a proper couple. You see, Katie was just angry that she couldn't have children. She was looking for someone to blame.

'I tried to reason with her and asked her how she could contemplate killing innocent people. I remember thinking how cold she'd become when she said that it didn't bother her. She felt nothing for those women. They were a means to an end. She said that they'd spent years in abusive relationships. So if they didn't value themselves, then why should she care about them?

'I tried to convince her that these women were just ordinary people trying to rebuild their lives and that what she was planning to do to them was wrong. We had a heated argument. The worst we'd ever had. I was so angry with her. Anyone else would have backed down and seen sense, but not Katie. She'd always had a stubborn streak. Once she got an idea fixed in her head, there was no talking her out of it.

'Later, I heard a dragging noise in the hall. It was Katie, lugging a suitcase. She told me my clothes were inside, and that

I had a choice. Either I supported her, or I could leave. I couldn't believe she was making me choose. She said that if I didn't help her, there'd be no going back. She didn't believe in giving anyone a second chance.

'It brought me to my senses. I knew that when it came down to it, there was no choice to be made. I couldn't face life without Katie. I was sickened by what she was proposing to do. But killing those women was a better option than spending the rest of my life without her.

'Katie had it all worked out. She insisted the bodies had to be buried on the estate so that the evidence would point to our mother's involvement in the deaths. She wanted you lot to poke about in our mother's life, as she'd be worried that her secret would come out. As there was no apparent motive for the murders, you'd have to find out as much as you could about our family. And if you were thorough, you'd discover what our mother had done.

'You see, Katie just wanted everyone to see our mother for what she is. She wanted her to be publicly humiliated, and face the consequences of what she'd done to us. I accept that what I did was wrong. I had a choice, and I chose Katie. I'm sorry those women had to die, but I'd do it all over again if it meant I could still be with her. She was the love of my life.'

Jemima sensed a slight change in Broadbent's body language and knew exactly what he was thinking. It was virtually impossible to not react when listening to Chris Walker tell his story. The man felt sorry for himself. He claimed to have tried to get Katie to back out of the murders, yet had still played an active role in the sadistic killings. And to say that he would do it all over again if it brought Katie back to him was blatant proof that Walker felt no remorse for what they had done.

Jemima discreetly nudged Broadbent's thigh with her knee, warning him not to react. They'd made it through Walker's emotional quagmire. Now they were about to be rewarded with the information they really needed to hear. That is, as long as Walker didn't renege on his promise, and clam up altogether.

They needed him to name the victims. Even if the women hadn't used their real names, there was a small chance that if they'd stayed at the refuge, the police would be able to discover their real identity.

'I know you don't believe me, but up until the very last moment, I tried to persuade Katie to take a softer approach,' said Walker. 'I suggested we tell David that Bernard was our biological father, but Katie insisted it would be pointless. We had no proof, and it wasn't as if we could force Bernard to take a paternity test. Without evidence, David wouldn't believe our mother capable of such a betrayal.

'Katie was adamant that murdering those women was the only way we could hurt our mother. She insisted that when the bodies were eventually discovered, all the lies from her past would subsequently come out.

'It was easy for Katie to get a foothold in the refuge. As Vanessa had vouched for her, everyone had been eager to believe that Katie was just another do-gooder. No one suspected her real motive for being there, and Katie loved the deception. She told me that she'd never felt more alive. She got a kick out of it. The women seemed to trust her, and she became a confidante to some of them.

'It was a high-risk strategy. If our mother had found out about Katie's involvement at the refuge, she would have banned her from the place. We both knew that our mother wouldn't allow either of us back into her life and certainly wouldn't let us have anything to do with the refuge.

'As it turned out, the plan was a slow burner. Katie had been part of the Friday team for almost eight months when our first victim presented herself. Natalie Youde was a twenty-four-year-old victim of domestic violence who was about to begin a new life in Coventry. Arrangements were in place for her to stay in temporary accommodation. They'd even found her a part-time job at a small retail outlet.

'Natalie was due to travel on the train from Cardiff Central to Birmingham New Street. From there, a connection would take her on to Coventry, where she would meet another volunteer who would escort her to a half-way house.

'Vanessa had responsibility for making travel arrangements for all relocations. She asked Katie if she'd accompany Natalie to the train station on the following Friday. They actually made it easy for us at the refuge. For some reason, the women were always kitted out in the same clothing whenever they relocated them, so Katie knew what Natalie would be wearing. She bought a wig that was a similar colour and style to Natalie's own hair and took a set of clothes from the storeroom at the refuge.

'Finding someone of a similar height and build to Natalie proved a little more problematic. But after a couple of visits to the students union at Cardiff University, Katie eventually managed to find a female student keen for a free train journey to Birmingham. Katie explained to the girl that she would be expected to put on a wig, wear a particular set of clothes, and take an empty suitcase with her. In return, she'd get a free ticket. When the girl questioned it, Katie passed it off as being a dry run for a short film she was about to make. The girl seemed satisfied with the explanation and was happy to get a free trip home.'

Jemima swallowed hard. It was awful to realise that Natalie Youde had lost her life at the very moment she was about to embark on a new beginning. The young woman had most probably believed that she had put the worst behind her, and had no reason to fear Katie Walker.

'The evening before we snatched her, I very nearly bottled it,' said Walker. 'Katie wasn't helping matters. She was hyper, yapping away like a dog with a bone. After a while, her words lost meaning, and the sound of her voice became unbearable. Her excitement made me feel sick. It even crossed my mind that we'd all be better off if I killed her instead. But I loved her too much.

'I was at my wits' end and knew I needed to put some distance between us. So I switched off my phone, got in the car and drove. I didn't want to go through with Katie's plan. I'd done my best to talk her out of it, but nothing I said made her change her mind. There was no reasoning with her. She'd always had a vindictive, unforgiving streak, and I knew she'd leave me if I didn't play my part.

'The journey was a blur until I found myself driving along the lane towards our parents' estate. I thought about turning up at the Hall and confronting them but decided against it. Katie was right. It wouldn't do any good.

'The electric gates were open, so I turned into the grounds and drove up to the turning area near the edge of the wood. I sat in the car for most of the night, trying to clear my mind so that I could make a decision about what I was going to do.

'It was a strange night. I remember that the moon was bright. There were plenty of stars. It was peaceful, almost magical, and I was grateful for the solitude. When I finally switched my phone on, I discovered that Katie had left me dozens of messages telling me to ring her. I didn't bother. I drove home instead. She was in bed when I arrived. It was almost four in the morning. Katie stormed into the room, slapped my face and demanded to know if I was backing out of the plan.

'I told Katie that if she'd asked me that question a few hours earlier, my answer would have been yes. But I'd mulled it over and had come to realise that nothing in my life made sense without her. I didn't want to go ahead with it, but if it was the only way I'd get to keep her in my life, I'd do whatever she asked of me.

'I could tell that Katie was nervous when she left Hermione's that morning. We'd been over the plan so many times. She drugged some fruit juice, put it in her bag and told me that she'd send me a text when she was about to leave. I was to meet her at a lay-by on a relatively quiet stretch of road. The deception was easy to pull off as our cars are identical, apart from the number plates.

'When we met up, Natalie was already unconscious. Katie grabbed the few pieces of luggage, opened the cases and emptied Natalie's possessions into the boot. Katie kept the suitcases, and we swapped vehicles. I headed back to Hermione's in Katie's car. Katie went to meet the student.

'Katie told me later that she was stunned at the similarities between the student and Natalie. The wig and the clothes were a perfect disguise. She said that if anyone were to check the station's security footage, they'd be hard-pressed to tell it hadn't been the real Natalie boarding the train. Katie ensured that they stood in full view of one of the surveillance cameras as they waited for the train to arrive. The girl was completely unaware that she was helping Katie to kill someone.

'As the train pulled out of the station, Katie waved goodbye to the fake Natalie. Afterwards, she headed back to the refuge to finish her shift. Everything had gone to plan. No one suspected anything was wrong.

'In the meantime, I drove back to Hermione's. Natalie was still out of it and would be for hours. We'd soundproofed the garage a few months earlier, just to be on the safe side, and improved the locking mechanism on the doors. There was no way anyone could get in or out of there. But I was still worried, so I tied Natalie to the seat, gagged her then locked the car and secured the garage doors.

'Katie returned shortly before two o'clock. She had three consultations booked in for that afternoon. I couldn't get over how calm she was. Nothing seemed to faze her. It was as though the events of the morning hadn't happened.

'Now that Katie was there to keep an eye on the place, it gave me time to set things up in the garage. Natalie was still unconscious, so I dumped her on the garage floor. I reversed the car outside and parked it next to Katie's. Then I set about getting things ready in the garage. I covered everything in plastic sheeting, set up the table we'd already modified to restrain her, then stripped Natalie, placed her on the table and strapped her down.

'It was a relief to shut Hermione's later that day. When everyone had gone home, we headed upstairs and changed into disposable overalls. Katie was eager to get started, but I still tried to get her to back out, as I knew there'd be no going back once we killed her. My latest wobble wound Katie up no end.

'It worried me that she wouldn't accept that what we were doing was wrong. She didn't place any value on Natalie's life. She insisted that this was our chance to make a stand and say enough's enough.

'She asked me how I felt about the fact that our mother treated those women better than she ever treated me. And Katie was right. I couldn't argue with that, as I can't recall a single occasion when my mother showed me any kindness. Katie insisted that our mother needed to be taught a lesson, and this was the perfect way to do it.

'I was worried about getting caught, but Katie was confident that we wouldn't be. We'd been careful, and there was no reason for anyone to suspect us, as we ran a successful business, and were respectable people. Everyone would think that Natalie had got on that train. Anything could have happened to her at Birmingham, where she should have changed trains. Katie said we were home and dry.

'I told Katie that I didn't know if I'd be able to live with myself. The thought of what we were about to do made me feel sick. I'd never killed anyone before. It was going to be messy, and it wouldn't be easy to dispose of the body afterwards.

'Katie insisted there was no going back. We couldn't let Natalie go, as she could identify us. We had to kill her. She said we had enough disinfectant to get rid of any traces of blood, and we'd wash the body to get rid of any evidence linking us to the murder. She assured me that as long as I was careful, no one would see me in the woods. And when the corpse was eventually found, everything would point to our mother, and we'd bring her world crashing down around her.'

'That is enough for now,' Walker's solicitor interrupted. 'My client has been cooperative so far, but he needs a break.'

'I'll arrange for some food to be taken to your cell,' said Broadbent.

'We'll resume in two hours,' said Jemima.

Chapter 47

Chris Walker was escorted back to the interview room. Once he had settled himself onto his seat, he took a sip from a fresh cup of water then began to speak.

'You must understand that I didn't want to kill those women,' he said.

Jemima was exasperated by his repeated attempts to make them believe that he had not been a willing participant in the murders. Walker had a choice and chose to end those women's lives. It sickened Jemima that he was trying to make them believe that he had been a victim of circumstances beyond his control. Despite having had a lengthy break, hours spent holding herself in check were both physically and mentally exhausting, and she was sure that Broadbent felt the same way too. She just hoped that neither of them did or said anything to make Walker clam up and so jeopardise the chance of a detailed confession.

'Natalie was still unconscious when we were about to start the ritual,' Walker continued. 'I remember thinking that I'd never been so scared in my life. My stomach was churning like a cement mixer. As Katie removed Natalie's gag, my hands were shaking so badly that I couldn't feel anything. The stainless steel dish I was carrying slipped through my fingers. As it crashed to the floor, the sound echoed throughout the garage.

'The noise shocked Natalie. She went rigid, as though a jolt of electricity had passed straight through her and brought her back to life. Not that she could move far, because of the restraints about her wrists and ankles. She opened her eyes, but couldn't see us at first because she was facing the ceiling. Though it didn't take her long to realise that something was wrong, and when she did, we had to get to work on her quickly.

'She kept screaming. The sound went through me. But I could see from the expression on Katie's face that she liked it. Natalie kept moving her head from side to side as she struggled against the restraints. Katie grabbed Natalie's head and told me to get cutting.

'I didn't have the stomach to cut her, but Katie insisted it had to be me as I was Zeus. Katie had already told me that I had to destroy Natalie's womb. She said we couldn't swap roles because she was Hera and had to use the pomegranate seeds.

'Katie kept shouting at me, ordering me to get it done. I think she was afraid that I'd back out. I'll never forget the feeling. Sweat was running into my eyes, making them sting. I took a deep breath, picked up the blade and gripped it so tightly that my hand hurt. My knuckles were white, and I couldn't stop shaking. My heart was beating so quickly that I thought I'd have a heart attack if I didn't do it soon.

'I wasn't brave enough to look at her. So I closed my eyes and plunged it between Natalie's thighs. I jerked backwards and almost lost my footing as a wet spray showered my skin. For some reason, I hadn't expected that to happen.

'By that point, I'd accepted that there was no going back. So I kept thrusting, and the blade ripped Natalie's flesh to shreds. I tried to block out what I was doing by thinking of Katie. I was only doing it for her. I told myself that if it made her happy, then it was the right thing to do.

'I remember thinking that every thrust took less effort than the previous one. When Natalie stopped screaming, I could hear a sickening squelching sound as the blade entered and came out of her body. I didn't know at that point whether she was dead, or unconscious. I didn't want to look at mangled flesh or a dead body, as they would prove that I was a murderer, and I wasn't ready to accept that yet.

'I kept going until Katie put her hand on my arm and told me to stop. I opened my eyes and looked at Natalie's face. I could tell that she was dead. Katie took the blade off me then picked up a container of pomegranate seeds, opened Natalie's mouth and poured them in. She pressed the seeds down with her fingertips until no more would fit inside. She closed Natalie's mouth then got a sponge and began to wash the body with a mixture of disinfectant and water.

'Katie probably thought I was pathetic as I curled up on the floor and kept crying. She shouted at me the way our mother used to. Katie ordered me to strip off, have a shower and change my clothes. She was going to clean up the garage while I buried the body. I couldn't understand how she could be so calm and matter-of-fact about what we'd done.'

Jemima was shocked. She glanced across at Broadbent and saw that he had turned pale. He had an aversion to blood, and Walker's description of Natalie Youde's murder had left little to the imagination.

Walker appeared to be oblivious to the effect he had had on them and continued with his ghastly monologue. 'Every woman we killed stayed at the refuge. Cheryl Thomas was our second victim. Katie said her real name was Holly Vetch. She turned up at the refuge as she wanted to make a new life for herself away from her hometown of Abergavenny. She overheard Katie talking to Vanessa about Hermione's. After that, Holly kept dropping hints about how she'd like it if Katie would train her up as a reflexologist.

262

'Katie hadn't planned to abduct her. It was a spur-of-the-moment decision. She was driving along a Cardiff street in the middle of the afternoon when she came across Holly quite by chance. There was hardly anyone around, certainly no one who knew them. So Katie pulled up, asked her if she wanted to take a look around Hermione's, and Holly got into the car.

'Katie told Holly that the car park was reserved for clients and drove straight into the garage. When Holly got out of the car, Katie rushed across, grabbed Holly's hair and thrust her face-first against the wall. She was out cold, and before Holly had a chance to come round, Katie had injected her with a sedative.

'Katie came to find me and told me what she'd done. I moved the car out and prepared the garage. Ninety minutes after everyone had left the premises, we started the ritual. Holly was dead before she had a chance to regain consciousness.

'As for the others, I just have a list of names. By that stage, I wasn't even interested in them. They were just more of the same. There was Rhian Morgan, Victoria Larkin, Emma Garvey, Lara Knight, Tara Fenton, Janine Baxley, and Chantelle Prince. I couldn't even tell you the order in which they died.'

'Were there any other victims?' asked Jemima.

'No, and there wasn't another burial site. You've found all of them. Shall I tell you about Vanessa and the baby now?'

Jemima nodded.

'So, when you turned up unannounced at Hermione's, we knew we had to act quickly. I'd never seen Katie so jittery. She always liked to plan things out, didn't like it when she was forced to improvise. We hadn't expected anyone to find the bodies so soon. And when they were discovered, everything happened so quickly. We hadn't thought that far ahead, and it soon became obvious to us that we'd lost control of the situation.

'Our plans changed when Katie realised that Vanessa was pregnant. Up until then, it had all been about Katie getting revenge on our mother. But the pregnancy changed everything, as Katie realised that it was going to be her only chance of motherhood.

'She'd planned to kill Vanessa and snatch the baby almost right from the start. It's why we got ourselves false passports and set up foreign bank accounts. If you hadn't stopped us that day, we'd have new identities and would be living our lives halfway around the world. You'd never have found us. We were so close to having it all. Katie almost got to make her dream come true.

'We'd always known that the bodies would be found. We'd planned it that way. That's why Katie insisted that I didn't bury them too deeply in the first place. But we hadn't anticipated the hot weather. It led to the corpses being discovered too soon. The timing couldn't have been worse. There were still loose ends to tie up for us to have a reasonable chance of leaving the country with our baby before you linked us to the murders. But as it was, Vanessa hadn't given birth.

'To stand a fighting chance of getting things back on track, we needed Vanessa to come to Hermione's. So Katie offered to give her a free Indian head massage and reflexology session. She told her it was a pre-birth treat. At first, Vanessa had been reluctant to accept the invitation. She said she was too tired and needed to rest. But Katie had sounded so upset on the phone that Vanessa finally agreed to come.

'She arrived just as Hermione's was about to close for the day. Whilst Katie administered the treatments, I closed up and checked that everyone had left the premises. I followed the usual daily routine, so no one suspected anything. We were on a tight schedule. So as soon as possible, I went into the garage and began to prepare for Vanessa.

'We'd kept the sound of panpipes playing in the treatment suite. It's got a hypnotic quality, guaranteed to relax. We had CCTV set up in the room, and I watched as Katie brought a dumbbell down on Vanessa's head. She'd been worried about doing that, as she knew she had to get it just right. You see, it had to be hard enough to knock her out, but not so hard as to cause permanent damage, as it could have affected the baby's chances of survival.

'Katie told me afterwards that she felt guilty about what she did to Vanessa. She hadn't cared about killing the other women. But then Katie hadn't liked them. Vanessa was different. Their relationship had been the closest thing to a real friendship that Katie had ever experienced, apart from her relationship with me. But their friendship was of secondary importance, as Katie wanted Vanessa's baby. The woman was about to make the ultimate sacrifice to enable us to have a child of our own.

'It wasn't easy to move Vanessa from the treatment suite to the garage, as she was a dead weight. The garage was set up as an impromptu operating theatre, and we secured Vanessa to the table. Katie cut the clothes away, and we just got on with it.

'We were both concerned about the effect Vanessa's head injury may have on the baby. The wound bled a lot. Far more than either of us had anticipated. I remember the hair nearest to her scalp was dark and matted with congealed blood. We hadn't exactly been gentle with her, but Vanessa hadn't shown any sign of regaining consciousness. Her stomach was huge. Our baby was inside this woman's body, and we were moments away from becoming a real family.

'And then it happened. Vanessa's stomach rippled. It was like that scene from *Alien*. We both jumped in surprise then laughed in relief, as it meant our baby was still alive. It was the moment I realised that I wanted this baby too. Up until that point, I'd gone along with things for Katie's sake. But suddenly, we were so close to seeing the baby for the first time. We were in touching distance of embarking upon the perfect family life. It was something I'd never believed was possible. And I couldn't wait to hold the baby in my arms and be its father.

'Vanessa began to stir as she felt the baby move inside her. She struggled to open her eyes, and tried to move her limbs, but couldn't. Vanessa asked us if the baby was coming. Katie told her it would all be over soon, and then injected her with a sedative, and that's the last time Vanessa spoke.

'When Katie picked up the scalpel to cut into Vanessa, she seemed so calm and confident. It was a complete transformation. She was back in control, determined to deliver the baby as quickly as possible so that the sedative didn't have a chance to harm it. I asked her if she knew what she was doing and Katie said that she did, as she'd watched a programme about it on TV.

'I warned her to be careful, as it's one thing watching an expert do something, but quite another thing doing it yourself. She just smiled and told me that there's a first time for everything. She said there was nothing for me to worry about as long as I handed her the instruments when she asked for them. So I shut up and did as I was told, as our baby's life depended upon us.

'Katie had nothing to do with Bernard's death. That was down to me. I couldn't let him walk away scot-free.'

Chris Walker broke down as he told them about the moment he learned of Katie's death. It had come as a shock when he saw an article in a discarded newspaper. Until then, he'd assumed she'd been arrested during the police raid on Hermione's. He said that things had become a bit of a blur after that.

Chris Walker was charged with eleven counts of murder. He insisted that he did not want a trial as he intended to plead guilty, so he was placed on remand until a judge became available to sentence him.

Epilogue

They marked the end of the case in the usual fashion with a few drinks down the pub. The mood was jolly enough. Yet for some inexplicable reason, Jemima felt like an interloper, as she sat there quietly nursing her rum and coke.

The lads had paired up and were focused on a highly competitive game of darts. They'd insisted it was just for fun, but the body language, banter, and occasional furtive look suggested otherwise. There'd been a small wager on the outcome. It was two-all with everything to play for on the final leg. Peters and Sanders had the edge, but Ashton and Broadbent were hot on their heels.

Kennedy and Trent were chatting away happily, chuckling every now and then, forcing Jemima to smile and make the occasional bland comment to keep up the pretence of being interested in what they were saying. She could tell that something was going on between them. There was more room at the table now that the other four were playing darts. Yet Kennedy and Trent remained huddled together.

There was a fleeting moment when Jemima thought she saw Kennedy's finger brush Trent's hand. He'd mentioned early on in the investigation that he'd known her for a while. And the events of that evening made Jemima think that perhaps their relationship was more than just a professional one.

Jemima experienced an unexpected pang of jealousy. Not because she had designs on Kennedy, or anyone else for that matter. But, witnessing an intimate moment of a couple who obviously enjoyed each others' company was another wakeup call about the state of her marriage to Nick.

The first seeds of doubt had been sown a few days earlier, when Chris Walker opened up to them about his feelings for his sister. It was apparent that he had been so in tune with Katie's emotions as to notice the change in her behaviour as she tried to come to terms with her lack of fertility.

To a certain extent, Katie Walker's predicament had mirrored Jemima's. Yet Nick had not once offered Jemima any emotional support or even commented on the fact that she was so obviously self-harming. And since experiencing that particular epiphany, Jemima questioned whether she had been wrong to believe that their marriage was rock-solid.

Perhaps her judgement had been poor, and Nick didn't love her as much as he professed to. It was something Jemima needed to address. Though for now, she thought it was better left alone, which was difficult as it was already eating away at her. But she was determined to bide her time, watch Nick more closely, and see where the evidence took her.

Chris Walker was sentenced to life in prison, and things at the station soon returned to normal. Trent, Ashton, Sanders and Peters had gone back to their usual posts, and the place seemed quiet without them.

'I've got some news,' said Kennedy, as he strode into the room.

Jemima could tell from the expression on his face that whatever he was about to tell them would be good news. 'What is it, sir?' she asked.

'It won't surprise you to hear that the case at Llys Faen Hall raised this team's profile within the force. A lot of eyes were on us whilst that was going on, and we acquitted ourselves splendidly. So much so that I've just been made aware that the

Chief Constable has found money in the budget for us to have a full-time detective constable.'

'That's great, sir. Got anyone in mind?' asked Jemima.

'Funny you should ask me that. How would you feel about Finlay Ashton joining the team on a permanent basis?' asked Kennedy.

'I'd love him to join us,' Jemima replied. 'He'd certainly add value with his particular skill set. And he'd fit in well.'

'My thoughts exactly. I'll go and make the call.'

A NOTE TO THE READER

Dear Reader,

Thank you for taking the time to read *Revenge*. I hope you've enjoyed this encounter with Detective Inspector Jemima Huxley and will want to join her in future investigations. But watch out, because there's a dangerous road ahead and she's going to face plenty of challenges along the way.

I love writing about Jemima because she's such a complex and troubled character, with many layers yet to be revealed. Like most people, Jemima's not always nice, but her heart is in the right place, and she definitely looks out for anyone who needs her help.

As Jemima's creator, even I've been surprised to discover certain things about her. It's as though I'm getting to know a new friend, warts and all. Hopefully, if you stick around, you'll come to feel the same way too.

Jemima's chosen career has placed her firmly in a male-dominated environment, and although she can hold her own, she sometimes finds it tough. She feels the need to prove herself and wouldn't dream of asking for help, even if she could do with it. But at least Dan Broadbent has her back, even though she often gives him a hard time.

I would be truly grateful if you would leave a review on **Amazon** and **Goodreads**. I love to hear from readers, so if you would like to contact me, please do so through my **Facebook page**, ask me a question on **Goodreads** or send me a message through **Twitter.** You can also see my latest news on my **website**.

Gaynor Torrance

www.gaynortorrance.com

Sapere Books is an exciting new publisher of brilliant fiction and popular history.

To find out more about our latest releases and our monthly bargain books visit our website: **saperebooks.com**

Printed in Great Britain
by Amazon

35919011R00163